D0205648

"LIKE WHAT YOU SEE?"

Donovan's knowing smile made Sarah's breath catch and her heart pound. Oh, he was dangerous. And oh, how tempted she was. But she had sworn long ago to control her disgraceful passionate nature, and no brazen rogue was going to change that.

"Mr. Donovan, I am trying to conduct business," she said primly. A drop of water dripped from his hair to his bare shoulder, and wound its way down his chest. She jerked her gaze back up to his. "Business," she repeated. "About the bed . . . "

"Want to try it out?"

Her mouth fell open. "I . . . are you out of your mind?"

"Nope." He gave her a wicked grin.

"Mr. Donovan, you are becoming distracted from the issue," she forged on. "If I could just have your attention for a few minutes—"

He grabbed her wrist and tugged. Before Sarah could blink, he'd pulled her against his warm, damp body. "Forget about business," he murmured, his breath whispering over her sensitive ear. "I'd say you have my attention right now."

Donovan's Bed

Debra Mullins

AVON BOOKS ◆ NEW YORK

This is a work of fiction. Names, characters, places, and incidents either are the product of the author's imagination or are used fictitiously. Any resemblance to actual events, locales, organizations, or persons, living or dead, is entirely coincidental and beyond the intent of either the author or the publisher.

AVON BOOKS, INC.
An Imprint of HarperCollins*Publishers*
10 East 53rd Street
New York, New York 10022-5299

Copyright © 2000 by Debra Mullins Manning
Inside cover author photo by Studio 16 / Cristopher J. Happel
Published by arrangement with the author
Library of Congress Catalog Card Number: 99-95335
ISBN: 0-380-80774-2
www.harpercollins.com

First Avon Books Printing: February 2000

Printed in the U.S.A.

WCD   10   9   8   7   6   5   4   3   2   1

This book is dedicated to
Sandy Ferguson and her daughter, Sarah Ann,
the real life Sassy,
and to
Nikoo McGoldrick,
for that night in the bar,
and to Jake,
for all the research

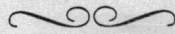

Chapter 1

Wyoming Territory
May 1882

Everyone watched the bed come through town.

The three old men sitting outside the saloon ceased their checker playing as it passed by in the back of Amos Carver's ancient buckboard.

"Would ya look at that," Mort rasped, pushing back his hat with gnarled fingers. "Big enough for a whole family."

"Or for one hot-blooded woman," Johnny said.

"Amen," Gabriel whispered.

The wagon continued down Main Street, sunlight gleaming along the bed's carved headboard. All activity in Burr came to a standstill, as if the entire town were bewitched by the fantastic sight.

1

Marianne Westerly, the preacher's daughter, gripped her mother's arm as they stepped out of Pearson's Mercantile. Her hushed comment carried the longing of a prayer. "Oh, Mama, look at the carvings."

Nearby, Ellie Pearson stopped sweeping the wooden walkway outside her husband's store to look with wondering eyes upon a bed splendid enough to birth a king. She caressed her ripening belly, where her unborn child slept. Her husband, Nate, stepped out beside her and slipped an arm around her shoulders. Resignation underscored his tender smile as he watched the unattainable pass him by.

The Tremont sisters even forgot their rumor swapping with the mayor's wife to stare in goggle-eyed amazement at the magnificent spectacle.

"Oh, my stars!" Emmaline Tremont exclaimed, then blushed when her sister elbowed her for staring.

From the window of the tiny newspaper office, Sarah Ann Calhoun also took note of the extraordinary bed. The morning sun imbued the walnut finish with warmth, as if the wood itself still lived. Old Amos Carver—spitting chaw and cursing at his mules from the driver's perch of his decrepit wagon—seemed an insult to the bed's majesty.

For a moment, half-forgotten dreams of white lace and baby cradles drifted through

Sarah's mind. Then she shook off the foolish notions. *It's just a bed*, she reminded herself. Just another of Jack Donovan's pretentious acquisitions. It meant nothing to her.

Nothing but an opportunity.

With a grin, she reached for her pad. Her duty as editor of the *Burr Chronicle* lay in reporting anything that might interest the town. And the town was very interested in Jack Donovan.

He had arrived in Burr almost a year ago and deposited a scandalous amount of money into the bank. Then he bought some fine grazing land and built up a ranch, filling his beautiful house with wonderful furnishings from back east. Rumors abounded about the source of his wealth. Some said he had discovered gold. Others said he was a notorious outlaw who had retired to enjoy his ill-gotten gains. But since he came to church every Sunday and never had more than one drink at the saloon, the matrons of Burr chose to overlook his mysterious origins. In fact, many a young lady had set her cap for Jack Donovan.

But not Sarah.

She stepped outside the newspaper office, resolved to put an end to the speculation once and for all. Jack Donovan and his mysterious past would evade her no longer. There was something about him, a dangerous edge, that told her that he wasn't exactly the law-abiding citizen he appeared to be. Once she discovered his secrets, she would finally make her father's dream come true: the *Burr Chronicle* would become one of the biggest newspapers in Wyoming Territory.

And her own demons would be silenced forever.

She watched Amos and his wagon disappear over the rise. Around her, the town began to bustle once more. Conversations picked up where they'd left off. Horses whinnied, leather creaked, and wheels rumbled over hardpacked dirt. Down at the church, a group of men resumed hammering the dance floor they were building for the spring social on Saturday night.

Sarah's shoes beat purposefully down the wooden boards as she went to fetch her horse. The time had come for Mr. Donovan's reckoning. She would have the answers to her questions this time, and she would use that bed to get them.

"There she goes," Johnny said, lifting his gaze from the checkerboard as Sarah strode past them toward the livery stable.

"Goin' after Donovan again." Gabriel spat into the spittoon beside his chair, then leisurely jumped one of Johnny's checkers and scooped it from the board.

"I never saw a woman more determined to

run a man to ground," Mort commented.

"You remember the time she followed him down to the creek, and there he was, as nekkid as the day he was born?" Johnny hooted. "I never saw a woman so churned up."

"And her stormin' through town afterwards, soakin' wet from head to toe. Tongues were flappin' that day for sure," Gabriel said with a grin. Johnny's double jump made the grin fade and he scowled at the checkerboard. "Makes a body wonder how she got herself so wet," he said absently.

"What about the time he was working in his barn and she cornered him in the hayloft?" Mort leaned back in his chair in preparation for a nap. "The boys who work for Donovan said she come runnin' out of that barn like a cat with its tail on fire. And with straw in her hair, too. Musta looked awful funny, 'specially with it bein' the middle of winter and all."

"What about the time she found him in the barbershop?" Johnny asked. "How do you figure she got shaving cream all over her like that, anyway?"

"Heaven only knows," Gabriel answered, snaring another of Johnny's pieces.

They settled into silence, the occasional clack of captured checkers blending with the rowdy music and whooping laughter coming from the saloon behind them.

Then Sarah came galloping past, and the

three men paused and gazed after her until she disappeared over the hill.

"So," Gabriel said, turning back to the checkerboard. He scowled as Johnny made his next move. "You figure on a June wedding?"

Mort slid his hat low and closed his eyes for the intended nap. "Yep."

"King me," Johnny said with a smug smile.

When Sarah caught up with Amos's wagon, he neither slowed nor looked back to see who followed him, though he gripped the stock of his shotgun with one hand. Sarah moved alongside the wagon, her bay keeping pace with Amos's mule, Gertrude.

"Morning, Amos," she said with a cheery smile.

"Mornin'." His gaze never wavered from the road.

"I see you got yourself a job."

"Yep." Amos turned his head and shot a wad of brown spittle sailing into the dust. He wiped his mouth with the back of his hand and tugged his worn hat down over flyaway gray hair.

Sarah waited, but the old prospector said nothing more. "You're working for Mr. Donovan?" she asked.

"Yep."

She rolled her eyes. She'd get more information out of Gertrude!

He swung his head around and looked at her. "Told me this would happen," he grumbled.

"What? Who told you what would happen?"

"Donovan." He spat another wad of tobacco juice into the waving grass beside the road. "Told me you'd be along."

"Did he?" Sarah's eyes narrowed. "What else did he say?"

"Told me not to say a word if any busybody, newspaper-writin' shrew started askin' questions."

With each word, her spine grew stiffer. "Did he indeed?" she asked through clenched teeth.

Amos chuckled, tobacco juice dribbling into his unkempt gray beard. "Yep. He's payin' me four bits to haul this here bed out to the ranch. He ain't payin' me nothin' to answer a lot of fool questions."

"I see." Gripping the reins with one white-knuckled hand, Sarah reached for her reticule. "Well, I'll pay you two bits to answer questions."

Amos scowled.

"Think, Amos." Sarah shook her purse. The jingle of coins brought a speculative gleam to the old man's eyes. "I'll pay you to talk to me. Just like a job."

"Humph." He squinted at her purse, then shook his head. "I'm not losin' four bits just 'cause you're nosy. If ya got questions, ya gotta talk to Donovan."

"As if I haven't tried," Sarah muttered. Jack Donovan had managed to elude her inquiries for five long months. "All right, have it your way. But I'm riding with you to the Donovan spread."

"Suit yourself," he said with a shrug.

When Amos turned his attention back to the road, Sarah's gaze slid to the bed.

Up close it was even more spectacular. Her imagination provided a clear picture of how it would look with a fancy coverlet spread across the mattress. She leaned closer to examine one of the bedposts. Cherubs carved from walnut clutched garlands of lifelike flowers that twined around the post. She imagined waking to a servant bearing hot coffee and biscuits. Slowly the servant's nebulous features gave way to a lean-boned face with a pair of wicked, dark eyes . . .

Startled, Sarah pushed the picture from her mind. Jack Donovan had no business slipping so intimately into her private thoughts—her interest in him was purely professional.

And the sooner she got her questions answered, the sooner she could forget about Jack Donovan.

"What do you mean, he's not here?" Sarah demanded, frustration roiling within her.

Standing on the front porch of Donovan's sprawling white ranch house, Matt Gomez, the foreman, gave her an apologetic smile. Men swarmed around them, unloading the pieces of the bed. As they traipsed up and down the stairs, she noticed more than one stifled grin, and Matt himself had a twinkle of humor in his brown eyes.

"I'm sorry you rode out here for nothin', Miss Calhoun. Heck, if Donovan had known you were comin' I'm sure he woulda put off his trip to Laramie."

"Oh, I'm sure." Her sarcasm wiped the good humor from the foreman's expression. "No doubt he heard I was coming and took off, the sneaky poltroon!"

"Sneaky what?" Matt thumbed back his hat. "Now, Miss Calhoun, there's no need for name callin' here. And just what the heck is a pol-troon, anyway?"

"A coward, Mr. Gomez." She smiled when he stiffened. "What else would you call a man who runs from a woman?"

"Smart," Amos snickered, helping one of the hands with the headboard. Masculine chuckles echoed his words.

"Donovan ain't a man to run from nothin'," Matt said, clearly offended.

"Well, apparently, Mr. Gomez, he is running from me."

The men grew very quiet. Sarah smiled triumphantly, certain she had the upper hand. Why, they even looked a little afraid of her.

"Good afternoon, Miss Calhoun."

Her stomach erupted into nervous flurries as she slowly turned. Jack Donovan stood a few feet behind her, legs spread, his saddlebags slung over his shoulder. His dark pants were covered in trail dust, as was his white shirt and black leather vest. While not the tallest man there, he still topped Sarah by several inches. He wasn't as broad in the shoulders as some of the other men, or as big in the chest or as beefy in the arms. His build was one of lean, whipcord strength that gave the impression of speed and agility. But then, he didn't need bulk to intimidate people. Most folks took one look at his black-as-hell gaze and cleared a path.

At the moment he wore his hat low over his eyes, but Sarah had only to glance at the firm set of his jaw to know that he was annoyed.

Then again, he was always annoyed with her.

"I didn't know you were back, Donovan," Matt said.

"Well, I am. Don't you men have work to do?" He jerked his head toward the wagon. The ranch hands leaped into action, moving the furniture with none of the easy banter of before.

"Well, Mr. Donovan, trust you to spoil a good time." Sarah glanced at the silent, bustling men, then turned back to Donovan. Propping her hands on her hips, she asked, "Are you going to talk to me today, or are you going to hide until I'm gone?"

He stared at her for a long moment, and Sarah found herself wishing she could see past his hat brim to his eyes. Then he strode past her and up the steps, where he shrugged off his saddlebags and dropped them on the porch.

"Mr. Donovan, I'm talking to you."

"I hear you, Miss Calhoun." He removed his hat and slapped it against his thigh to get rid of the dust, then pinned her with a heated look. Her pulse skipped. But it must be irritation that had put that smolder in his eyes, not some other emotion.

"Come inside if you want to talk," he said, baring his teeth in a smile that made the dimple crease his left cheek, yet gave her the impression of a wolf about to pounce. "Unless you're nervous about being alone with me."

"Certainly not." She took a deep breath to fortify herself, then walked up the steps and into the wolf's lair.

He followed her inside. She could smell him, a distinctively masculine scent intermingled with that of horses and sweat and leather. He stayed close behind her, and everything female in her responded to the threat of his proximity, as if he were a predator and she, his prey. She could almost feel the heat of his body against her back, and her flesh prickled with awareness. Should he decide to pounce . . .

Ruthlessly, she repressed the shameful emotions. She was here to work, not to conjure improper fantasies about Jack Donovan.

She took a moment to calm herself by admiring a set of silver candlestick holders, and Donovan ignored her while he hung his hat on the wall. Then he grabbed her arm and pulled her toward the kitchen.

"Come on," he ordered.

"Mr. Donovan!" She tugged at her arm, but he didn't let go until they reached the kitchen water pump. Then he simply released her and turned his back on her. "Mr. Donovan," she said again. "You . . . what are you doing?"

Donovan draped his vest over the back of a chair and started to unbutton his shirt. "I'm washing up, Miss Calhoun. And if you want to talk to me, you have about five minutes to do it."

"But you . . . you're . . . Mr. Donovan, I must insist that you put your clothes back on right now!"

He arched his brows at her and stripped off his shirt. "I didn't realize you were so shy. Not after that day you followed me to the creek."

"And you pulled me in!"

The wretched man actually smiled. "It seemed to be the best way to get rid of you."

He hooked the shirt over a chair and turned to the pump. Giving the handle a couple of strong plunges, he bent over and stuck his head beneath the spurting water.

Sarah stared at his muscled back, the smooth expanse mottled by a scar or two that hinted at hard living. Her gaze slid to his tight backside straining against the seat of his pants, and back up to his sinewy arms. She swallowed hard. The scandalous cravings she had fought to suppress surged to life again. Damn him.

He stood up, raking back his wet hair with both hands. With the inky locks slicked back like that, the angular planes of his cheekbones seemed more pronounced, and his eyelashes looked ridiculously long, almost like a child's. But it was no child that studied her with that hungry obsidian gaze—it was a man who had seen too much and felt too deeply. There was danger there, but vulnerability, too. And that paradox was why she couldn't seem to stay away from Jack Donovan.

That, and her own prurient impulses.

"Like what you see?" he asked with a knowing smile that made her breath catch and her heart pound. Oh, he was dangerous. And oh, how tempted she was. But she had sworn long ago to control her disgraceful, passionate nature, and no brazen rogue with secrets in his fathomless eyes was going to change that.

"Mr. Donovan, I am trying to conduct business," she said primly. A drop of water dripped from his hair to his shoulder and wound its way down his lightly furred chest. When she realized that she was staring, she jerked her gaze up to his. "Business," she repeated. "About the bed . . ."

"Want to try it out?"

Her mouth fell open. "I . . . are you out of your mind?"

"Nope." He gave her a wicked grin. The boyish dimple in his cheek contrasted sharply with the very adult twist of his lips.

"Mr. Donovan, you are becoming distracted from the issue," she forged on, smoothing her skirts with shaking hands. What would it be like to smooth that firm, bare flesh? She squelched the wanton thought. "If I could just have your attention for a few minutes—"

He grabbed her wrist and tugged. Sarah yelped as she stumbled forward, grabbing at his muscular arms, but he caught her with his hands on her ribs, his thumbs just beneath her breasts. Before she could blink, he pulled her close against his warm, damp body and dipped his head close to her ear.

"Forget about business," he murmured, his breath whispering over her sensitive flesh. She shivered despite herself.

"Mr. Donovan." It was getting difficult to think clearly, to breathe properly. "If I could just have your attention . . ."

"I'd say you have it." He smoothed a hand over her hip, then patted her bottom. "Let's go to bed."

"No!" Ignoring her sizzling nerve endings, she shoved him in the chest with both hands. He let her go. "Jack Donovan, you are contemptible!"

"And you, Sarah Calhoun, are wet."

Sarah looked down at the front of her blouse. Her eyes widened in horror as she realized that the thin white lawn was almost transparent now. Her nipples stood proudly and unmistakably erect. She quickly crossed her arms over her breasts.

He laughed. She scowled at him, then grabbed his leather vest off the chair and shrugged into it.

"I'll get to the bottom of all your secrets, Jack Donovan," she warned. Cheeks flushed but head held high, she turned and stalked from the kitchen.

Donovan watched her go. His gaze followed the honey-blond braid trailing down her back, and came to rest with masculine appreciation on her trim backside as she stomped from the room. The woman might be a pest, but she had curves in all the right places.

He shook his head. The attraction between them burned fierce and hot whenever they met, and doing outrageous things to her was the only way he could think of to keep her at a distance. Despite her high-necked collars and arrow-straight spine, or maybe because of them, he always felt the urge to lay her down on the nearest flat surface and satisfy the hunger that gnawed at him every time she came near him.

Maybe it was the way she pursed those kissable lips in disapproval, or the way her eyes got so big and round when she was shocked. And he sure as hell liked that pink flush that spread from her cheeks down her neck when she was flustered. One of these days he'd follow that blush to see just how far it went. He wanted to unbutton that starched blouse, unfasten the serviceable, drab-colored skirts, and loosen her braid while he made her ache for him the way he did for her. He'd never wanted a woman so badly in his life.

But he couldn't have her.

Sarah was too caught up in the *Burr Chronicle* to make room for hearth and home. Now that the ranch was in working order, it was time he found himself a wife. But he needed a woman who would be content to cook and keep house and raise children. He knew instinctively that Sarah would be a wildcat in bed, and he certainly enjoyed getting both her temper and her body all fired up, but he had no desire to compete with the newspaper for her attention. Besides, the woman was too darned smart. She'd figure him out in a heartbeat, and that was the last thing he wanted. Not to mention that a newspaperwoman would always be shoving her nose in other people's business and bringing attention to herself—and him. Close scrutiny was something he could not afford to risk.

Nope—the one woman he'd never marry was Sarah Calhoun.

Chapter 2

On Saturday the town of Burr buzzed with anticipation over the coming festivities. Wyoming Territory had suffered a hard winter, and the advent of spring lightened everyone's heart, even though the weather was still seasonally cool. The dance was a way to celebrate.

Sarah stood in her room, listening to the enthusiastic shouts that drifted to her. Since the Calhoun house stood back to back with the newspaper office, sound carried easily from Main Street. Excitement crackled around Burr like a blanket of lightning.

Sarah spread her brown poplin dress on the bed. She, too, was looking forward to the event. She intended to corner Jack Donovan and try again to discover what secret lurked in his shady past. Her intuition told her it was something big, a story that would elevate the

Burr Chronicle from a tiny weekly newspaper to one that would circulate across the territory.

For a moment she reveled in her daydream. Her task promised to be difficult, since the man was simply impossible. Every time she had tried to get him to talk to her, he did something to prick her temper. In the barn, he'd tossed a forkful of hay at her, and at the barbershop, he'd smeared shaving cream all over her. Other occasions over the past several months made her burn just to think about them. Obtaining answers would require both fortitude and persistence, and she had to keep him from goading her. Gladly, she accepted the challenge.

A soft knock sounded at her door.

"Come in."

The door swung open, and her mother peeked in.

"Oh, good, you're not dressed yet." With a flourish, June Calhoun bustled through the doorway. "Look at this. Isn't it lovely?"

Sarah stared as her mother held up a beautiful, sky-blue satin gown. Ecru lace edged a squared neckline that dipped lower than any dress Sarah owned. The same lace rimmed the hem and sleeves, occasionally graced by tiny blue bows. It was a fabulous creation, designed for evening wear.

"That's Susannah's gown," she murmured in recognition. "It'll never fit."

Her mother beamed. "I altered it for you,"

she said, holding it up against Sarah. "You'll look stunning!"

Her mother's blue eyes sparkled with a pride Sarah hesitated to extinguish. After the death of her husband, June Calhoun had started taking in sewing to try and make ends meet. In the past three years she had gone from simple mending and tailoring to designing many of the gowns worn by the women of Burr. The satisfaction her work brought had helped deal with the grief of losing her husband.

Sarah fingered a bit of lace wistfully. "You did a fine job, Mama."

"I wanted you to have something to wear besides that plain poplin of yours."

Sarah glanced from the dress on the bed to the one in her mother's arms. "I think I should wear the poplin," she said gently. "It's not as conspicuous. After all, I'm going for the sake of the paper . . ."

"Nonsense!" Her mother spread Susannah's dress on the bed beside the sturdy poplin. Tucking back a graying strand of dark blond hair, she considered the two garments. Even Sarah had to admit that the fancy gown stood out like a peacock next to a broody hen. "There's no reason you shouldn't have hopes and dreams just like every other young lady your age," her mother said.

Old memories rose to taunt Sarah, reminding her of everything she could not have. "There's a very good reason," she replied with a hint of bitterness. "Luke Petrie, remember?"

"Him?" A wave of her hand dismissed Sarah's comment. "That was years ago."

"People in this town have long memories. If I arrive at the dance all decked out in silk and lace, everyone will be talking for weeks." Sarah took her mother's hand. "Mama, I'm not Susannah. She could have carried this off."

"She certainly could. Your sister never let idle tongues bother her." Smiling, June pulled her hand from Sarah's and took up the brown poplin. "I'll just put this away."

"Mama ..." Sarah's protest fell on deaf ears as her mother marched out of the room in possession of her best dress.

Despite her mother's determination to find her a husband, Sarah had long ago accepted that no man would have her. Not after the indiscretion three years before, which had caused her father's death.

Since then she had become the most respectable of citizens, dressing in somber colors, never showing a hint of bosom or a flash of ankle. She had dedicated herself to McHenry Calhoun's small newspaper, vowing to make it the best in the territory. And she'd never shown any interest in a man, which would have given rise to gossip. After a while, she'd come to the conclusion that she had no need of a man in her life at all.

Her tactics had worked. The scandal had finally died down. Despite the lingering blot on her name, the women of Burr no longer crossed the street when she passed. Male and female alike afforded her the respect due a businesswoman. But appearing at a social event in such a daring gown would no doubt fire the rumors all over again.

Bitterness pricked at her heart. How she wished she didn't care what people thought. Mama was right: Susannah certainly didn't.

With a long sigh, Sarah sat on the bed and thought of her vivacious older sister. Suzie's dramatic beauty had made the young men of Burr fall all over themselves in pursuit of her. She had left behind a trail of broken hearts the day she'd departed to follow her dream of a singing career in San Francisco.

But broken hearts were quite different from broken lives.

Sarah smoothed her hand over the azure satin. Not only had her mother worked hard to alter this gown, she had also quite annoyingly appropriated the only other suitable dress for the dance. Yielding to the inevitable, Sarah stood and began to undo the buttons of her sturdy calico.

So people would talk. Just as long as one of them was Jack Donovan.

*   *   *

Music and laughter rang out through the night, accompanied by the thud of feet on the wooden dance floor. Lamplight flickered over flushed and smiling faces as couples whirled around to a lively reel played by Mort on his squeezebox, Johnny on his banjo, and Gabriel on his harmonica.

Donovan stood on the sidelines. Dressed in black except for his silver embroidered waistcoat and white shirt, he felt as out of place as a gambler at a prayer meeting.

Wanting to fit in, he began moving through the crowd, exchanging greetings with everyone while managing to remain solitary at the same time. He sized up the unmarried ladies of the town, waiting for some jolt, some gut instinct that would tell him he'd found the right one. But despite all the flirtatious smiles and sidelong glances from the females surrounding him, not one of them set off that spark that told him she was the one.

He made the rounds twice and ended up back on the sidelines, discouragement seeping through his confidence. He ran a finger along his tight collar. The way some of the girls' mamas were looking at him was downright predatory. He was more comfortable out on the trail, alone with his thoughts, than here in "civilization."

"Look at her." The malicious whisper caught his attention. He watched Emmaline Tremont, one of the two young women standing in front of him, duck her head close to her sister's ear. "How can she appear like that in public?"

"Flaunting herself," Juliana Tremont responded with smug derision. "I told you she had the heart of a harlot."

"I knew she hadn't changed," Emmaline hissed. "Not after what she did . . ."

Donovan frowned as the two kept at their scornful muttering. Even though the Tremont sisters were the biggest gossips in town, he had considered Juliana, the younger sister, a candidate for the position of his wife. Now he crossed her off his list. No wife of his would take pleasure in another's misfortune.

Emmaline gave her sister a knowing look. "Those Calhoun girls are nothing but trouble."

Calhoun. Donovan flinched as if a snake had bitten him. They couldn't be talking about Sarah, could they? Miss I-Don't-Need-a-Man-the-Newspaper-is-My-Reason-for-Living Calhoun? Miss Buttoned-Up-to-the-Neck-Not-a-Hair-Out-of-Place Sarah Calhoun? No, he must have mistaken the name.

"How could June let her come out like that?" Juliana sniffed.

"Every man here will be wanting to follow her home," Emmaline warned sagely.

Curious, Donovan moved to see past the two sisters. Gone was the prim and proper newspaper editor, and in her place stood a vision of golden seduction. The blue dress Sarah wore defined her womanly shape in a way no man could fail to notice. The low-cut bodice showcased her full breasts and a waist that appeared no wider than the span of his hands. He'd always thought she was fine-looking, but tonight her beauty stunned him. Add guts and brains to that lovely package, and here was a *real* woman.

Something primitive uncurled inside him, making his muscles tighten and his loins stir in hunger. *She was the one.*

No! He jerked his thoughts from that track. The last person he should be considering for a wife was nosy Sarah Calhoun. *Smart* Sarah Calhoun. No way, no how, could he ever consider her for a bride—no matter how tempting she looked in that dress.

The Tremont sisters continued to malign Sarah, each insult throwing another log on the fire of their malice. His protective instincts warred with his survival instincts as he resisted the urge to defend Sarah. But it was the word "whore" that finally decided the matter. Survival be damned. He could handle the sassy Miss Calhoun, but he couldn't stand by and listen to her be called names that she sure as hell hadn't earned, even though he'd given her ample opportunity. Donovan cleared his throat, and the two women turned to face him.

"Good heavens!" Flirting for all she was worth, Juliana patted her dark hair and smoothed her hands over her skirts. "Mr. Donovan, you gave me such a fright! I surely didn't hear you come up behind me."

"Sorry, Miss Juliana." He noticed for the first time the lines that bracketed her mouth. While he had known she was past the first bloom of youth, he had not realized that the harsher planes of her face came from her spiteful character.

Emmaline asked, "Have you just arrived, Mr. Donovan?"

"Nope. I've been here a while now." Donovan watched with satisfaction as Emmaline's pleased expression faded.

"Really?" Juliana cast a nervous glance at her sister.

Donovan bared his teeth in a smile. "Yes, I've been standing right here, staring at the most beautiful woman in town."

Juliana blushed. "Why, Mr. Donovan . . . !"

"I guess I'll have to get up the gumption to go talk to her. Pardon me, ladies." With a polite nod, he pushed past the Tremont sisters. Their indignant gasps added to his amusement as he skirted the edge of the dance floor and went to stand before Sarah.

Her blond hair was swept atop her head, leaving wispy ringlets to brush over her ears and neck. In the lamplight, her skin looked like fine porcelain.

She looked up at him with eyes the same shade as a Montana sky. For a moment he couldn't look away. Something, a challenge met and answered, compelled him to stay when he should have walked away. A becoming blush crept into her cheeks as his gaze slid approvingly over her, from top to toes and back again.

"Well, Miss Calhoun," he said. "You wanted my attention. Looks like you've got it."

Sarah's skin rippled with gooseflesh beneath that dark, compelling stare. "I seem to have everyone's attention," she replied. "Have you come to confirm the rumors?"

He didn't answer, just held out a hand. "Dance with me."

She hesitated, conscious of the whispers and knowing looks that surrounded them. She looked from his extended hand to his face, wondering if she dared give in to temptation and dance with the devil.

She wanted to dismiss Donovan as just an ornery man who thrived on annoying her, but tonight, she couldn't help noticing how different he was from every other man in Burr. In his black coat and tie and silver embroidered waistcoat, he was dashing enough to make any woman's heart beat faster. His face had too much character to be called handsome and too many sharp edges to fit the definition of conventional good looks. But Donovan was hardly conventional.

Still, he had tried to blend in by at least appearing the gentleman. His overlong black hair normally had an unruly curl to it, but tonight he had tamed it by slicking it back. As he smiled, a dimple appeared in his left cheek.

All in all, he looked very civilized for a wolf mingling with a bunch of sheep.

"The longer you wait, the more they'll talk," he said as she continued to waver. "Are you afraid?"

"Certainly not!"

His lips parted in a wicked smile that weakened her knees and enticed her to explore the forbidden. "Then we dance."

He pulled her into his arms before she could protest. Mere inches separated them, and she could swear she felt the heat of his body envelop her. The aura of danger that surrounded him both attracted and frightened her, and the surety with which he held her made her feel both safe and captured. She closed her eyes, her body warming and responding in a way she hadn't felt in a long, long time.

"For a woman who's been trying to get me alone for almost a year, you sure don't talk too much."

Her eyes popped open, and her annoyed gaze jerked up to his. "What a ridiculous thing to say. You know good and well I only want to interview you for the *Chronicle*."

"I do?" His lazy tone could not disguise the insinuation behind the words.

"Mr. Donovan, you have a way of making an innocent situation sound perfectly indecent."

He shrugged, apparently unfazed by her displeasure. "What else is a man supposed to think when a woman chases him like a hound after fresh meat?"

Her cheeks heated. "You, sir, are not a nice man."

"True enough." He dipped his head close to her ear and whispered, "But you seem to be the only one who knows it."

His breath caressed her neck, prickling her flesh with awareness. She moved her head, and he straightened. The look in his dark eyes was edgy and predatory. There was quiet power seething beneath his deceptively harmless veneer, but his hold on her remained gentle.

Like recognized like, she thought suddenly. As someone who fought hard to suppress her own darker impulses, she could hardly overlook the same in another.

"People are curious about you," she said, trying to get the conversation back on track.

"Good. Let them stay that way."

She blinked at his brusqueness, but forged

ahead. "I mean, look at you. You dress like a gambler—"

"I've done some."

"Oh, really?" But not professionally, she thought. He wasn't glib enough, not smooth enough, and certainly not polished enough. He lacked the easy sophistication of a man used to blending into social situations—a skill a gambler would have developed out of necessity.

She could imagine Jack Donovan as a lawman, a miner, or even an outlaw. He had an element of danger, a sense of self-containment, found with that sort of solitary occupation, but there was no way he had ever been a gambler.

Which left the question of where his wealth had come from.

At her speculative glance, he laughed. "Miss Calhoun, you're like a tick under my skin about my past."

"Human nature, Mr. Donovan. When a man like you comes to town, flaunting money the way you have, people are bound to talk."

"Flaunting money? And what do you mean, a man like me?" The cool, self-possessed Donovan actually seemed disconcerted.

"You're an eligible, wealthy bachelor whose existence seems to have begun the day you came to Burr. You spend money like it's water, but no one knows anything about you. Of course you're bound to attract attention."

"A man's past is his own business, Miss Calhoun. That's an unwritten law." Warning underscored his tone as he growled, "But I'm not a wanted man, so the good people of Burr needn't worry about being murdered in their beds."

"Who said anything about murder?" She held his gaze, eyebrows raised in challenge.

He didn't look away. "I won't discuss my past. Ask me about something else."

"It's my business to uncover secrets, Mr. Donovan."

"Take it or leave it."

She deliberated a moment, torn between pressing for more or settling for what he was willing to offer. "Very well, I'll take it. For now. Would you be willing to discuss your ranch?"

"Sure thing." Pride lit his face. "I just bought some stock. In a few weeks the Triple D will be up and running."

She nodded with polite interest. "The outbuildings are quite impressive, but I'm really interested in the fancy furniture you bought. Take the bed, for instance. Most of the men I've known would be content sleeping in a bunk or a bedroll."

He stared at her with masculine interest, smiling when a flush heated her cheeks. "So, Miss Calhoun, you've been thinking about my bed."

Her blush deepened, and she grew annoyed with herself. "It just doesn't seem like the kind of thing a man would buy for himself."

"You're right. I didn't buy it for myself. I bought it for my wife."

She stumbled, and his strong arms immediately tightened. "Your what?"

"My wife. I mean to find one here."

"Oh." She didn't like the sprig of hope that grew in her breast. "And have you found one yet?"

"No. But I have a list of three or four names to choose from."

"A list?" she choked. "Like a list of supplies you buy at the mercantile?" Good heavens, the man had spent a fortune building the house of any woman's dreams and furnishing it as extravagantly as any Boston manor. The bed alone must have set him back quite a bit of money, yet he didn't seem to care which wife would soon reside in it!

"I'm looking for certain qualities in a woman," he continued, oblivious to her growing ire. "I made a list of some of the unmarried ladies hereabouts who might have them."

"And what are these *qualities*?" She could barely maintain a civil tone.

"Well, my wife has to be a hard worker, used to ranch life. She'll take care of my house and trust me to provide for her. And she has to like children. I aim to have a lot of them."

"So what you're saying is that she needs sta-

mina, obedience, and good breeding poten-
tial."

"That's right." He smiled.

"Mr. Donovan, you might as well just go buy
yourself a horse!"

The smile disappeared. "Now just a minute
here—"

"You can't shop for a wife the way you
would a brood mare! A woman needs to be
loved, to feel important in a man's life. To
be his partner. You can't marry someone just
because you think she'll be easy to break to the
saddle!" Furious now, she jerked out of his
arms. "I can't stomach your company another
minute."

Strong fingers closed on her arm before she
could take a step. "You walk away from me
now, you'll just start up all that talk you're trying to avoid," he warned. "You want a piece
of me? Let's take it someplace private."

She stared at him, battling the urge to stomp
off, consequences be damned. "What do you
mean, private?"

He pulled her back into his arms and began
dancing her toward the edge of the crowd.
"Don't worry about your virtue, Miss Calhoun.
We'll stay within screaming distance." He
grinned, and she wanted to smack that dimple
right off his cheek.

He swept her to the edge of the platform and
then gallantly took her hand to help her down

the steps. Given his strong grip on her fingers, Sarah wondered if he was holding her prisoner.

Only a few heads turned their way as he escorted her with a firm hand on her elbow toward the church a few yards back. She knew she would have attracted much more attention had she given in to impulse and stormed off the dance floor, and was grudgingly grateful that he'd rescued her from her own impetuous nature.

Donovan led her around the side of the building, away from prying eyes but close enough to be heard should she call for help. Then he released his grip on her elbow, crossed his arms, and looked down at her.

They were alone. Above them stars glittered like diamonds against a sky of dark blue velvet, and insects chirped mating songs far prettier than the music they had left behind. Donovan stood with his back to the moon, his face cast in shadow, his masculine stance making Sarah restlessly aware of her own smaller feminine stature.

"Now, what was that you were saying, about me not knowing a woman from a horse?"

His voice rippled over her, soft, dangerous. For a moment she couldn't think for the fluttering in her belly. "That's not what I meant," she whispered finally.

"I know what you meant." He reached for

her. She tensed, but all he did was slide his hands down her bare arms. His callused thumbs rasped over the vulnerable flesh of her inner elbows, the sensitive palms of her hands. The pure sensuality of the gesture sent heat spiraling through her, making her tremble in a response she couldn't deny.

His fingers tightened over hers as he sensed her reaction. He took a step closer, slowly raising his hand to her chin. Her breath caught. She thought he would kiss her—finally, after all these months—but he only stroked the backs of his fingers over her throat.

"A woman," he said with slow deliberation, "has soft skin. Silky hair." He tugged gently at a wispy curl, his knuckles brushing her ear. "And a sweet mouth, meant for kissing. I don't ever recall wanting to kiss my horse."

"I should hope not." Her words were barely audible. Where had her anger gone? she wondered. He touched her with the skill of a man who knew women well, yet the knowledge excited instead of repulsed her.

"Now you ..." He stroked his thumb along her lower lip. "You, Miss Sarah Calhoun, are a different kettle of fish altogether. I've been thinking entirely too much about that sassy mouth of yours."

"You have?" She couldn't think, couldn't breathe. Her body hummed with readiness, poised for whatever he asked of her.

"Yeah." He cupped her face in his hands, spearing his fingers into her hair. A long blond coil dropped over her shoulder as he dislodged her hairpins. "Sweet Lord, what a sassy mouth."

"I've thought about you, too," she admitted in a shy whisper. Slowly she raised her hands to his lean waist, exploring the taut muscles.

"I shouldn't be doing this."

"I shouldn't either . . ." The words dissolved against his mouth.

She'd been kissed before, but never like this. His lips were soft, his touch gentle. His tenderness aroused her faster than hot passion would have done. She pressed closer to him, molded her mouth more precisely over his, shivering with delicious excitement as he held her face in his hands and savored her.

"God." He broke the kiss, but barely, his mouth hovering within an inch of hers. "I had to know how you would taste."

She smiled, her gaze drifting to his mouth. "Really?"

"Hell, yeah." He nuzzled her cheek with his lips. "But we have to stop. I have to think about finding a wife, much as I'd like a tumble with you."

She stiffened as his words cut through the desire that tangled her thoughts. For a moment she had actually thought—"*What* did you say?"

"I said I'd sure enjoy a little slap and tickle with you, sassy girl, but my future wife might not like it."

"You low-down skunk!" Stung to her feminine core, she jerked away from him. "So I'm good enough for a romp in the hay, but not good enough to be on that list of yours? Have you been listening to the gossips, Mr. Donovan?"

"I don't care about gossip." He moved to brush a strand of hair out of her face, but Sarah turned from his touch.

"Then why do you consider me good enough to bed, but not for your precious list?" Passion flared into anger, all the better to dull the pain in her heart. "I work hard at my newspaper, and I love children."

He leaned close. "You know good and well why you're not on the list, Sassy."

"My name is Sarah."

"Sassy suits you better. Truth is, you're prettier than an Arizona sunset, but you're too ornery for your own good, and you love that damned paper more than you'll ever love a man. I need a woman who puts me before anything else. Your husband would have to lie down on the printing press just to get your attention!"

She slapped him. Stunned at her own action, she could only stare as he raised a hand to rub his cheek.

"See what I mean?" He smiled, but the derision in his expression seemed directed more toward himself than her. "We mix like fire and oil, sassy girl. That kind of explosion makes for hot loving, but it doesn't fit into a marriage."

What a fool! "Good evening, Mr. Donovan. I hope you find what you're looking for—though I can't help but pity her." Without waiting for a response, Sarah left him standing there in the dark.

Chapter 3

∞

Monday morning, Sarah set the type for the article herself. As each piece clicked into place, a smile of pure satisfaction tugged at her mouth. This story ought to see that Jack Donovan got just what he *thought* he wanted, and exactly what he deserved.

Wealthy Bachelor Seeks Wife

Jack Donovan, Burr's most eligible bachelor, has declared his intention of taking a bride. He has designed his beautiful home with the future Mrs. Donovan in mind, going so far as to purchase furniture from back east, including an ornate bed that any woman would covet. The bed dates back a hundred years and looks big enough to sleep a family of six, though Mr. Donovan's expressed desire for children may exceed that number. Carved into the rich walnut posts and headboard are cherubs and flowers of exquisite workmanship. The future Mrs. Donovan looks to be one lucky lady.

Mr. Donovan has indicated that his future wife must be a woman suited to the rigors of childbirth and ranching. The eager bridegroom can be reached at the Triple D ranch, just outside Burr, Wyoming Territory. Only qualified ladies need apply.

The *Burr Chronicle* hadn't been in Pearson's Mercantile even two hours before Millicent Castor paid a visit to the newspaper office. Sarah looked up as the door blew open, unsurprised at the identity of her visitor. "Good morning, Mrs. Castor."

"Good morning, Sarah." The mayor's plump wife struggled against the door a moment and heaved a sigh when it gave up the battle and clicked into the latch. Outside the wind howled in protest.

Sarah stood and came out from behind her desk. "What can I do for you today?"

"I came to put a notice in the *Chronicle* about the town council meeting next week."

"Certainly." Sarah handed her a notepad and pencil. "Just write down what you want it to say."

The mayor's wife started to write. After a moment she asked, "So, dear, how are you these days?"

"I'm fine, Mrs. Castor."

"Good, good." Still scribbling, Mrs. Casto.

glanced at Sarah from the corner of her eye. "And your mother?"

"She's well."

"That's fine, then." She finished the notice and handed the pad and pencil back to Sarah. "Do you hear from your sister?"

"She writes. Mama sends her the *Chronicle* regularly."

"Why, isn't that nice? Susannah can have a little bit of home come in the mail." Mrs. Castor smiled, revealing the dimples nearly hidden in her chubby cheeks. "You've done a good job with your newspaper, Sarah. I read it from first page to last, every issue."

Sarah paused in making notes about the typesetting of Mrs. Castor's announcement. Covertly she studied the woman, noting the sparkle in her brown eyes and the flush in her cheeks. Her bountiful bosom fairly quivered with excitement. Given that the mayor's wife was the biggest gossip in town, Sarah wondered what bit of hearsay had brought the portly woman to her doorstep.

"I'm glad you enjoy the *Chronicle*."

"Oh my, yes!" Mrs. Castor lowered her voice to a conspiratorial whisper, though no one else was present to overhear her. "I especially like the piece you did on Mr. Donovan. Such a handsome man. And so closemouthed about himself."

Sarah tensed at the mention of Jack Donovan. "Thank you."

"How ever did you get him to open up, dear?" Mrs. Castor paused expectantly, her brown eyes snapping with anticipation.

"Well, I—"

"You can tell me." The mayor's wife patted Sarah's hand. "I promise, I won't tell a soul."

"There's nothing to tell." Feeling as if she were caught in a mud slide, Sarah grasped for words that would not implicate her in unfounded rumor. "I simply asked him a few questions."

"I'm certain there's more to it than that. Won't you tell me which one of our girls that handsome man has his eye on?"

Stung that she was obviously not considered one of "our" girls, Sarah said tightly, "Everything I know about Mr. Donovan's marital plans is in the article."

"I don't believe that for a second, Sarah Ann Calhoun, and I am well and truly hurt that you won't confide in me. Me, who's known you since you were born!" With a sniff, Mrs. Castor wiped at an imaginary teardrop with her forefinger.

As Sarah started to protest, the door to the office slammed open and the Tremont sisters hurried inside in a whirl of windblown skirts and petticoats. Juliana brushed the dust from her dress, while Emmaline shoved the door shut.

"Good afternoon, Emmaline. Juliana." Mrs. Castor favored both women with a huge smile. "Fancy meeting you here."

"Hello, Mrs. Castor." Emmaline nodded her head at the mayor's wife and turned her attention to Sarah. "Good afternoon, Sarah. Juliana and I just stopped by to invite you to the sewing circle tomorrow."

Sarah eyed the sisters with caution. Juliana was an unpleasant woman Sarah's age who fancied herself a great beauty. Emmaline, five years older, prided herself on her arrow-straight posture and impeccable manners. The Tremonts had been Sarah's greatest detractors during the scandal, and Emmaline had been a longtime rival of her sister, Susannah. Given the facts, the timing of this invitation to the close-knit sewing circle seemed extremely suspicious.

Sarah realized that everyone awaited her answer. "Why thank you, Emmaline, but I really should work on the *Chronicle* tomorrow."

"Oh, come now, Sarah." Emmaline smiled, a mere straightening of her thin lips that narrowed her eyes. "We'll have tea, and Juliana is going to make her famous lemon cake. Isn't that so, sister?"

"Why, yes." Juliana gave Sarah a look that could have scorched her hair. "Please do come,

Sarah. We have so much to talk about."

"If you mean what I think, don't waste your breath." Mrs. Castor heaved a dramatic sigh. "Sarah is keeping all the details about Mr. Donovan's wedding plans to herself."

"Mrs. Castor, I told you—"

"How selfish of you, Sarah." Despite her smaller stature, Juliana somehow managed to look down her nose. "Of course, perhaps Sarah just wants Mr. Donovan for herself."

"Juliana!" Emmaline exclaimed, splaying her hand over her scrawny bosom.

"I only said what everyone else is thinking."

"That will be enough," Mrs. Castor announced. "Juliana, don't be ridiculous. Everyone knows that Mr. Donovan is interested in more than simple companionship."

"There are certain kinds of companionship that all men are interested in." Juliana wrinkled her nose and looked Sarah up and down; then her pointy features took on a sly cast. "I saw you go off with him Saturday night, Sarah. And then you came back with your hair all mussed. I suppose now we all know how you managed to describe his bed in such intricate detail."

"Everyone saw that bed when it came through town, Juliana," Sarah retorted. "I'm just more observant than most."

"I'd say you got a closer look than the rest of us." Juliana tucked a strand of dark hair back beneath her bonnet and gave Sarah a look of pure challenge. "As close as the mattress perhaps?"

Silence descended. Sarah glanced from the spiteful glee on Juliana's face to Mrs. Castor's look of breathless anticipation. Emmaline's eyes narrowed as they all awaited her response, surrounding her like crows picking over a carcass. She should have expected it after she let her anger get the best of her and wrote that article. She had learned the hard way not to let her emotions overrule her intellect, yet she had done just that. Her throat tightened as she realized that all her hard work to repair her reputation over the past three years had been for nothing. The slightest hint of a man in her life brought the whole scandal to life again.

"Nothing to say, Sarah?" Juliana taunted.

Sarah glared at the smaller woman. Though she felt like crying, she refused to let someone like Juliana Tremont belittle her.

"Your manners are deplorable, Juliana," she replied with a coldness that made the other woman gape. "Now, if you ladies will excuse me, I have work to do." She took up the notepad that held Mrs. Castor's announcement and dismissed the three by turning her back.

A stunned silence followed, tension thickening the air until Sarah could barely breathe. Tears stung her eyes, but she refused to give in to them. For three years she had allowed these women to dictate her way of life. She had played by their rules, never once straying from the path of respectability they set forth, and all to make up for a single error in judgment. Yet despite years of impeccable behavior on Sarah's part, they still turned on her at the first hint of impropriety.

No more.

The words seared her brain like a cattle brand. No more would she let others control her life. She reached for the tray of type, her movements pure reflex as she began to set the announcement for the mayor's wife.

"Sarah Ann Calhoun," Mrs. Castor finally said, her voice hoarse with shock. "I would not have believed such rudeness from you."

Emmaline chimed in. "I take back my invitation to the sewing circle, Sarah, unless you apologize to my sister at once."

"Yes, Sarah," Juliana put in. "Do apologize."

Sarah didn't look up from her task. Juliana Tremont was free to speak of beds and mattresses with impunity while she, Sarah, could not so much as wear the wrong dress without being censured. She was tired of paying for sins she had committed three years ago. She had a new life now, and a purpose. She needed to concentrate on that and let the rumors slip past her like dandelion seeds on the wind. She needed to stop caring so much what people said.

But it was easier said than done.

Sarah dared a quick glance behind her. Juliana's face was beet-red, but Sarah couldn't say whether it was from embarrassment or anger. Emmaline whispered in Juliana's ear while Mrs. Castor patted the younger woman's arm in sympathy.

"Come, sister," Emmaline finally said. "We're leaving." The swift tap of footsteps and the scrape of the door punctuated her words. After a moment the slower treads of Mrs. Castor followed. Sarah looked up in time to see the three of them pass her window, heads bowed as they whispered among themselves. With a sigh, she put down her work and covered her face with shaking hands. Already she could imagine the rumors blowing through town.

In refusing to apologize to Juliana Tremont, she had taken control of her life. She only hoped she would not regret it.

Late Thursday afternoon, Donovan rode into town, tired, dusty, and thirsty. As he passed the church, Mrs. Tillis stepped outside and rang the bell, dismissing the students from their makeshift classroom. Eight months big with child, the blacksmith's wife would obviously not be able to teach for much longer.

The clanging of the bell was drowned out by the excited shouts of the children as they flooded from the church. Shrieking and calling to one another, they raced in all directions, some in groups and some alone. Beneath him, Donovan felt the gelding tense. He pulled up on the reins and patted the horse's neck as a stampede of youngsters galloped past. The animal shuddered, tossing his head and snorting, but all four hooves remained on the ground. Compared with the adventurous ride into town, Donovan considered that a huge improvement.

Murmuring reassurances, he continued to stroke the bay's satiny neck. As the last of the children scurried past, the horse settled down, though his ears flicked back and forth as if on the alert for another onslaught. Donovan set him to an easy walk down Main Street.

It felt good to have his own mount again. His last horse, Seven, had been a bay, and the best damned horse he'd ever had. They'd been through a lot together. But Seven was gone now, the victim of a bullet from a madman's gun. So when Matt had told him about a homesteader who wanted to sell a spirited bay, he'd gone out to meet with him. And he'd come back with Senseless.

Senseless was exactly that. A beautiful animal, the gelding reminded him of Seven in a lot of ways, except that he was a lot more high-strung. The ride back had been an adventure, what with the darnedest things rattling the horse. But he was a fine animal for the most part, and Donovan was pleased with his purchase.

He had intended to hitch up outside the saloon, but one glance at the crowded hitching post changed his mind. He saw a good place a couple of doors down, just outside the mercantile and across the street from the newspaper building. As he dismounted and looped the reins around the post, he couldn't help but glance over at the office of the *Chronicle*. He wondered if Miss Sassy Calhoun was still put out with him. He grinned. That woman had a fire burning inside her. He just couldn't help stoking it now and again.

"Well, hello there, Mr. Donovan."

Senseless snorted and shifted at the unfamiliar voice. Donovan patted the bay reassuringly and turned to see the Turner twins, Minnie and Mabel, standing just outside the mercantile. As usual, they were dressed identically, today's ensemble consisting of blue sprigged muslin dresses with matching flower-decked bonnets. The pretty blonds were barely sixteen, but since they were the daughters of Ross Turner, one of the wealthier cattle ranchers, they already had a flock of suitors around them. Even so, Donovan hadn't bothered to add their names to his list. Out west many girls married at a young age, but he wanted a woman who could pull her weight, not a schoolgirl who would cry for her papa when the going got rough.

Besides, the Turner sisters tended to do everything as a set. And he didn't even want to think about what that might mean.

"Well, hello to you, Miss Minnie, Miss Mabel." He reached up and touched his hat brim. The two girls beamed at him with identical smiles that bordered on adoring. He slowly lowered his hand, puzzled by their behavior.

"We were hoping to see you, Mr. Donovan." The speaker—he thought it was Mabel—fluttered her eyelashes at him in an unmistakable attempt at flirtation.

He blinked, unable to believe his eyes, and glanced at the other twin. She fixed him with a worshipful blue gaze and stated proudly, "That's right. I made Papa bring me to town just so I could see you. Then *she* decided to come along."

"Is that so." He tried a glare—the same fierce expression that had made armed men back away with shaking hands. But the girls appeared oblivious to the subtle shift. Reckless youth, he thought with a sigh.

"It was my idea." Minnie attached herself to his arm, and he glanced with shock from her small fingers gripping his shirtsleeve to the look of ardent admiration on her face.

"No, it was *mine*." Mabel leaped forward and latched on to his other arm. "I would make a better wife. *She* always burns the biscuits when it's her turn to cook supper."

Minnie glared at her sister. "Well, at least I don't giggle all the time. You'd probably drive him crazy with all your little-girl antics." Giving Donovan a look from beneath her lashes, she said throatily, "She's just a child. *I'm* all woman."

He was out of his depth. He knew it and had no idea what to do about it. "Where's your father?"

"Oh, he's down at the bank." Mabel sighed and linked her elbow through his. "He'll be there for *hours*." She smiled meaningfully.

Donovan cleared his throat and took a step away. Unfortunately, that brought him into contact with Minnie, who was on his right. He flinched as he felt her press her budding breasts against his arm. Jerking his head around, he grew even more alarmed at the blatantly passionate look the girl gave him.

"I sure wouldn't mind a closer look at that gorgeous bed of yours, Mr. Donovan," she murmured.

Mabel gaped at her sister, blue eyes wide with shock. "Minnie Jean Turner!"

Minnie cast her twin a superior look. "Oh, go play with your dolls!"

Enough was enough. Donovan slipped from

Minnie's grasp and dodged out of the way as Mabel surged forward, face red.

"You take that back!" Mabel yelled.

"You're such a child." Minnie sniffed.

Unsettled by the commotion, Senseless shifted and bumped Mabel. She squealed as she tripped and flew into her sister. The two of them landed in the dirt, a flurry of petticoats and screeches. Senseless snorted, further startled by the noise, and tossed his head. At that moment, Donovan could have kissed the animal.

"You ladies had best get out of the way," he said, moving to help first one, then the other, to her feet. "Senseless here gets a mite riled at loud noises."

Mabel clutched her skirts and scrambled for the walkway. Minnie brushed off her dress, then leveled a contemptuous look at the bay. "When we get married, that horse is going to *go*." She shifted her glare to Donovan, then stalked after her sister, who had fled toward the bank.

Donovan took off his hat and combed his fingers through his hair. "What the hell was that about?" he muttered. With a shrug, he replaced his hat, patted Senseless on the flank, and slipped him a piece of carrot from his pocket. "Thanks, pal. I think you just saved me from a heap of trouble."

Still bemused, he set off for the saloon. Now he *really* needed a drink.

By the time Donovan got to the saloon, two more marriage-minded females had accosted him. One had offered to cook him supper; the other had offered something of a more intimate nature. And both had remarked on how much they liked his new bed. What the hell was going on?

Stopping outside the swinging doors, he took off his hat and slapped it against his thigh to shake the dust loose. The checker players, sitting in their usual spot outside the Four Aces, looked up from their game.

"Hey, there, Donovan," Mort said.

"Mort. Johnny, Gabriel." The latter two nodded in greeting and went back to their checker game, but Mort tilted his chair onto its hind legs and gave him a wide smile.

"Haven't seen ya around." Mort clenched a toothpick between his teeth, his blue eyes twinkling. "Heard ya were in the market for a prime filly."

"Actually I just bought a gelding." He indicated the bay, whose ears twitched as a wagon rumbled by.

Mort squinted at the horse, then chuckled. "Well, that's not what I meant, but that's a fine piece of horseflesh, Donovan. It surely is."

"He's a beautiful animal," Donovan agreed, admiring the way the sunlight played over the horse's coat. "He's a bit high-strung, though. I'm gonna have to work with him."

"That so?" Mort chewed on his toothpick and grinned like he knew some secret.

Donovan replaced his hat and gave the oldsters a nod. "See ya around."

The two men engrossed in the checker game grunted in response. Mort touched his hat brim, still wearing that all-knowing grin. Donovan shook his head and went into the saloon.

The squeak of the doors swinging behind him melded with the familiar sounds of cards being shuffled and bottles clinking against glasses. Conversation hummed steadily, like a heartbeat, and cigar smoke tinged the air with wisps of gray fog. For a moment he was fifteen years old again, watching his mama all done up in satin and feathers, singing songs that no one could hear.

He closed his eyes against the painful memories. The liquor. The men. The murder. It was a time in his life he wanted to forget, yet those incidents had led him to where he was today. His entire identity had been forged from spilled blood and steel-edged lust.

"Hey there, boss!" Amos called to him.

The past dissolved into the present.

Donovan made his way across the room and edged up to the bar next to Amos. "Everything all right at the ranch?" he asked.

"Yep." Amos tossed back a shot of whiskey and reached for the bottle.

"Must be, if you're here instead of there."

Amos grinned as he poured another shot. "Right as rain, boss. Get yer horse?"

"I did." Donovan signaled the bartender. "He's got a lot of spirit."

Amos smiled, a gleam in his eye. "Betcha he does." He gulped down another mouthful of whiskey.

Coralee, one of the saloon girls, sidled up to Donovan and smiled with blatant invitation. "What'll ya have?" she purred, pressing her scantily clad bosom against his arm.

"Harve's getting it." Unlike many of the girls, Coralee was actually pretty, with big brown eyes and bouncing chestnut curls. Any other time, Donovan might have considered taking her up on her unspoken offer. But he was fed up with women for the day. "Another time, maybe."

She drew a slender hand across his chest. "I'll hold ya to that." She lowered her voice to a whisper. "Maybe we can have a tussle in that purty bed of yours. I sure would like that."

Before he could respond, Harve brought Donovan's usual bourbon and shooed Coralee off with an impatient hand. "Get off with ya, Coralee. This one ain't interested."

With a pout, Coralee turned on her heel and stalked off in a flurry of satin and feathers. Despite himself, Donovan enjoyed the view of her retreating rump. Then he turned to Amos. "Something going on around here I don't know about?"

"Naw. Word got out 'bout you lookin' for a wife is all. Was in the paper."

"Is that so? Well, that might explain a few things." Stifling a grin, Donovan took a sip of the bourbon. So, Sarah had advertised that fact, had she? Good. So far his list of eligible women was a mighty short one. He thought back to the incident with the Turner twins, then shrugged. It was worth a bit of bother if he ended up finding the right wife.

"Yep," Amos said. "Folks been talkin' since the paper come out on Wednesday."

Better yet, Donovan thought, finishing off his drink. If the paper got out to some of the surrounding spreads, he might get lucky and find himself a rancher's daughter instead of a spinster from town. He placed his empty glass on the table and tossed down some money beside it. "I'd better get Senseless out to the ranch. See ya later, Amos."

"I'll come with ya." Amos left his half-empty glass on the bar, hitched up his britches, and trailed along behind. It was unusual that Amos would leave a single drop of whiskey untried, much less half a glassful, but Donovan didn't comment. He walked out of the saloon and headed for Senseless.

But his horse was gone.

He stopped and stared at the empty spot on the hitching post where he'd tied the bay. Rage rose, hot and fast. Who had stolen his horse? A year ago, no one would have dared . . .

He turned and stalked back to where Amos was making conversation with Mort, Johnny, and Gabriel.

"Mort, did you see who ran off with my horse?" Donovan demanded.

"Nope." Mort chewed on his toothpick. "Saw him loose himself from that hitchin' post and go off down the road yonder."

"Why didn't you call me?"

"Well, Johnny here had just kinged Gabriel, and—"

"Never mind." Donovan had the suspicious feeling that everyone was laughing at him, and he knew this group well enough to understand that demanding answers would get him nowhere. "Which way did he go?"

"Thataway." Johnny pointed down Main Street. "He was walkin', not runnin'. You could probably still catch him."

"Thanks." Donovan set off after his errant horse.

Chapter 4

Sarah locked up the back door to the newspaper office and turned toward home. She walked along the back fence that set the Calhouns' property away from the town by rote, her mind in turmoil.

The newspaper article had not generated the results she had intended. The gossip mill was grinding away with speculation over the article. No doubt everyone was wondering if Sarah intended to be a contender for the position of Mrs. Jack Donovan. For two days she had seen the pointed looks and overheard the urgent whispers as she walked by. And each incident chipped away at the fragile confidence that she had managed to rebuild since Luke Petrie.

It was as if the last three years had never happened.

The one redeeming feature of this entire

mess should have been Donovan's annoyance. She had imagined several scenarios, all involving a snarling, irate Donovan bursting into her office and venting his displeasure with much shouting and pulling of hair. And she would fend off his vituperations with witty, biting comments that would set his teeth on edge until he went mad with frustration.

But she'd been denied even that pleasure. Rumor had it that the man was out of town—he didn't even *know* about the article.

As she strolled toward the back of the Calhoun house, a whinny drew her attention, and she glanced over at the corral.

"Oh, no!"

Sarah picked up her skirts and ran over to the huge bay gelding standing outside the fence. Her own bay filly whickered at the other horse from inside the corral.

"Senseless?" she asked incredulously. Reaching out to grab his reins with one hand, she stroked his neck with the other. "What are you doing here?"

"That would be my question."

Startled, Sarah saw Donovan approaching from the front of the house.

"I thought you were out of town," she blurted.

"Keeping track of me, sassy girl? I'm flattered."

"That's not what I meant," she snapped.

When he extended a hand for the gelding's reins, she held them out of his reach. "What do you think you're doing?"

"Taking back my horse." He leaned over her, his broad chest a whisper from her face, and snagged the reins from her hand.

"Your horse? This horse belongs to Cutter Johnson."

Still standing only inches away, he arched a brow at her. "Accusing me of horse stealing now, Sassy?"

"Of course not. And don't call me Sassy."

"Sarah, then. I'm thinking that if anyone's a horse thief around here, it's you."

"*Me?*"

"You're the one standing here with my horse. What am I supposed to think?"

"You bought this horse from Cutter Johnson?"

"You bet I did."

She closed her eyes and let out a long sigh. Things had just gone from bad to worse. "Well, Mr. Donovan, you just bought yourself a passel of trouble. You can expect this to happen any time you're in town."

"You plan to steal my horse whenever I come to town?"

Her eyes flew open, and she scowled up into his grinning face. That darned dimple conflicted with the wicked laughter in his eyes, giving his face a mischievous cast that she found all too attractive. "Don't be ridiculous. Senseless used to belong to me, and he has a tendency to think this is still his home."

Donovan glanced from Senseless, to the bay filly in the corral that was almost his exact match, and back to Sarah. "He used to be yours?"

"Yes. My mother and I had to sell Senseless three years ago when my father died. We needed the money. First we sold him to Mort Tanner."

"Mort? Short guy, blue eyes, hangs out at the saloon?"

"Yes, Mort." Sarah took a deep breath. "Well, that didn't work out. When Senseless was ours, he developed a liking for my mother's molasses cookies, so he ran away from Mort all the time and ended up here. We finally had to give Mort back his money, and we sold Senseless to Cutter Johnson, who lived much farther away. We thought that might solve the problem. And until now, it did."

Donovan was frowning at her. "So you mean to tell me that anytime I come to town, my horse is going to wander over here?"

She twisted her hands together. "Probably. That's why I named him Senseless."

He stared at her for so long that she had to battle the urge to shift her feet like a schoolgirl caught playing with her mama's jewelry. Finally he just shook his head. "Woman, since I met you, all sorts of crazy things have happened to me."

A flush slowly warmed her cheeks. "Surely you don't blame me for this."

He shrugged. "I'm just saying life has gotten a lot more interesting since you started chasing after me."

Her jaw dropped. "I never—!"

"You did," he asserted, the corners of his mouth twitching.

"Mr. Donovan, you know that's business!"

"And what's with this Mr. Donovan stuff? You can call me Jack, after all we've meant to each other."

"I barely know you!"

"And I'll call you Sarah," he continued, as if she hadn't spoken. "Though Sassy suits you better. 'Specially after that kiss you laid on me the other night."

"That *I* laid on *you*? You were the one—"

"You sure are pretty when you get riled." He caressed her cheek, making her protests fade to incoherent splutters. "Makes me want to carry you off to the nearest hay pile and see how hot you can get."

"Mr. Donovan . . . Jack . . ." she spluttered.

"I like the way you say my name." He stepped a little closer until her breasts just touched his chest. "I bet there's a hay pile in that stable over there, isn't there?"

Her heartbeat thundered in her ears. He

seemed to give off some kind of heat that enticed her closer and made her want to forget that he considered her good enough to bed, but not good enough to marry. Already her breathing had gotten faster, and she took a step away, hoping the distance would help her regain some control.

"That kind of talk is inappropriate, *Mr. Donovan*."

"Come on, Sarah." His voice deepened to a gentle coaxing. "You and I both know that there's fire inside you just dying to get out. I don't know why you're so afraid of it."

"I'm not afraid of anything, least of all a man who dresses like an outlaw and has no concept of social graces!"

"Social graces, huh? At least I know who I am, sassy girl. Can you say the same?"

She clenched her hands into fists. "Please take your horse and get off my property. And I'll thank you to keep your innuendoes to yourself in the future."

"Innuendoes, hell! I was saying it straight out. You were made for loving, Sarah, but you've got yourself locked up so tight that even the sunlight can't get close."

She pressed her lips together. "That's the second time you have insulted me. Please leave."

He shook his head. "No insult intended. I just expected a woman like you to recognize the truth when you heard it. Guess I was wrong."

"I don't like your version of the truth, Mr. Donovan." She met his gaze, hoping the hurt didn't show in her eyes.

"Then let's hear yours, sweet Sarah. It's locked up inside you somewhere, but you've been living other people's truth for so long that I doubt you'd recognize your own anymore." He turned to leave, then paused. "And by the way, I sure do appreciate you writing that newspaper article about me. Should make wife hunting mighty easy now."

His arrogant tone made her want to scream. "I hope you get *exactly* what you want, Mr. Donovan."

"I always get what I want, Sarah." He tugged his hat brim. "Have a nice day now."

He left her there, her emotions churning, her pride smarting, as he walked away with his horse, whistling.

Damn his handsome hide.

A week later, Donovan walked into his darkened house, having left the rest of the hands at the bunkhouse after a long, dusty day of herding his new cattle. Moonlight streamed in through the window, but he didn't really need the light. He was at home in the shadows.

He hung his hat on the peg near the door and ran both hands through his sweat-drenched hair. He could do with a bath, but felt too tuckered to haul out the tub and heat the water. The kitchen pump would have to do.

He stripped off his shirt, appreciating the relief as the cool night air struck his perspiration-damp flesh. Dropping the filthy garment to the floor, he stuck his head under the pump, letting the cold water wash the grime from his skin. Despite how tired he was, he much preferred a long, hot, dusty day herding cattle to what had transpired in the week since sassy girl had published her newspaper article.

Jack Donovan knew the rhythm of the hunt as well as he knew the beat of his heart. He knew the smell of the chase, the taste of it. In his former profession, he had always been the predator.

This was the first time he had ever been the prey.

He muttered a curse, then doused his head under the water again and scrubbed at his face with both hands, as if to wash away the memory.

It didn't work. He straightened, water streaming down his cheeks and neck, and scowled into the darkness. Darn that woman. She plagued him night and day, in person or not. Everything led him back to Sarah, even his damned horse.

He swiped his hands over his hair, squeezing the water from the ends, then glanced down at the part of him that was still clothed. With a shrug, he bent down and pulled off his boots. It was nearly midnight, and no one was here but him. He might as well wash all of him at once.

As he peeled off the garments and dropped them on the floor, his gaze fell on the pies sitting on the table—all six of them—and the accompanying notes. Six different flavors of pie, baked by six different women, all interested in marrying up with him. He clenched his jaw. That darned Sarah—she made him hotter than a steam engine in the middle of July, but she was still all wrong for him.

He turned back to the pump, naked and aroused despite himself. Damned woman. Everywhere he turned now, he bumped into marriage-minded females. They cajoled, flirted, and fainted. They stopped him on the street, rode out to the ranch, and followed him around town. The only place they never followed him was into the saloon, but he had a feeling that might be next. He had even taken to bringing Matt or Amos along with him everywhere to help keep them at arm's length. The gifts of food were only a small part of what had turned into a full-fledged, hound-dog pursuit of Jack Donovan.

At first he had been amused by Sarah's article. Now it was getting increasingly annoying.

He gave himself a quick rinse, then gathered up his dusty clothes and padded naked through the dark, empty house. He was downright shocked at the behavior of some of these "good" women. Their chase held none of the subtlety of a true hunt. If they'd been out on the trail, they wouldn't have been able to trap so much as a field mouse. They were too noisy, too clumsy. Hell, he'd met saloon girls with less obvious wiles.

He climbed the stairs to the bedroom, shaking his head. He was beginning to wonder if there was a single woman in town, aside from the soiled doves, who didn't resort to plots and plans to get a man's attention.

There *was* one, he realized as he pushed open his bedroom door. Sarah Calhoun. And that was that.

With a sigh, he tossed his clothes over a chair. At the rate things were going, his bed was going to be mighty empty for a while yet. He couldn't have Sarah, and he hadn't found anyone else who tickled his fancy the way she did. And as for the others . . .

He stilled a shudder. As much as he wanted a wife, he just couldn't stand the thought of being tied to that sort of manipulating female for the rest of his life. Sarah was the only one who didn't try to finagle her way into his affections. He only teased her about it because some stubborn part of himself wished that she would.

He lit the lamp and turned to his cold, lonely bed.

"Evening, Jack Donovan."

He stopped short and stared at the woman reclining on the mattress. She smiled, revealing a tiny space between her two front teeth that he might have found charming any other time. As it was, he could only stare in stupefaction as she sat up and lazily smoothed a hand over her auburn hair.

"I was beginning to think you weren't coming home." She slid him a warm, dark-eyed look.

"Mrs. O'Brien?" he finally said, still stunned.

"Katie." She rose to her knees, the sheets tangling around her bare legs. "You can call me Katie. I'll call you Jack."

"Katie?"

Her hot gaze slid over him, jolting him with the reminder that he was naked. He grabbed his shirt off the chair and wrapped it around his waist. "What are you doing here?"

"I thought you might be tired of all those silly young things chasing after you," she said, slipping from the bed. Her sheer lawn shift revealed a lush, full figure designed to make a man's mouth water. "I thought you might want more womanly company for a change."

"I . . . uh . . ." Words failed him as the sultry widow approached. She was pretty and willing. So what was he waiting for? "Mrs. O'Brien . . ."

"Katie," she whispered, stroking her hands over his bare shoulders.

He backed away until his spine bumped the bureau. She followed, pressing against him. "Mrs. O'Brien . . ." he said again.

"Am I right?" With a gleam in her eye, she slowly trailed one hand down his chest and past his stomach.

He grabbed her wrist before her fingers made contact.

"I never figured you for a shy one," she murmured. "I hope you're not offended, but I feel a woman needs to try out a husband before she marries him."

He had to give her credit: she knew what she wanted.

"You're very honest," he said. He couldn't help wishing Sarah were more like the earthy widow. He knew that deep down inside prim-and-proper Sarah, hot-blooded Sassy was just itching to escape.

"Fair's fair," Katie said, distracting him from his thoughts. "I get to try you out, and you get to try me out." She grinned. "And by the way, I left my pie on the table with the others."

He laughed. As he looked down into her soft, brown eyes, he wondered why he was hesitating. Katie O'Brien fit all his requirements. She was a rancher's widow, used to hard work, and an accomplished cook. On top of that, she had already proved her fertility by bearing her late husband a son. And she was attractive. Any sane man would take her up on her offer and rush her to the nearest preacher.

He must be insane—it was the only answer.

"I'm sorry, Mrs. O'Brien, but I have to turn you down." He slipped from between the woman and the bureau and managed to snag his pants from the chair.

"I can change your mind." Before his astonished eyes, she slipped off her shift. Her voluptuous figure would have enticed a monk. He stared appreciatively, but she stirred no desire in him at all.

She wasn't Sarah.

Just the thought of Sarah had him harder than an ax handle in seconds. He shifted his hold on his pants so the garment blocked his arousal from Katie O'Brien's sharp-eyed view.

Damn it all. Sarah Calhoun was the *wrong woman*.

But so was Katie O'Brien. And damned if he understood why.

"Jack?" The widow reached for him, but he dodged her touch.

"I'm sorry, Mrs. O'Brien," he said as he backed out the door. "A woman like you deserves a man who appreciates her. I'll go saddle my horse and see you home."

Sarah stared at the ceiling of her bedroom. She should have been asleep hours ago, but her restless mind refused to allow her peace. Jack Donovan had turned her quiet, simple life into chaos.

She flung back the covers and slid from the bed. Since he had deigned to notice her at the spring dance, her life had become the cynosure of speculation and rumor. Moving to the window, Sarah rested her head against the frame. She had worked hard to repair her tarnished reputation. She had gone from the passionate young woman in love with the wrong man to the proper and respectable businesswoman who ran the town paper.

That newspaper had saved her life. But the cost . . .

Grief rose like a heavy fog from within, obscuring the present and revealing scenes from the past to torment her. Images of her father guiding her small hands as he taught her how to set type. Visions of her sister, always so beautiful, always the one entertaining beaux while Sarah worked long, lonely nights with ink staining her skin. Then Luke Petrie had arrived, and that was when everything had started to go wrong.

How desperate she had been, Sarah thought,

moisture welling in her eyes. A man had finally noticed her. Her, Sarah, the "smart" sister. She had believed every lie Luke Petrie told her; gave him her heart and her virginity. In return, he had murdered her father.

And whether the townsfolk ever chose to forgive her or not, she would live with the guilt for the rest of her life.

A sob escaped her. She ruthlessly quelled it, pressing her lips together. She knew her disgrace had doomed her to a life without a husband or children. Very few men would take on a woman with a past, and she wasn't yet desperate enough to accept an offer from the sort of man who would. She had buried the part of her that longed to be a wife and mother, and concentrated on making her father's dream come true.

While other small-town newspaper editors put together their papers in old barns or even outdoors, Mac Calhoun had spent all his savings to build the tiny office of the *Burr Chronicle* right on Main Street. He brought in extra money between issues by printing up advertisements for other businesses. He had sworn that the *Burr Chronicle* was going to be the most popular paper in the territory, and Sarah owed it to him to see that happen.

She swiped a tear away and tried to distract her thoughts by focusing on the view out the window. Below, a shadow moved in the night.

Sarah pressed her face against the window-pane and stared at the area where she had seen the movement. Gradually, as the clouds cleared a path for the moonlight, she began to make out the shape of a man sitting on a horse.

He shifted in the saddle, and she knew it was Jack Donovan.

Her pulse sped up. Why was he here, beneath her window, in the middle of the night? It was like some tale from a dime novel.

He just sat there, so still she might have mistaken him for one of the shadows if Senseless hadn't chosen that moment to toss his head. Then he urged the horse forward, came fully into the moonlight, and looked straight up at her bedroom window.

She knew she should step back. She was in her nightgown, and she knew he could see her. It was the height of immodesty. But for some reason, she couldn't move . . . or didn't want to.

You were made for loving. She heard his words again as if he whispered them in her ear, and a tremor shook her. He didn't know how right he was, and how hard she fought that part of herself.

She knew well the fires that burned inside her. Her passionate nature had long been a failing. Her own heated emotions had caused more harm than good, especially when she gave them rein. Case in point—when she had gotten so annoyed at Jack Donovan that she wrote that article, which had started the gossip about her all over again.

But worse than her temper were the terrible longings that plagued her, the secret cravings that frequently held her captive late at night as she longed for a man's touch.

At heart she was a wanton, and she hated herself for it.

Yet here she stood, proving her true nature by brazenly displaying herself for the pleasure of the man below. She should be in bed asleep, like any other respectable woman. But she couldn't pull herself away, couldn't break the silent communication that stretched tautly between them.

She knew he desired her; he had made that very plain. But she hadn't wanted to admit her own reciprocal feelings. The stirrings invoked by his kiss two weeks ago had become stronger and more disturbing each time they met, and those passions awoke now, flushing her body with heat.

She could feel his eyes on her. Her body reacted, making her nipples hard and her knees weak. She closed her eyes and took a deep breath to slow her pounding heart. Then she raised one trembling hand to the windowpane, wishing she touched warm flesh instead of cool glass.

But giving in to these dangerous feelings

would mean disaster. Donovan had made it abundantly clear that he wanted her only as a bedmate and not as a bride.

She knew now what he was doing beneath her window in the middle of the night. He knew the most hidden, darkest part of her. He had seen deep into her soul and knew her for what she was . . . a slave to her own passions.

And still, she wanted nothing more than to go outside and step into his arms and let loose the fires that consumed her.

He knew he shouldn't have given Senseless his head.

Donovan looked over the Calhoun house. It was well built and painted white, with a wraparound porch and real glass windows. Someone had planted flowers along the walkway, and lace curtains fluttered in the night breeze. It was more than just a house; it was a home.

A pale flash of movement in one of the upstairs windows caught his eye and he glanced up. A woman stood in the window, the moonlight making her nightgown glow white and her hair glint with gold.

Sarah.

His body reacted to the sight of her, and he cursed. Why her, damn it? Why did he react so fiercely to the one woman in town who *wasn't* after him? The one woman he couldn't have?

She was pretty, but so were a dozen other women. And come to think of it, he had never been partial to blonds. He liked brunettes with big, dark eyes. The widow O'Brien was more his type of woman. But for some reason, it was Sarah Calhoun who made him hot. Blond, blue-eyed Sarah, with her starched petticoats and her single-minded determination. There were times when he was sure she would figure out who he had been and print the story in the paper, destroying his chance of starting over. If he had any brains at all, he would stay as far from her as possible.

But here he was, sitting outside her house like some lovesick cowhand hot for the boss's daughter. Of course, love had nothing to do with it. It was a physical thing between him and Sarah. It would eventually fade.

He hoped.

He was so close to having what he wanted. He couldn't let anything get in his way now.

With a jerk of the reins, he turned his horse around and galloped off into the night.

Chapter 5

Bessie Beaumont had three big brothers, all ugly as sin and devoted as lapdogs. Each brother had a shotgun and the skill to nail a squirrel at fifty paces.

And all three of them were on Donovan's tail.

He ducked down the alley next to the barbershop and peered out to scan the terrain. His blood was thundering through his veins, and a particular exhilaration gripped him. It had been almost a year since he had played this game. He realized that he missed the sharp-witted challenge of the chase ... even when he was the one being pursued.

The Beaumont brothers were questioning Ellie Pearson across the street. The three mountain men were equally huge and equally unwashed. He couldn't tell who was Beau, who was Buford, and who was Ben, and he

really didn't want to get all that friendly with
the family anyway. While the brothers were occupied, he slid around the corner and made for
the door of the barbershop.

"There he is, Buford!" Bessie screeched from
across the street. "Get him!"

Donovan cursed as he darted through the
entrance, the whooping Beaumonts hot on his
trail. Mort and Johnny, waiting for the barber,
looked up, and Gabriel lifted his head from the
barber's chair as Donovan stood in the middle
of the shop, glancing around for an exit.

"Hey there, Donovan," Mort greeted him.

"Is there a back door?" Donovan demanded
of Ned Gorman, who stood with the razor
poised above Gabriel's lathered face.

"Sure is," Ned answered. "In the back."

Donovan bolted as the Beaumont brothers'
footsteps thundered on the wooden walkway
outside.

"Get him, Ben!" Bessie wailed over the din.
"You fetch me my husband right now, or I'm
fixin' to cry and ruin my complexion for the
weddin'!"

Donovan made it to the back room and
found the door. He slipped through and
clicked it shut behind him as he heard Beau's
voice—or was it Ben's?

"You seen a low-down polecat come through
here, barber? Now, Bessie, don't cry . . ."

"I want my husband!" she whined.

Bessie Beaumont's yowling rendition of feminine tears spurred Donovan to the next building. He yanked open the door, shot inside, and closed it with a barely audible scrape. He paused for a moment, listening, but the Beaumont boys were occupied with calming down their distraught sister. He grinned, the thrill of the hunt still singing in his blood.

"Mr. Donovan? What are you doing?"

Her smooth, familiar voice kicked up the speed of his pulse. Thrumming with excitement, roiling in the juices of primitive instinct, Donovan turned and met Sarah's inquiring, blue-eyed gaze.

Time seemed to slow. He watched her breasts rise and fall with her breathing. She trembled as his stare lingered there, and her eyes widened. Everything he had felt last night came back with a vengeance, but now he didn't care about the hows and whys.

"I saw you last night." She jolted at the roughness of his tone, but he ignored her trepidation and reached for her, capturing and holding her fluttering fingers with his. "I saw you standing there in your nightdress, and I know you saw me."

She opened her mouth, but no sound came out.

"You saw me, Sarah." He tugged her closer. "And you stood there and you showed yourself to me. And you wanted me."

He lowered his head, claiming her mouth in a possessive kiss.

Sarah stiffened with shock as his mouth joined with hers, the attraction between them sizzling like grease on a griddle. She lifted her hands to his shoulders to push him away, but the warmth of his touch seduced her. The unbridled desire that drove him matched her own confusing emotions. Even as the voice of reason screamed not to give in to danger, her lips parted beneath his, and she melted into his embrace.

It all seemed so simple, so basic. She closed her eyes in pleasure as the familiar fires licked at her, urging her closer to him. Her body had reacted the moment she saw him slip through the back door of the *Chronicle*. The way he moved mesmerized her. Swift. Stealthy. Soundless. Like a mountain cat stalking prey. There was a wild look in his eyes that set her heart to pounding, and her senses hummed, her body awakening with those traitorous longings that tortured her at night.

And right now she didn't care about anything except that he keep touching her.

His big hands smoothed down her back, pressing her hard against him as he swept his tongue into the softness of her mouth. She opened to him, offering him everything, her own long-rejected passion exploding from within like the steam from a locomotive.

Anything could happen, and she wanted it to. Ignoring the tiny voice of morality that whispered through her mind, she grabbed fistfuls of his hair with both hands and kissed him with every ounce of passionate hunger that enslaved her.

A shriek rent the air. "Fetch me my husband now! I'm fixin' to be Mrs. Jack Donovan afore sundown!"

Sarah broke the kiss and stared at him. "What was that?"

"Damn." He eyed her mouth with such carnal intent that she shivered. "Bessie Beaumont. She wants to marry me."

"What?"

"No time to explain." He grabbed her hand and yanked her toward her desk. "I need you to hide me until the Beaumonts leave."

She watched with amazement as he took off his hat, dropped to all fours, and crawled beneath her desk. "Are you out of your mind?"

He stuck his head out and glared at her. "You listen here, sassy girl. The Beaumont boys are bound and determined to drag me to a shotgun wedding unless you help me. And seeing how it was you who got me into this fix, I reckon you can get me out of it. Now sit down."

"You can't blame me for this! The Beaumonts can't even read."

"Sit, Sarah."

She gaped. "I can't sit at my desk with you under there! It would be so . . . so . . ."

He grinned at her, every inch the rogue with his dark hair tumbling over his forehead and the single dimple creasing his cheek. "What's the matter, sugar? Don't you trust me?"

"I . . . I . . ."

The front door to the newspaper office swung open, and the Beaumont brothers squeezed through. Donovan ducked back under the desk.

"Afternoon, Miss Sarah," Ben, the eldest, said. "We're looking for Mr. Donovan on account of he's gonna marry our sister this afternoon. Have you seen him?"

Sarah glanced from their shotguns to their slow-witted but determined expressions. With a graceful, casual movement, she slid into her chair and folded her hands atop her desk.

"I'm sorry, boys," she said with a charming smile. "I haven't seen him all day."

The Beaumont brothers shuffled and shifted and scratched their heads, clearly at a loss.

"Are you *sure* you ain't seen him, Miss Sarah?" Beau, the biggest of the lot, asked, pushing back his dusty, battered hat. "We saw him run this way."

"Mr. Donovan and I don't exactly get along," Sarah said.

"That's not what I heard." Bessie pushed past her brothers and stood with her hands on her pudgy hips, her scraggly red-brown hair falling in her eyes. Her overendowed bosom heaved with outrage. Though her head barely reached her brother's chest, Bessie glared at Sarah with all the fierceness of a grand Amazon princess.

Sarah raised her eyebrows. "I don't know what you heard, Bessie—"

"I heard that you got your eye on my man, Miss Prim-and-Proper. And I'm here to tell ya that I don't take kindly to no Jezebel sniffin' around my husband."

The insult stung. "Believe me, Bessie, I wouldn't *dare* come between you and Donovan." Beneath the desk, hard fingers pinched her calf. She kicked in retaliation, only to have her foot imprisoned in a strong palm.

"See that you don't," Bessie huffed. "And don't you be goin' around callin' him Donovan, you hear? His name is *Mr*. Donovan to you!"

"Mr. Donovan," Sarah muttered as she felt her shoe slide from her foot.

"That's right. And I'll be Mrs. Donovan, soon as we find that . . . soon as we find my darling man." Bessie smiled, revealing yellowed teeth in dire need of a scrubbing.

"You'll tell us if you see him, won't ya, Miss Sarah?" Buford asked.

Out of sight of the Beaumonts, one masculine finger slowly traced the sole of her stockinged foot from heel to toes. Heat streaked through her body and knocked every sensible thought from her head.

"Yes-s-s-s-s-s," Sarah all but moaned.

"Thank you kindly, Miss Sarah," Buford said as he and his brothers turned to leave.

Bessie marched up to the desk just as the rascal underneath it slipped off Sarah's other shoe and began to rub both her feet with warm, powerful fingers. His thumbs pressed into the arches, and his hands massaged and squeezed the tender flesh.

"I got my eye on you," Bessie announced dramatically. She leaned on the desk and shook a finger in Sarah's face. "You see to it you keep your distance from my husband."

Lean hands slid up her calves and kneaded the muscles there. Sarah could only nod at Bessie's warning, lest a moan of pleasure escape her lips instead of words.

"Come on, Bessie." Ben took his sister by the arm. "Maybe he went by the saloon. We'll find him." He pulled her out the door.

The second they were gone, Sarah shoved back her chair and stood, anger simmering along with passion through her veins. "They're gone. You can go now."

He clambered out from beneath the desk and got to his feet, watching her with smoldering dark eyes. "I figure I'm not in much of a hurry."

The low timbre of his voice made her pulse skip, but the Beaumonts' crudeness had reminded her of her resolve to resist the untamed side of herself. "If you hurry, you can slip out before they see you."

"You trying to get rid of me, sassy girl?" He cocked his head to the side. "After the way you all but crawled up inside me before?"

"Get out." She pointed a finger at the door. "Get out now."

"You started this." Anger tinged his voice and sent a warning that she rashly ignored.

"No, *you* started this—you with your precious list. I told you that you can't choose a wife the way you would a brood mare, but you didn't listen."

"*You're* the one who wrote the article that has every woman in Wyoming tracking me like a horse thief," he retorted. "I can't turn around anymore without finding some woman mooning after me or fainting on me or even trying to seduce me!"

"You poor thing," she sneered.

"You were mad because I told you that you weren't the sort of woman I intend to marry. You wrote that article in a temper tantrum!"

Sarah fisted her hands. "That's right, you low-down polecat. You told me straight to my face that I was good enough for you to take to bed, but not good enough to make your wife. I imagine the whole town told you about the scandal, so you thought I was an easy mark."

"I never thought you were an easy mark, and I never listen to gossip," he snapped back. "I told you, I can't marry a woman with a job. I need to marry a woman who will give all her attention to being a wife and mother. We both know that's not you, Sarah, no matter how hot we get each other."

"You said I'm not good enough to be your wife," she repeated. "So I'll thank you not to be putting your hands on me anymore."

He stared at her for a long moment. "I never said you weren't good enough, Sarah. You're just not the *right* woman."

"That's almost the same thing." Her chin jutted proudly as she met his stare.

"Fine." He shoved his hat on his head, then handed her the shoes he held in his other hand. "I believe these are yours?"

She snatched them from him. "Out!"

"I'm going." He started to the door, but paused and glanced at her over his shoulder. "But I'll be back, sweet Sarah. And we'll see what's what."

Sarah snarled an unladylike curse and flung her shoes at the door as it closed behind him.

Women. Who could understand them?

Donovan heard the two thuds against the door just after he closed it, and he couldn't help but grin. Her shoes, no doubt. Any other woman might indulge in a fit of maidenly tears, but his sassy girl had a temper like a tornado.

The grin slipped from his face. When had she become *his* Sassy?

He turned to head down to the saloon, where he'd left Matt and Amos. And stopped abruptly when a shotgun barrel jabbed into his gut. He lifted his gaze to Buford's—or Beau's?—beady-eyed face.

"Goin' somewhere, Donovan?"

Donovan took a step back and came up against another shotgun that poked him in the kidney.

"Doesn't look like it," he said. His mind swiftly calculated the odds, even as he noted a dozen possible weak points. There were two of them—no, three, he corrected as the third brother walked up with Bessie in tow. And the girl wasn't much of a fighter, but she sure was a heck of a screamer.

The thought of listening to her caterwauling until death parted them was enough to make a man long for a bullet in the brain.

"Ya got him!" Bessie breathed with admiration.

"Sure did." The Beaumont behind him shoved him hard with the shotgun, making Donovan wince. "Anything for you, Bessie. You know that."

"Let's go get the preacher and get you married up afore sundown," another brother suggested. He glared at Donovan. "And you'd better make my sister the happiest woman in Wyoming Territory, you got that, Donovan?"

Donovan nodded, his fingers curling into his palms. He could take them. He knew he could. Easily. He had fought and won in worse situations. But the Beaumont brothers weren't the brightest fellows he'd ever encountered, and they were likely to start firing at anything that moved if he made a break for it. And that meant that innocent people might get hurt.

He could let them take him to the church, which stood apart from the main buildings of the town. Then he would take them down and make his escape. His body tensed, poised for the slightest opportunity.

He wasn't about to marry Bessie Beaumont, shotguns and brothers be damned. But neither would he be responsible for the deaths of innocent people.

Never again.

Sarah worried her bottom lip between her teeth. She had peeked out the window of her office to watch Donovan walk away, only to witness his capture instead. And now she was torn.

She glanced over at the Winchester rifle that hung on the wall. She knew how to use it. As a woman who often worked alone late at night, she had felt it a wise precaution to have some means of protecting herself. Burr was a quiet town for the most part, and when the sheriff had died nearly two years ago, they hadn't even bothered to replace him. Yet a woman could never be too careful, as she had learned three years ago.

She felt her throat close up and willed away the painful memories. Donovan was in danger. There were three of them, and the Beaumont brothers all topped Donovan by at least three or four inches and outweighed him by fifty pounds. She had no doubt that one-on-one, he could handle himself. But three-to-one odds stretched the limits of any man's ability.

She had to help him.

Her mind whirled as she hurried to the wall and lifted the rifle down. She hated guns. Hated the coldness of the metal that felt like death in her hands.

But as angry as she was at Donovan for his arrogance, and at herself for responding to his kiss, she couldn't let the man die.

She walked to the door and opened it. The Beaumonts had made it as far as Doc Mercer's, and they were obviously bringing Donovan to the church.

Her hands were steady as she checked to be sure the weapon was still loaded. She *hated* guns. A gun had killed her father. And she had sworn that day, bent over her father's body with his blood staining her hands, that she would never again love a man who lived by the gun. The thrill of danger that lured such a man exacted too great a cost on those around him.

Sarah raised the rifle and sighted down the barrel, aiming at one of the Beaumont's gun hands. She would not kill a man, but she would darned well slow him down.

"Boss!" Waving, Amos hurried past.

Sarah lowered the rifle.

"Boss, wait!" Matt was hot on Amos's heels.

"Bessie!" A wiry young man with a prominent Adam's apple hurried after both of them.

Sarah blinked in surprise. What was Homer Beasty doing here?

Bessie stopped and whirled. "Homer?"

"Bessie." Homer stopped and took her hands in his. "Bessie, say it isn't so. Tell me you're not going to marry this ... this ..."

"Am so." Bessie sniffed and gave Homer a look. "A girl's got to get a husband any way she can."

"Well, I won't have it!" Homer stood straight as a fence post and glared at Donovan. "I love you, Bessie, and I'll fight for you if I have to."

"Oh, Homer." Bessie sighed, obviously moved by his declaration.

"You." Homer pointed a thin finger at Donovan. "Defend yourself!"

Homer rushed his rival. Sarah waited, expecting Donovan to win the skirmish with little effort. Instead, Homer got him on the chin with a left hook that sent Donovan sprawling.

"Homer!" Eyes wide with admiration, Bessie hurried to the young man's side and attached herself to his elbow. "My goodness, I never realized how strong you are!"

"A man's got to protect what's his. And I've loved you so long that I think of you as mine." Homer glanced at the fallen Donovan, then turned his earnest expression on his lady love. "Bessie, my darling, will you marry me?"

"Oh, yes!" Bessie all but smothered the young man as she flung her arms around him. "Yes, I'll marry you, Homer Beasty!"

"Then let's do it right now. I'm not taking any chance of losing you." Homer led Bessie toward the church, her brothers trailing along behind with confused looks on their faces.

Donovan sat up and rubbed his jaw. Locating his hat, he grabbed it and got to his feet.

"Why'd you let him deck you?" Matt asked. "You coulda laid him flat without breakin' a sweat."

Donovan grinned. "But then I'd be on the way to the church with Bessie Beaumont."

Amos chuckled. "Pretty smart fella, ain't ya?"

Matt chuckled as he finally got the joke. "Better than a shoot-out, anyway."

"My thinking exactly, Matt. I'm lucky he showed up when he did."

"Pshaw, that weren't no luck," Amos snorted. "I knew Homer was sweet on Bessie. Everyone expected them to marry up afore now, but Homer never got up the gumption to ask."

"Amos and I rode out to get him," Matt said with a grin. "We figured you could use the help."

"I'm obliged to you both." Donovan looked past the two men to the *Chronicle* building. The Winchester seemed suddenly heavy in Sarah's hands as their eyes met and held. Then he placed his hat on his head and looked at his companions. "Whiskey all around, I'd say. And Amos, I figure I owe you another four bits."

"Yeeehaw!" Amos did a little jig as the three men turned toward the saloon.

Sarah watched them go. He knew, blast him. He knew that she would have helped him. She closed the door and hung the rifle back on the wall.

It made her crazy, the way that man could see right into her soul.

With a little sigh, she turned to her only trustworthy companion these days. Her printing press.

Chapter 6

"Mama, I wish you would stop this."

"But that blue dimity would look *lovely* on you, Sarah."

"Mama, we've talked about this before."

June Calhoun sighed. "I don't know why you do this. You'll never catch a husband dressing like a spinster."

Having heard this particular lecture many a time, Sarah pressed her lips together and increased her pace. The church was coming into view, and the crowd milling around outside indicated that the town meeting had yet to begin.

"Sarah Ann Calhoun, don't you dare ignore me," June said sternly, quickening her pace as well. "I just want to see you happy."

"I am happy, Mama." She tossed a quick smile at her mother, despite her annoyance. "I have you, and I have the paper. I don't need anything else."

"The newspaper was your father's dream, not yours." June shook her head. "I remember how you used to daydream about getting married. You would even make up names for your children. You wanted a dozen."

"Things change."

Her mother continued as if she hadn't heard, her voice soft with nostalgia. "Remember that wedding ring quilt? You worked so hard on it. I think it's still in your hope chest in the closet. You swore you were going to lay it over your marriage bed on the night of your wedding."

As her mother kept talking, Sarah's mind wandered to that quilt. She had worked on it with all the enthusiasm of the young girl she had been, bedazzled by dreams of happily-ever-after. She remembered laying it in her hope chest, imagining the night when she would present it to her new husband as a wedding gift.

That night would never come now.

"Sarah, are you listening to me?"

"Yes, Mama. Look, we're here." She said a silent prayer of thanks as Honoria Westerly, the reverend's wife, called out to them.

"June! Sarah! Over here!"

"Good evening, Honoria." Sarah's mother smiled as she greeted her closest friend.

"Evening, Mrs. Westerly," Sarah said politely.

"Marianne is over there with Lorinda Baines,

Sarah," Honoria said. "I'd appreciate it if you could keep her distracted while I talk to your mother about making her a new dress for her birthday."

"Certainly, Mrs. Westerly." Sarah had barely turned away before Honoria launched into the details of the gown she wanted Sarah's mother to create.

She wandered toward the group of young women gathered near a buckboard wagon. Pieces of conversations drifted to her as she made her way through the crowd. Ellie Pearson, heavy with child, deep in conversation with Doc Mercer and his wife. The rumble of male laughter and good-natured ribbing from the cattlemen who lingered on the stairs of the church. The widow O'Brien calling after her young son, Kevin, as he chased the Tillis boys through the crowd. As she approached her destination, giggles and girlish voices rose above all else. Marianne Westerly spotted her and waved her over.

As Sarah moved beside Marianne, she heard Lorinda Baines expounding on the secrets of married life. Only two weeks ago, Lorinda had married Ethan Baines, a local horse rancher. Now the unmarried ladies, including Emmaline and Juliana Tremont, listened with rapt fascination as Lorinda revealed things only hinted at by their mothers.

"Well, Ethan is the most wonderful man,"

Lorinda said. "He's very gentle and he treats me like a china doll."

"I hope my husband is like that." Marianne sighed.

"I should hope that he's gentle!" Emmaline sniffed. "A man should act the gentleman with his wife at all times."

"Well, not at *all* times," Lorinda responded with a sly smile.

A burst of giggles followed her statement. Sarah looked down at her folded hands. Out of all the women there, she alone knew exactly what Lorinda Baines meant. While a woman wanted a husband to treat her with care and respect, there were times, such as the marriage bed, where a rogue was more desirable than a gentleman. A tendril of longing twined around her heart, and she suppressed it, refusing to submit to the shameless hunger that plagued her almost constantly now.

"I can't *wait* to get married," Marianne whispered with excitement. "I do so want to know what *it* is all about. Mama refuses to discuss the matter."

"I should hope so!" Emmaline said. "Such things are inappropriate for a young girl's ears."

"You just say that because you don't know yourself, Emmaline," Lorinda teased. More giggles erupted as Emmaline flushed a bright red.

"The marriage bed is sacred and should not be whispered about in such a manner," Emmaline snapped.

"Speaking of beds," Juliana said with a glance at Sarah, "I wonder if Jack Donovan will be coming to the meeting tonight."

"Oh, isn't he the handsomest man!" Marianne exclaimed. "And he actually *wants* to get married. Not like some men around here."

"I hear he's the richest man in town. Gold mines," Lorinda added sagely.

"I heard he used to be an outlaw," Marianne contributed excitedly. "But he seems like such a nice man."

"And that bed." Juliana fanned herself. "Goodness, just the thought of it makes me all trembly."

"Juliana!" Emmaline chided. "A lady does not speak of such things."

"Oh, Emmaline." Juliana dismissed her sister and looked at Sarah. "What do you think, Sarah? After all, you've seen more of that bed than anyone."

The insinuation was unmistakable. Marianne and Lorinda gaped, and Emmaline placed a hand to her bosom. Juliana just watched Sarah, a malicious glitter in her eyes.

Sarah felt the heat creep into her cheeks. "In the course of business, yes, I did get a good look at it. And it's beautiful. I can't wait to see who he marries."

"Neither can I." Juliana stared at Sarah.

Sarah met her gaze, then looked at the other women. "If you ladies will excuse me, I believe the meeting is starting." She walked away with her head held high.

"Well, we know who Jack Donovan *isn't* going to be marrying," Juliana said, loud enough for Sarah to hear. Furious whispers followed her words.

"Sarah." Marianne hurried up to her and fell into pace when she didn't slow. "Don't let Juliana hurt you. She never has a kind word for anyone." She smiled.

The preacher's daughter was a beautiful brunette with soft gray eyes and a roses and cream complexion. She was sweet and compassionate, and purity shone from her gentle smile like a light from heaven.

Sarah had once known such innocence. Now she felt tarnished next to Marianne's sterling virtue.

"Don't worry about it," she said. "I'm going to fetch Mama so we can get a good seat."

"If you're sure you're all right." Marianne's flawless brow crinkled with concern.

"I'm positive." Sarah squeezed Marianne's arm in reassurance. Marianne Westerly was the one woman in town that Sarah could honestly call a friend.

"All right then. I'll stop by sometime this week, and we can have a nice long visit."

"You do that."

The other woman smiled and hurried back to her group. Sarah sighed as she watched her go, feeling old beyond her years. Marianne Westerly was everything she herself had once been. Marianne loved to cook and sew and longed for the day when she would bear children. She would make some man a wonderful wife.

Donovan should probably propose to *her*.

Her mouth trembled as tears threatened unexpectedly, and she pressed her lips together. Ruthlessly, she repressed the dreams of husband and family. That would never happen for her. She would be alone until she died. And that was the way things were.

"Yoohoo! Sarah, over here!"

She spotted her mother standing near the church steps with one of the ranchers and waving for Sarah to join them. June's never-ending campaign to matchmake for her daughter was born of love, if futile. Resigned, she slowly made her way over.

June took her arm as soon as she was within reach and tugged her closer. "Look who stopped to say hello, Sarah."

Sarah smiled politely. "Hello, Mr. Turner."

Ross Turner took off his hat, revealing light brown hair threaded with silver. His dark eyes were warm as he said, "Good evening, Sarah. I was hoping to see you tonight."

"Oh?" She glanced at her mother. June beamed at her, which immediately put her on her guard. "Uh ... what a nice thing to say. How is your family?"

"Fine, fine. Ross Junior's been helping a lot with the cattle, but I think the twins are still feeling the loss of their ma. Girls that age need a woman's guidance." He smiled and added, "If you know what I mean."

Sarah was shocked by the admiration in his voice. Though in his forties, Ross was still as fit as a man half his age, and one of the wealthiest men around. His wife had died two years ago from influenza, leaving Ross to raise his son and three daughters on his own.

And now he was smiling at her, Sarah Calhoun, like a suitor come calling on Sunday.

"Young girls do need a woman to talk to," June interjected into her daughter's silence. "Before you know it, they'll be married and gone from the house."

Ross flashed her mother a grateful smile. "Don't I know it. Little Betsy keeps begging to dress like her sisters. And the twins are barely sixteen, but the boys have already come sniffing around. I've got a mind to keep my rifle handy."

June laughed just as Reverend Westerly stepped out of the church and began ringing the bell that signified that the town council meeting was about to begin. Ross took Sarah's hand.

"Perhaps I could call on you next Saturday evening, Sarah?" He squeezed her fingers meaningfully.

Sarah hesitated, still stunned that such a decent man would even consider courting her.

"Sarah!" June urged in a whisper.

"Of course," Sarah finally said. "Around seven o'clock?"

"Seven," Ross agreed. He squeezed her fingers again and released her hand. "I'll look forward to it. Until then, Sarah." He tipped his hat. "Mrs. Calhoun."

Sarah watched him make his way through the crowd. Her mother took her arm and tugged her forward with the rest of the crowd that was moving into the church.

"Ross Turner, Sarah! You *must* allow me to make up that blue dimity for you now. You certainly can't wear those drab browns and grays that you insist on, not when a man like him comes courting!"

"If you want to, Mama." Sarah reached the church steps and stood aside so that her mother might go before her. She bumped up against someone and glanced behind her. The apology died on her lips as she met Donovan's dark-eyed stare.

A tingle ran down her spine. He didn't smile

or say a word. Just looked at her with those all-knowing, velvet-brown eyes.

"Oh, Sarah, this is wonderful!" June was saying. "I told you so many times that you deserve the same opportunities as any other girl. Haven't I been saying that? Goodness, Sarah, there's every chance you might become Mrs. Ross Turner by the end of summer!"

Startlement flashed across Donovan's face before his expression settled into impassivity. Sarah opened her mouth, but slowly closed it again. She owed Donovan no explanations, especially not in the middle of a crowd of busybodies. She had every right to take the opportunity to become a wife and have a family. And if certain people didn't like it, too bad. She gave Donovan a curt nod, then turned back to her mother.

"Come, Mama. I want to get a front-row seat." She urged June up the stairs, steering her toward the open double doors of the church. Just before stepping through, she glanced back at Donovan.

He was gone.

Town meetings were a new experience, Donovan thought as he seated himself in the back. In his former profession, he had never been welcome at one. But now, as a respected—and wealthy—member of the community, he was pretty much expected to attend.

The five members of the town council—Doc Mercer, Mr. and Mrs. Castor, Reverend Westerly and Mortimer Tremont, the undertaker—sat at a table in front of the church. The rest of the townspeople settled into the hard pews as Arnold Castor, the mayor of Burr and a well-to-do banker, called the meeting to order.

Donovan let his mind drift as issues were brought up and discussed and decided upon. There was a bit of a ruckus when the Ladies' Auxiliary for the Betterment of Burr suggested that the saloon should be closed on Sundays, but otherwise his thoughts remained uninterrupted as he thought about what June Calhoun had said.

Ross Turner was planning on courting Sarah.

He told himself that it was none of his business. He liked Ross. Having spent years learning to size up people at a glance, Donovan had decided that Ross was a decent, hardworking man and a leader of the community. Turner knew how to treat his men and his cattle, and Donovan had the highest respect for him.

But he wasn't sure if he liked the idea of Ross's hands on Sarah.

"Doesn't matter what you like," he muttered to himself. "She's got a right to get married if she wants to."

He tried to be happy for her—but somehow he couldn't.

"What I want doesn't matter," he grumbled

under his breath. The young couple sitting near him eyed him strangely. Donovan stared at them until they flushed and turned away.

You aren't going to marry her, the voice persisted. *You might as well stand aside and let another man have her.*

Let another man touch her. Let another man bask in the heat of her passionate nature. Let another man—like Ross Turner—bury himself in her sweet body.

He shifted in his seat and silently cursed as he physically reacted to the image of Sarah naked and writhing in a man's arms. Except the man in his imagination wasn't Ross Turner: it was himself.

"Damn," he muttered. Too bad his body didn't realize that Sarah Calhoun wasn't the right woman to become his wife. To distract himself, he turned his attention to the meeting.

"The issue of a school has been brought before the council by the Ladies' Auxiliary," Arnold Castor was saying. "As president of that group, Mrs. Castor will elaborate."

Millicent Castor rose to her feet from her seat at the council table. "Thank you, Mr. Castor." She looked over the crowd and folded her hands at her waist. "The ladies of this town would like to suggest that a school be built and a proper schoolteacher hired to teach our children. The population in and around our little town is growing, after all, and we need to make room for newcomers."

"Let the newcomers build their own school!" a man's voice called out.

"Now that's the wrong attitude," Mrs. Castor chided. "Our own children will benefit from this as well."

"What about Mrs. Tillis?" asked a woman with a baby on her lap. "My younguns like Mrs. Tillis."

"Mrs. Tillis has been doing a fine job as our schoolmarm," the mayor's wife said with a smile, "but she has given us her resignation so that she can take care of her six children, including the little one on the way."

There were murmurs in response to this.

"Who all's gonna pay for the school and a new teacher?" asked Nate Pearson.

"That's one of the things we have to decide," Mrs. Castor responded.

"I don't like it." Ross Turner stood and folded his arms as he faced the council. "I don't see the need for a fancy school building when the church does just fine. And if there are too many children, then keep the girls home. What are they gonna use all that book learning for anyway? They're gonna grow up and get married, after all."

"No!" Sarah leaped to her feet, put her hands on her hips and looked Ross straight in the eye. "I could just as easily tell you to keep the boys home, Mr. Turner, since a body doesn't need to know how to read in order to rope a calf."

A riot of laughter and voices exploded at her words, and Donovan swiped a hand over his mouth to hide a telltale grin. He couldn't help but be amused that the target of her ire this time was Ross Turner.

The noise got louder. Arnold Castor banged the gavel on the table, but no one paid any mind as Sarah continued to debate with Ross.

Ross Turner was a powerful man, and many people who were unsure about the school issue were nodding in support of him for that reason alone. Donovan agreed with Sarah that all children should be given the opportunity to get an education. He knew from his own childhood how valuable schooling could be. If he'd been given the chance to go to school as a boy, things could have turned out much differently for him.

"The town does not have the money to be hiring teachers or building a school," Ross said firmly. "The church does just fine, and I'm sure we can find someone else to teach the children."

"We can raise the funds," Mrs. Castor interjected. "We have several proposals ready—"

"There's no need," Ross insisted. "And I think most people here will agree with me. Things are fine just as they are."

There was a general murmur of assent. Sarah

looked around at the crowd. "But there *is* a need for this," she insisted. "Would you truly deny your female children the chance to learn?"

"They don't need no book learnin'," someone said.

"Mr. Turner's right," spoke up another man. "Them gals are just gonna up and get married anyway. They don't need that stuff."

"Listen to Miss Calhoun." Donovan rose to his feet. All heads turned his way, but he looked over the sea of curious faces and met Sarah's gaze. "Women deserve education the same as men do," he said. "How else are they going to write letters to their relatives or read stories to their youngsters? Or be sure they're not getting cheated at the mercantile? No offense, Nate."

Nate Pearson grinned, and some people laughed.

"Women are just as much a part of our town as men," Donovan continued. "They're the root of it. They raise our children and take care of our homes. They nurse the sick and prepare the food and do a lot of other things that we men usually don't notice." He paused. "More than ten years ago, when this territory was first established, we showed the world how we value our women by giving them the right to vote. Women have served on our juries, and we've even had a woman justice of the peace. If our women are uneducated, the children of our town will grow up believing that women are less important than men. And as we already know here in Wyoming Territory, that just ain't so."

The women in the room burst into applause. Donovan looked back at Sarah. The expression on her face was a mixture of gratitude and admiration. For the first time since they'd met, he broke eye contact first. He wasn't sure what had prompted him to speak his inner thoughts so publicly. Perhaps it was the memory of the young boy he had once been, alone and uneducated in the world. Or perhaps it was the thought of his mother, and what she might have done with her life if she'd been able to read and write.

Or maybe he'd just wanted to show Sarah that there was more to him than she thought.

"All well and good," Ross said as the clamor started to die down. "But who's going to pay for all of this? I hope you aren't counting on charitable donations."

"Don't worry, Mr. Turner," Sarah said. "You don't have to contribute if you don't agree."

Ross frowned at her.

"Very true, Sarah," Mrs. Castor agreed, sending a cool smile Ross's way.

"I'll pay for it." Heads swiveled his way again, and Donovan fought the urge to step back. He was used to lurking in the shadows, not basking in the light of so much attention.

"You'll pay for it?" Sarah repeated, her tone dumbfounded.

"We'll make a deal." Donovan looked at the council. "If the town can raise the funds to build the schoolhouse, I'll pay the teacher's wages for the first year. After that, it's up to you."

"We could appoint a school board," Mrs. Castor said with excitement. She glanced at the other four council members. "We could have fund-raisers during the year if we need to."

The members of the town council murmured to each other, and Donovan looked over at Sarah again. She smiled at him, a soft, genuine smile, and his heart turned over.

Arnold Castor stood. "The council agrees with Mr. Donovan's suggestion, but we need to take a vote. All in favor, raise your hands."

Hands shot into the air. Most were women, Donovan noticed, but several of the men who had been ready to follow Ross Turner's advice had now switched sides.

"All opposed?" Hands went up again, but many fewer than the first time. "It's settled then," Mr. Castor said with a bang of the gavel. "The town council will support the Ladies' Auxiliary for the Betterment of Burr in their effort to raise funds to build a schoolhouse. And the council gratefully accepts Mr. Donovan's offer to sponsor the teacher for the first year."

A cheer went up, and the gathering exploded into a babble of voices. Donovan found himself inundated with people eager to thank him for his generosity. He shook hands and returned pleasantries, somewhat overwhelmed by the attention. He had found a place among these people, he realized with astonishment. They considered him part of the community—just as he had always wanted.

But even as he reveled in the small victory, even as he thrived on the backslaps and hearty thanks, he was shaken by the knowledge that he would have done it all for nothing more than Sarah Calhoun's approving smile.

Chapter 7

People followed Donovan out of the church, still stopping him and thanking him for his generosity. Mrs. Castor herself had trapped him beside the church stairs and was showering him with effusive gratitude.

Sarah took a deep breath, uncertain why her hands were trembling and why her heart was pounding so fast. That he had supported her in so important an issue stunned her. But that he honestly believed in the cause was truly astonishing.

Donovan finally managed to separate himself from Mrs. Castor, and Sarah grabbed her chance. He crossed to where his horse was tied to a tree, waving in response to greetings and accepting hearty pats on the back with a smooth yet distant smile. She could tell that he wanted to get away from the adulation, but there was something she wanted to say to him first. Grasping her skirts, she hurried over to him, stopping a few paces away as he untied Senseless.

"Mr. Donovan."

He paused, the reins dangling from his hands. "Evening, Sarah."

"I want to thank you for what you did in there." She clenched her fingers into the sturdy brown material of her skirt.

He shrugged. "I did what I had to; nothing more."

"You did something wonderful," she said, stepping closer. "You can't know how I feel right now. You've done this incredible thing, supported my argument in there and offered to pay a teacher's wages for a whole *year*—"

"I had my reasons, sassy girl, and I'm sorry to say it really had nothing to do with getting in your good graces."

She flushed. "I didn't think it did."

"The fact is, I never got schooling when I was a boy. If I had . . ." He let the words trail off. "The town needs a school. And since I'm going to be getting married and having my own younguns, I reckon I should be sure that they have the chance for the education I never had."

"Whatever your reasons, I'm grateful to you," Sarah said with a soft smile.

"I don't want your gratitude, Sarah." His expression tightened as he reached out and traced a finger along her jaw. "Fact is, I don't know what I want from you."

She touched the hand that caressed her face. "Friendship?"

He gave a harsh laugh. "Is that possible?"

"It has to be," she said. "By your own intentions, it's all we can have."

He rubbed his thumb against her cheek. She closed her eyes and savored the contact for the briefest moment before looking at him again. "I think we need to make a new start, Donovan."

"If it isn't too late."

"I don't think it is." With an effort, she took a step back, away from his touch. "I'm sorry I was so bullheaded about prying into your past. You were right when you said that a man's past is his own business. I won't pester you anymore."

He blinked. "I . . . don't know what to say."

"You don't have to say anything," she responded. "Your secrets are safe from me."

"Sarah." He came forward and took her hand. "Since you're giving something to this . . . this peace treaty of ours, I want to do the same thing."

"You don't have to." She tried to pull her hand away, but his grip was too firm.

"I want to." He paused, scanning her face. "I promise not to tease you anymore, sweet Sarah. I know you haven't had it easy, and I think lately I've made things worse for you."

She flushed and looked away. "It hasn't been that bad."

"Nevertheless, I promise not to do it anymore." He turned her face until she met his gaze. "Friends don't make each other uncomfortable, right?"

"I . . . I suppose."

"Good. Then we're agreed." He took his hand from her cheek and held it out for her to shake. "Friends?"

The sincerity in his expression squeezed her heart. She so badly needed someone who would not judge her. Someone like him, who saw through the facade she maintained every day to the real woman beneath.

Somehow that prospect didn't seem so scary anymore.

"Friends," she agreed and shook hands.

Friends.

Donovan watched Sarah walk away with a sense of wonderment. Something amazing had just happened. She had agreed not to pursue his past anymore. He had agreed not to try and seduce her when they both knew he had no intention of marrying her. They had settled their differences like civilized people and agreed to get along.

In a way, it didn't seem odd that they could be friends. Deep down, they'd always understood each other. No, what felt strange was that he already missed the pleasure of touching her, of teasing her and watching her get riled up and embarrassed. But a promise was a promise. And Jack Donovan kept his promises.

He turned to mount his horse.

"Not so fast, Donovan."

Ross Turner approached him, and Donovan wondered if the man had witnessed his discussion with Sarah.

"I wanted to wait until Sarah was gone," Ross said, answering his unspoken question. "There's some things I want to say to you."

Resigned, Donovan looped the horse's reins around the tree branch again, then turned to face Ross. "Go ahead."

Ross frowned. "I never had any problem with you before, Donovan, but it looks like that might be changing."

"I'd hate to see our friendship ruined over a schoolhouse." Donovan felt something untamed uncoiling within him. He tried to maintain an expression of polite attention.

"It's not the schoolhouse," Ross answered, stepping closer. "The town can build a dozen schoolhouses for all I care, as long as they don't expect the cattlemen to pay for it."

"That's a sorry attitude to have," Donovan said, his muscles tensing. "But I figure every man is entitled to his opinion."

"This isn't about opinions, Donovan." Ross

narrowed his eyes. "This is about you and me. And Sarah."

Donovan raised his eyebrows. "What about Sarah?"

"I've lived here for over twenty years, Donovan. I've known Sarah since she was born. And I don't cotton to a newcomer like yourself toying with her affections."

"I'm not *toying* with anything." His voice lowered ominously, despite the twinge of guilt. "That's an insult to both me and Sarah."

"Sarah's a good woman," Ross returned. "She's had a hard time of it, and her judgment in the past hasn't always been sound. I mean to make sure that she doesn't make another bad decision."

Donovan scowled down at the shorter man. "Who's to say she will?"

Ross thrust a finger at him. "You're new here, Donovan. Nobody knows where you came from or who your family is. I find that mighty suspicious."

"I'm not wanted anywhere. That's all you or anyone else needs to know."

"That's not good enough. I mean to find out about you, Donovan. And if I don't like what I find out, you can be sure I'll be saying so. Publicly."

Donovan didn't even blink. If he had a penny for every threat made against him, he'd be even richer than he already was. "Is it really

Sarah you're concerned about, Ross?" he asked softly, baring his teeth in a smile that made the other man step back. "Or is it that you don't like the fact that someone else in town has just as much influence as you do?"

Ross's face reddened, but to his credit, he didn't explode. He jabbed his finger at Donovan again, though he kept his distance. "You just watch your step, Donovan. And I'll be watching you."

Ross spun on his heel and stalked away.

Donovan watched him go, tension coiling in him like an angry rattler. He had just managed to get Sarah off his trail, and now he had Ross Turner to worry about. With a muttered oath, he turned and mounted his horse. He kicked Senseless into a gallop, heading down Main Street and out of Burr.

He urged the bay faster, the countryside passing by in a blur. Already the sun had settled behind the mountains, casting a golden glow across a sky painted with pinks and oranges and lavenders. He barely noticed.

He rode as if pursued by screaming Indians. Senseless hit his stride, eating up the ground yards at a time, and Donovan urged him on.

Finally the ranch came into view. Donovan slowed up and eased Senseless into a gentle walk.

The house glowed warmly, gilded by the setting sun, and the outbuildings shone white against the dark mountains. Donovan stared at all of it, suddenly overwhelmed by his accomplishment.

Who could have known that the bastard son of a saloon girl would end up like this? Who could have foreseen that the greatest tragedy of his life—his mother's murder—would lead him down a path that would bring him here, to his own land, his own home?

How he had longed for a home. A place to belong. Every night as he lay on his pallet above the saloon, listening to his mother in the next room with the men who paid her for "company," he had dreamed of having a real home. One with a cheery fire and a mother who baked cookies. As he grew to manhood, that dream had shifted. He started craving his own land, his own house. And a wife who would cook his meals and bear his children. And maybe bake cookies.

Now he had the land and the home. All he needed was the woman.

After Sarah had approached him this evening, he had started to wonder if he hadn't been a little too vehement about not considering her for a bride. Heat like they had generally didn't just go away. Perhaps they could have worked something out.

But now he had another problem. He hadn't lied to Ross; he wasn't wanted anywhere. He had never committed a crime or been to jail.

But he *had* killed. In the name of justice.

He thought back to the sixteen-year-old boy he had once been. That man in a child's body who had discovered his mother dead one morning, strangled by a no-good son of a bitch who had a taste for knocking around women. That youngster who, fired up on more grit than sense, had taken a horse and tracked down his mother's murderer.

And he had killed him, when the bastard had come at him with a knife as long as his forearm, stabbing the man with his own weapon.

He remembered being sick. He had lost his dinner, then dragged the dead criminal back to town on a litter tied to his horse. The man had been too big for him to lift over the back of the animal.

He brought the body to the sheriff, with the idea of seeing justice done for his mother's murder. The sheriff hadn't cared one bit about the untimely death of a whore, but it turned out the dead man was wanted for robbing a stage. Donovan found himself wealthier by five hundred dollars and wiser in the ways of the world.

When the sheriff had asked his name, Donovan had been too humiliated to tell the lawman that he was the son of the disdained whore. He had met the sheriff's gaze squarely and said, "Blade."

And Blade he had become.

For the next fifteen years, he had pursued fugitives from justice. He had become wealthy from the bounties he collected and become legendary for the blade he wielded so well.

Until a year ago.

He closed his eyes as if to shut out the images that crowded his brain. His last bounty. The one that had gone so horribly wrong.

He had lost everything that night. The hostage. His horse. His confidence.

He knew then that it was time for Blade to retire. He took back his real name, and collected all his considerable savings from several banks. Then the bounty hunter Blade rode west one day, never to be heard from again.

And Jack Donovan had arrived in Burr, determined to build his dream.

Chapter 8

∽⎯⎯ꙮ⎯⎯∾

Town Council Votes to Build School
Ladies' Auxiliary Sponsors
Box Social to Raise Funds

At the town council meeting on Friday, May 12, the council voted to build a schoolhouse and hire a teacher for the children of Burr.

To raise the funds necessary, the Ladies' Auxiliary for the Betterment of Burr has decided to sponsor a box social at one o'clock on Sunday, May 21, at Miller's Pond. All the unwed ladies in town are asked to prepare a picnic dinner to be auctioned off to the bachelors of Burr. The gentlemen will receive not only a meal for their donations, but they will also share the company of the ladies who prepared their respective baskets for the afternoon. There will be tables set up for anyone who does not intend to participate in the auction. The proceeds will go toward the cost of building materials for the schoolhouse.

During the meeting, there was some argument as to whether Burr can afford both a teacher's salary and the materials for construction. However, thanks to the generosity of Jack Donovan, this is no longer an issue. Mr. Donovan has offered to personally pay the teacher's salary if the town can construct the building.

"Mama, how many times must we discuss this?" Sarah snapped the reins over Matilda's back and steered the buggy toward Miller's Pond.

"I still think you should have made up a basket, Sarah." June smoothed her skirt of pale green gingham. "I'm certain Ross Turner would bid on it."

"Mama . . ."

"Sweetheart, the man has come to sit on our porch with you these past two Saturday evenings. And he's talking about marriage. Of course he would bid on your basket."

Sarah sighed and didn't answer, not wanting to prolong the discussion. Ross Turner *had* come calling these past two Saturday nights. They had sat on the porch and carried on conversations that mostly centered around Ross and cattle. It had been pleasant to listen to a man talk about his dreams while watching the sunset, though cattle was not necessarily her favorite topic of conversation.

She couldn't deny that Ross was attractive.

And he *had* mentioned marriage. But there was no spark between them. No fire.

Nothing like what sizzled between her and Donovan.

She should be glad of that. She should be thrilled to be free from that carnal side of her that tormented her with improper hungers.

With Ross she could have all those things she had always dreamed about: a home of her own and children. But the cattleman had made it quite clear that no wife of his would work. That meant she would have to sell the *Chronicle*.

She had worked out her feelings of guilt over her father's death by taking on his dream, but somewhere along the way, she had made the paper her own. She enjoyed her job, and it would not be easy to put it aside.

But, amazingly, she was actually considering it.

Miller's Pond came into view. The Millers had moved on long ago, after a fire had burned down their farm, but the name still clung to the place. The overgrowth had all but buried the ruins of the burned buildings, leaving a pretty meadow that was ideal for picnics, with a watering hole shaded by trees that had become Burr's favorite fishing and swimming spot. A lone shed standing at the edge of the woods was all that remained of the farm.

Reverend Westerly stood in the back of

someone's buckboard, a pile of picnic baskets at his feet. Mrs. Westerly sat in the seat of the buckboard with a small wooden box, no doubt for the collection of funds. Everyone milled around, socializing and laughing and smiling.

"It looks like we haven't missed anything," June said as Sarah stopped the buggy beneath a maple tree.

"Good. I want to talk to a few people before they start the auction." Sarah climbed down and tied the horse's reins around a branch.

June scrambled out the other side. "You do that, dear. I'll just go talk to Honoria." She took a bulky, cloth-wrapped bundle from the back of the buggy and hurried away.

Sarah frowned after her mother for a moment, wondering what she was carrying. Probably someone's new dress. Without another thought on the matter, she grabbed her notepad and pencil, then walked across the meadow.

"Looks like a fine crowd of folks showed up for the auction," Matt said.

"Sure does," Amos agreed. "You fixin' on buyin' one a them baskets, boss?"

Donovan glanced sideways at the two men walking beside him. "I don't think so, Amos," he replied.

Matt chuckled. "Hey, Amos, I reckon the gals would pay Donovan to pick one of those baskets, the way they've been after him lately."

"Yessiree," Amos agreed. "The boss did his share by offerin' to pay for that teacher. I reckon he don't have to participate if he don't want to."

"You can both stop talking about me as if I'm not here," Donovan growled.

"If ya don't aim to buy a basket, boss, why are ya here?" Amos asked.

"It seemed like the right thing to do," Donovan answered. "Besides, I *am* looking for a wife." He sent them a hard glance. "You two can stop trailing me like a couple of hound dogs. Get on and enjoy yourselves."

"You got it, boss." Amos grabbed Matt by the arm and dragged him off.

Donovan chuckled, then scanned the crowd. His restless gaze settled on a familiar face. Had he been searching for her? Sarah's dark blond hair shone in the sunlight as she spoke earnestly with Reverend Westerly. For an instant their eyes met. She gave Donovan a little smile, then turned her attention back to the preacher.

He stared at her, struck by the way the breeze stirred her hair, the way her laughter carried across the meadow. One smile shouldn't make his heart clench like that, he thought with a twinge of alarm. One look shouldn't steal the thoughts from his head or the voice from his throat.

By all that was holy, why couldn't she be the right woman?

The preacher said something to Sarah, then walked away. She glanced over at Donovan, and once more, their gazes touched. He started walking before he even realized he had moved.

"Good morning," Sarah said as he drew near.

"Morning." The delicate scent of lavender drifted to him. He had a sudden image of her taking a bath, smoothing lavender-scented soap over her long limbs and soft skin.

Damn.

"Going to bid on a basket today?"

"Why, do you have one to bid on?" he teased, reminding himself that they were friends and nothing more.

"Of course not," she answered, her cheeks reddening.

"That's too bad."

Her blush deepened. "I'm here for the newspaper, and nothing more."

"You think some man wouldn't bid on your basket?" Unable to resist, he stroked a finger down her flushed cheek. "You should look in the mirror sometime, sassy girl."

Sarah stepped away from his touch just as someone called her name. She glanced over her shoulder. "My mother needs me. I'll speak to you later, Mr. Donovan."

"Sure." He watched her walk away, his gaze

following the sway of her bottom beneath her dark brown skirt.

"Why, Mr. Donovan!" All warm smiles and sparkling eyes, Mrs. Castor came over and took his arm. "Imagine, a handsome man like yourself standing here all alone."

"Good afternoon, Mrs. Castor." Still distracted, he watched Sarah make her way through the crowd until she reached her mother, who stood with Ross Turner.

The mayor's wife followed his gaze. "Well, now, isn't that sweet? Ross Turner and Sarah Calhoun. Who would have thought?"

Donovan turned to look at her. "Pardon?"

"Well, certainly you've heard the news. It seems as if there's a match in the making over there, yes indeed."

"So I've heard," he muttered.

"June is thrilled to bits. Of course, Sarah will have to sell the newspaper. A man like Ross won't tolerate his wife working."

Sarah, sell the newspaper? Impossible. "When did all this happen?"

Mrs. Castor stared at him. "Why, everyone knows that Ross Turner has come to call these past two Saturdays. It was only a matter of time." She glanced again at the couple in question. "Because of Imogene and all that."

"Imogene?"

Obviously thrilled to have an interested ear, Mrs. Castor launched into the role of narrator.

"Imogene was Ross's cousin. When his wife died a couple years back, Imogene came out to look after the children. I think it was supposed to be a temporary arrangement, but she just stayed on. She was a tender-hearted girl, but . . . well, she was a bit plain, and she liked her sweets a little too much, if you know what I mean."

"What does Imogene have to do with Sarah?"

"Well, everyone knows how Ross is about money," Mrs. Castor continued, "and since no one ever expected Imogene to marry, I suppose it suited Ross to have her stay on and save him the trouble of hiring someone to care for the children. Then that peddler came through town last fall, and that was the end of that."

Fascinated by the miserly flaw in the otherwise perfect Ross Turner, Donovan prodded, "Then what?"

Mrs. Castor stared at him in surprise. "Why, hadn't you heard? Imogene ran off with the peddler and left Ross high and dry with no one to manage his household. His boy Ross Junior is old enough to go out on the range, and the twins can certainly keep house, but what about little Betsy? She needs a mama, being only eight years old and all."

"So rather than hire someone to care for the children, he decided to get married," Donovan concluded.

"Well, I'm certain that wasn't his only reason," Mrs. Castor said diplomatically. "But it sure is nice that he chose Sarah. After all, it's not as if she's had any prospects—"

"There's nothing wrong with Sarah." Irritated with himself for lending an ear to gossip for even a short time, Donovan ignored the look of disappointment on the woman's face and tugged his hat brim. "If you'll pardon me, ma'am."

He walked along the edge of the crowd, keeping an eye on Sarah and her suitor. Pausing at the table that had been set up for those not participating in the auction, he got himself a glass of lemonade from a giggling young woman and went to a secluded spot beneath a shady maple.

Across the meadow, Ross placed a proprietary hand on Sarah's elbow.

A mother for little Betsy? Red-hot fury surged through Donovan. The strength of his desire to go over there and break Ross's arm stunned him. What was wrong with him?

He sipped at his lemonade, barely tasting the tart sweetness of it. All right, so the situation bothered him. He had been so certain that Sarah would never make time in her life for a husband—yet Ross had asked her to marry him, and now Sarah was thinking about selling the newspaper. Donovan hadn't even bothered to try and court her; he had just spent months convincing himself that she was the wrong woman for him. He had never imagined that she might be willing to compromise.

Maybe it was because Sarah was a woman, and he wasn't used to having to figure a woman's mind. His job had demanded that he study a man until he knew how the fellow's mind worked. What his secrets were. His fears. His dreams.

He hadn't done that with Sarah.

But what did he know about decent women? The only women with whom he'd had any sort of relationship had been good-time girls.

And in the meantime, Sarah was considering changing her entire life around for a chance to catch a husband. Without the newspaper, Sarah would change. She would turn into one of those giggling females who talked about nothing but fabrics and furniture, who grew old too quickly from too many babies in too few years.

The thought of Sarah lying with Turner in the marriage bed was enough to make his stomach clench.

He couldn't let her do it. If she was so set on selling the paper and getting married, then she could damned well marry *him*.

The reverend held up the third basket and announced the name of the young lady who had prepared it. Masculine voices shouted bids as the woman in question flushed and giggled with delight.

"Isn't this exciting?" June asked. "I haven't been to a box social since I was a girl."

"It serves the purpose of raising the funds, which is the important thing," Sarah conceded. She glanced at the tall rancher standing beside her. "Don't you think so, Mr. Turner?"

"Tomfoolery," Ross snorted as the victorious winner came forth to claim his basket and his companion amid cheers from the crowd. "But I have to give the town credit for what it's trying to do."

Sarah sighed. Her mother was determined that she take Ross's interest seriously, and she was trying. But the man's narrow-minded thinking constantly disappointed her.

"Isn't that her fiancé?" June asked, stretching on tiptoe to see over the crowd. "Oh, how romantic."

"I certainly hope you don't expect me to participate in this foolishness," Ross said to Sarah.

"Of course not," she responded. "I didn't even prepare a basket."

"This next basket was made up by Miss Sarah Calhoun," Reverend Westerly called. "May I have the first bid?"

Ross stared at her.

"I didn't make anything!" she protested. "There must be some mistake."

Ross scowled. "Since the whole darned town knows I'm courting you, I suppose I have to make a bid or else look like a fool. I'm certainly not going to let anyone else spend the afternoon with you."

"But I didn't—wait a minute." She glared at June. "Mother?"

"I didn't see the harm." June rolled her eyes. "Young people these days."

"What's done is done," Ross said.

"Very well." Sarah glared at her mother as Ross called out his bid.

"I have fifty cents," the reverend announced with a stern look at Ross. "Do I hear one dollar? One dollar for this delicious ham dinner and the company of Miss Sarah Calhoun?"

Ross looked around threateningly, as if to warn off anyone else.

"One dollar."

Sarah jerked her head around at the familiar voice. Donovan leaned against a tree on the other side of the crowd, his arms folded across his chest. He watched her for a long moment with that black-as-hell gaze, then grinned and tugged his hat brim in salute. She flushed.

"What the hell does he think he's doing?" Ross's color rose, deepening his ruddy complexion to an apoplectic red.

June smiled with delight. "Apparently, he's bidding on Sarah's basket."

"One dollar. I have one dollar. Do I hear two?" Reverend Westerly called with a wide grin.

"Damn it." Ross glared at Sarah. "This is going to end up costing a pretty penny, and all because of Donovan. Two!" he yelled.

"Mr. Turner, your language!" June admonished.

Sarah raised her brows. Ross had shown her nothing but charm and geniality these past two weeks. She had never witnessed this side of him.

"Two dollars," the reverend said with a grin. "That's a fine donation to the school fund from Ross Turner. We have two dollars. Do I hear any more?"

"Two dollars," Ross muttered in disgust, digging for his money.

"Going once . . ."

"Two dollars, Sarah!" June exclaimed, her eyes bright. "That's a fine donation."

"Going twice . . ."

"Thirty dollars."

The crowd gasped.

Ross turned pale.

June squealed.

Sarah stared at Donovan.

The preacher cleared his throat. "Did you say two-thirty, Mr. Donovan?"

"No, Reverend. I said thirty dollars." Donovan held Sarah's gaze. Somewhere in the back of her mind, she thought she heard the howl of a lonely wolf.

"Thirty dollars. My goodness." Awed at a bid that amounted to a month's pay for most people, Reverend Westerly edged a finger along his collar and cleared his throat. "The bid is thirty dollars," he said loudly.

"Thirty dollars," Ross whispered. He swallowed, glanced at Sarah, then shoved the money back into his pocket. "I don't even have that much with me."

"Going once . . ."

Ross wasn't going to bid any more, Sarah realized.

"Going twice . . ."

He could have put his word on it and matched Donovan's bid, but he didn't.

"Sold to Mr. Donovan, for the price of thirty dollars!"

Sold to the devil for thirty dollars.

Sarah stepped forward, prepared to do her part to help the school fund. Ross grabbed her elbow.

"Sarah Calhoun, I hope you don't intend to go through with this!"

Sarah tugged her arm free and frowned at the red-faced rancher. "I have to go through with it, Ross. Even though I didn't make the basket"—she sent a sharp look at her mother, who ignored her—"I still have to do this, for the school."

"Sarah, I will not have you make a laughingstock of me. You will *not* go off alone with Donovan, and that's that."

She clenched her fingers tightly as her temper sparked to life, but she made an effort to remain calm. "I must go. Our neighbors expect it."

His face grew even redder if possible, but he had no answer. Appearances were everything to a man like Ross. Sarah turned her back on him and started walking toward Donovan, who had the basket in hand, a grin on his face.

Sarah pasted on a false smile for the sake of the crowd, all the while plotting to give Jack Donovan a piece of her mind.

And nothing else.

Chapter 9

"The nerve ... the utter gall ... !" Sarah spluttered. "Who gave you permission to interfere in my life?"

"I'm not interfering. I only bought your basket."

"It's the same thing."

Donovan sighed. He walked with Sarah through the meadow, looking for a place to sit and eat the dinner he had just purchased for thirty dollars.

Thirty dollars, he thought with a shake of his head. He could have bought a brand-new saddle for that amount of money! But it was worth it to get Sarah to himself. And it hadn't hurt to beat out Ross Turner, either. But he didn't think Sarah agreed with him.

Given her current temper, he decided to wait until she settled down before he mentioned the change in their relationship.

"I don't see why we have to go so far from the others," Sarah carped, stomping along with her sturdy brown skirt clenched in furious fists.

"Because I want to talk to you," he replied, feeling amiable. "And I really don't want any of those busybodies to get wind of what I have to say. Do you?"

Sarah snorted. "The last thing I want is gossip, but you and your grandiose gesture have assured that the rumor mill will be working overtime for the next week."

"Well, if I hadn't bid that much money, Ross Turner would be the one carrying this basket." He grunted and shifted his grip. "What the heck is in here anyway? Enough food to feed the whole town?"

"I have no idea what's in there," Sarah replied primly. "I didn't make it; my mother did. And as for Ross, why should the prospect of a picnic with him disturb me?"

"Because he's wrong for you. Look at the way he took off when I won your basket." Donovan stopped beneath a shady tree behind some bushes that would hide them from curious eyes and prying ears.

She pressed her lips together in annoyance. "Why Ross left is none of your business. Besides, who are you to say who's wrong for me and who's right?"

He put down the basket and withdrew a checkered tablecloth, then handed her an edge.

"I'm your friend. We are friends, aren't we?"

Sarah sniffed in disapproval as she helped him spread the cloth over the ground. "Friends don't embarrass friends."

"I wouldn't know. As you've pointed out, I'm a little short on social graces."

She made a sound of exasperation. "I don't know what sort of people you're used to, Mr. Donovan, but in most social circles, friends help each other."

"I am trying to help you. I need to talk to you alone, and this was the only way I could do it."

She sighed and shook her head. "Mr. Donovan—"

"Jack," he murmured with a warm, intimate smile. He touched her shoulder. "We've surely known each other long enough."

She eyed him warily, then nodded.

"Now sit down so we can eat."

She sank down onto the blanket as he started unloading the picnic basket. She watched his lean, competent hands and wondered what he wanted to talk to her about.

Donovan sat down on the blanket across from her and took off his hat, placing it on the ground next to him. His black hair was slicked back from his face, casting the sharp blade of his nose and his angular cheekbones into prominent relief. Sarah curled her fingers into her palms and fought the urge to touch him as he took an apple from the basket, pulled out a knife, and began to peel the fruit.

"What did you want to discuss?" she asked, trying to distract herself from her own sensual thoughts. "The school project?"

"Nope." The red skin fell away from the apple in one long coil. He held the freshly peeled fruit out to her. "Apple?"

Sarah blinked at the speed with which he had pared it. Taking it from his hand, she stared at the smooth surface. Any other man would have left nicks and jabs in the fruit, but Donovan had sliced the peel off in one quick, clean motion that left a smooth path from the knife. She glanced up at him, but he was peeling another apple with the same easy skill.

She wondered where a man learned to use a simple blade with the proficiency of a master woodcarver.

He glanced up as a second long curl of red peel dropped to the blanket. "What's the matter?"

She answered his question with one of her own. "Isn't it the woman who's supposed to tempt the man with an apple?"

He paused in raising the fruit to his lips. "I don't know about apples, sassy girl—but *you* sure tempt a man." He bit deep into the juicy pulp and paused, taking what seemed to be an indecently long time to finally scoop the bite into his mouth. The glint in his dark eyes made her shiver.

She cleared her throat. "I ... um ... I thought we had agreed that you weren't going to tease me anymore."

"I'm just giving you a compliment. You're a pretty woman, Sarah Calhoun."

She blushed. "Thank you. You're a very attractive man."

"Thank you kindly, Miss Sarah." He grinned, stretching out to lie on his side, his lone dimple easing the hawklike sharpness of his features. He propped his head on one hand and bit into the apple again with strong white teeth. The other men attending the box social had come dressed in their Sunday best, but Donovan had chosen to wear black pants, a white shirt, and a black leather vest. He looked nothing like one of the wealthiest ranchers in the area. At first glance she would have mistaken him for a cowhand or a drifter.

Or an outlaw.

Sarah averted her gaze from his lean body, so close and warm, and tried to ignore where her thoughts led. But she had to admit the idea of Jack Donovan as an outlaw definitely appealed to her. Even if he'd never broken a law in his life, he had that element of danger about him that secretly thrilled her. Determined to regain control of her wild fantasies, she bit into her apple. The tart sweetness of the fruit exploded on her tongue.

"You realize if we keep this up, we might actually get along," he drawled.

"I don't like to fight," she said.

"Yes, you do," he replied with a grin. "It keeps life interesting. Besides, it's your nature."

"It is not!" she responded hotly. He burst into laughter and she grinned sheepishly. "All right, so maybe it is. It must be the Irish bloodlines."

"I'd say it's just you, Sarah."

She sighed. "It's not very ladylike, is it? This temper of mine."

"I don't know about ladylike, but I'd rather be with a woman than a lady any time." He bit into the apple and chewed, his movements lazy, his gaze watchful.

"Ladies *are* women."

"There are women who are ladies, and there are women who are women. Ladies bore me. They're always fainting and blushing and worrying what everyone else thinks of their hair. Women, on the other hand, aren't afraid to just be. They don't get caught up in all that nonsense."

"Whether that's true or not, a woman must watch out for her reputation," Sarah said. "I've seen what happens when that reputation is a bad one, and it's nothing to laugh about."

He shrugged. "A woman should worry more

about what she thinks of herself than what others think of her."

"Easy for a man to say," she scoffed. "It's usually a man who ruins a woman's reputation to begin with."

"Sometimes," he conceded.

"Most of the time," she responded bitterly.

He stopped eating and pinned her with that wise, dark-eyed gaze. "Something you want to talk about?"

"No." She brushed away his concern with a wave of her hand. "I'm sure you've heard the whole story by now."

"Some people don't pay all that much attention to gossip," he said quietly. "And maybe everyone isn't talking about you as much as you think they are. There *are* other things going on in this town."

She flushed. "You think I'm self-centered, don't you?"

"No, I think you've been hurt. But it really doesn't matter what I think, sweet Sarah. It's your opinion of yourself that matters." He bit off the last chunk of apple and tossed the core into the basket.

"I like myself," she said thoughtfully. "Well, most of the time. I like what I've built with the newspaper."

"You picked yourself up from a fall and got right back on the horse," he pointed out. "That takes a lot of guts. A lot of women might have just given up and let someone else take care of them."

"I guess that's where my temper proved an asset," she mused. "I got mad, and I was stubborn enough not to let them beat me."

"Atta girl." He sat up and rummaged in the hamper, pulling out two thick ham sandwiches. "Too bad you're thinking of giving all that up."

She took the sandwich from his hand. "I'm not giving anything up."

"You'd be sacrificing the newspaper for a wedding dress," he said, unwrapping his sandwich. "And that would eventually eat away at you. You deserve better, Sarah."

"Ross is a good man. And it's my choice." She started to eat her sandwich, thinking the matter finished.

"I just want you to make the right choice. Who's to say that Ross will be the only man to ask you to marry him?"

She frowned. The man was like a dog with a bone. "I'm getting on in years, Jack, and there are very few men who would look beyond the . . . troubles . . . in my past like Ross has done."

"Getting on in years?" He threw back his head and roared with laughter. "How old are you, Sarah? Twenty-one, twenty-two?"

"Don't you know better than to ask a woman her age?" she snapped. "Never mind—obviously you don't. I'll have you know that I turned twenty-three last month."

"I'm thirty-one, sassy girl, and believe me when I tell you that you've just begun to live."

"No one can predict the future, Jack Donovan. I'm certain you felt older than your years at my age, just like I do."

He sobered. "It's true that I grew up long before I should have. Take my advice, sweet Sarah, and enjoy your youth. Life has a way of taking it from you, whether you like it or not."

The raw emotion in his voice stirred something in her. She touched his hand. "Where are you from, Jack? You've never said."

He looked down at her fingers on his, then glanced up at her face. "Kansas."

"You have family there?"

"No." He shook his head. "The only family I ever had was my mother, and she's been dead for years."

"It's devastating to lose a parent." Sarah hesitated. "How did she die?"

He paused, and she thought he wasn't going to answer. Finally he said "She was murdered."

"Oh, Jack, I'm so sorry."

He shrugged. "It was a long time ago."

"My father was murdered, too." She gave a wry smile. "I guess that gives us something in common, doesn't it?"

"I guess it does."

Silence stretched between them.

"Did they ever catch who did it?" she asked finally.

"Yep." He glanced at her, and she shivered, seeing the wolf looking out of those deep brown eyes. "I caught him, and I killed him. Guess that would be called justice, wouldn't it?"

She didn't know what to say, so she didn't say anything, merely sat there with her hand on his. After a moment, he turned his hand palm-up and twined his fingers with hers.

Birds called to one another and rustled through the bushes. A fat bumblebee buzzed drunkenly by, circling the tree trunk and hovering briefly over Sarah's ham sandwich before whizzing off in search of the flowers that dotted the meadow. The distant rumble of voices and occasional burst of laughter reminded them that they weren't alone, despite the relative isolation of their picnic spot.

"I . . . knew the man who killed my father," Sarah said softly. "I was in love with him. But after what he did, I helped the sheriff catch him."

The squeeze of his hand was reassuring. "At least with my mother, it was a stranger. I was barely sixteen, but I went out and tracked him down. I didn't mean to kill him; it just happened that way. I don't know what I might have done if I had actually been friends with the murderer. It must have been very hard for you."

"It wrecked my entire life. But I had the newspaper to help get through the worst of it. And now it's all I have left of my father, really—his dream."

"You kept it alive." He squeezed her hand. "I'm sure he's proud of you, Sarah."

"Thank you for saying that." She smiled at him, tears stinging her eyes. "You don't know how much I needed to hear that."

"Aw, now don't start crying on me." He searched his pockets and came up with a crumpled bandanna. Using the corner, he dabbed at the drops that skimmed her cheek. "Why do women always have to cry? Don't you know that tears make a man loco?"

She laughed through the tears, then took hold of the hand that had soothed them away.

"Thank you, Jack." She pressed a kiss to his knuckles. "You're the best friend a woman could have."

He grew still. "Just don't be inviting me to any quilting bees."

"*I* don't even attend the quilting bees," she said with a grin. "But you're welcome to come to supper anytime you have a mind to."

"Now that's an invitation that warms my heart. But what about Ross? He won't take kindly to another man sitting at your supper table."

"You're my friend. He'll just have to get used to it," she said fiercely.

"That's my Sassy." He grinned and tugged a wisp of hair that had escaped from her braid. "Go get 'em."

"I told you not to call me that ridiculous name." She flushed and hoped he would think it was from annoyance and not pleasure. Though she thrilled to the nickname, she would rather die than admit it.

"I told you, it suits you. Deep inside the prim and proper Miss Calhoun beats the heart of my sassy girl."

"Oh, stop." She gave him a playful shove, and the light of battle came into his eyes.

"So, you want to play, do you?" He gave her a devilish smile and tucked his bandanna away in his pocket.

"Now, Jack . . ." She scooted backward on the blanket. He reached for her and she squealed, batting his hand away before he could grab her wrist.

"Oh, no, you don't . . ." he growled.

With a screech of laughter, she threw her apple core at him, then rolled to her feet and ran. He was only a step behind her. He grabbed hold of her braid, bringing her to a stop, and pulled her backward into his arms. She whirled to face him, pushing against his chest with both hands and giggling.

"No, you don't, Jack Donovan! Stop!" The

fierceness of her commands wilted beneath the force of her laughter. She slapped the palms of her hands against his chest in a lame effort to break his hold. "Stop, I say!"

He grinned down at her like an outlaw. "Make me."

He started walking her backward, his arms locked around her.

"Jack Donovan, you let go of me right now, or I'll . . . I'll . . ." Her words spluttered to a stop as he tickled her ribs, and she started whooping with laughter again.

"Or you'll what?" he asked with a chuckle. "You don't look so tough now."

She writhed desperately, trying to escape the torment of his fingers dancing along her side as he continued to ease her backward until she came up against the tree. He planted his hands on either side of her head and smirked down at her. "Give up?"

She panted and blew a few loose tendrils of hair from her face. "Never."

He edged one hand down and flexed his fingers just over her ribs. "You sure?"

She nodded, her lips parted in a grin. "I never give up," she gasped.

"Stubborn Irish." He wiggled his fingers against her side. "Are you sure—"

She shrieked and jabbed his arm with her elbow, then pivoted to make a run for it. Her action knocked his hand from her waist, and as she turned, his palm skidded up to land on her breast. Both of them froze.

To her horror, her nipple hardened beneath his touch. She jerked her gaze to his and saw the knowledge of her body's betrayal in his face. Watching his hand with the intensity of a predator, he slowly rubbed his thumb over the rigid little nub. She gave a tiny whimper in the back of her throat as a jolt of arousal spiked through her.

He trailed the backs of his fingers across her breast, seemingly fascinated with her body's response. She reached out to stop him, to push him away, but instead found herself guiding his hand until the plump flesh rested in his palm. She let her head fall back against the tree, her eyes half shut, as she enjoyed the waves of pleasure that washed over her.

He raised his other hand to give the same attention to her nipple's twin.

She made a purring noise and arched her back, eager for his touch. He eased one leg between her thighs, then lowered his mouth to her throat. She moaned, and his arousal pressed into her hip with arrogant demand. She slid her arms around his waist and pulled him closer.

He flicked open the buttons of her blouse and parted it to her waist, revealing her lace-edged shift. He dipped his head, skimming his mouth over the tops of her breasts. She dug her fingers into his back, curving into him as his lips and tongue explored the sensitive flesh now revealed to him. Soft noises escaped her throat as he nipped at her neck and shoulder.

His fingers crept beneath her blouse and hooked the straps of her shift off her shoulders. The material gapped around her bosom, and he smoothed aside the cotton and lace until her breasts were bared to the May sunshine.

A breeze caressed her flesh, puckering her nipples even more. He smiled and traced one pale pink circle of flesh. Then he bent and took it in his mouth.

She slammed her head back against the tree, but the pain was lost in the desire that surged through her body.

"Sweet heaven," she gasped.

He looked up at her, holding her gaze as he suckled her nipple. The hungry passion that glowed in his eyes matched her own, and something snapped. She speared her hands into his hair and pulled his head up to kiss him with all the greedy ardor that raged through her.

His deep-throated groan ripped a similar noise from her. She pressed the palm of her hand against his arousal, eagerly stroking. He stiffened, then grabbed her skirts and yanked them up to her knees. His roughened hands caressed the backs of her thighs before he lifted her, shoving her higher against the trunk of the tree, curving her legs around his hips.

"Jack!" she cried out, gripping his shoulders, her body singing with passion.

He froze.

"Christ Jesus," he swore. "What the hell am I doing?"

He stepped back and lowered her to the ground, then jerked the edges of her blouse together. "Get dressed," he snapped.

Dazed, Sarah slowly straightened her clothes as he walked several yards away and stood with his back to her, his hands on his hips and his head bent. What had *he* been doing? Sweet Lord, what had *she* been doing? She must have lost her mind, to practically make love with the man in full view of the entire town.

But oh, how sweet the madness had been while it lasted.

Once she got her clothes properly buttoned and tucked, she reached behind her and pulled the tie from the end of her braid. Being shoved against a tree and half devoured had played havoc with her normally neat hairstyle—and people would definitely notice.

She finger-combed her loosened, waist-long hair and eyed Donovan's stiff back. Should she go to him and make sure he was all right, or just get the comb from her reticule and see to her hair? She hesitated, nibbling her lower lip, then made her decision. Resolutely, she headed for Donovan.

She knew he heard her come up behind him, because he stiffened.

"Jack?" She paused, but he didn't face her. "Listen to me. It's all right. I'm not angry or anything . . ."

"*You're* not angry?" He spun to face her, his expression fierce. "*I'm* angry, at myself. That almost got out of hand."

"It's all right, Jack. I know you made a promise to me, but we all make mistakes."

"A mistake? Hell, no." He gave a harsh laugh. "Wrong time and wrong place, definitely—but not a mistake. I'm just mad at myself for losing control."

She blinked, confused. "What?"

"Do you really think I'd risk everyone seeing us together after what you just told me?"

"I guess not." She felt very cold, as if she'd fallen into a frozen lake. She should have known he'd reject her after hearing about her past.

"I've been trying to be a gentleman, yet here we are, all over each other like a couple of minks," he continued. "Damn it, I lose my reason every time I touch you."

"It's not my fault you can't control yourself," she returned, hot anger dispelling the coldness of his rebuff. "As I recall, Jack, *you* were the one to bid on *my* basket."

"I know that! Damn it, woman, you make me do crazy things."

"No one made you do anything you didn't want to do."

"It's not that. I mean . . . Damn it, Sarah, it just isn't decent!"

"Decent?" The breeze blew long strands of hair across her face, and she impatiently brushed them aside, the picture of control even as her heart cracked a little more. "You're quite correct, Jack. Decent people do not behave like I just did."

"That's not what I meant—"

She held up a hand. "You've made your point. I quite understand."

"I don't think so." He gestured at her. "I can't seem to help myself around you, Sarah. Women like you make a man forget how to be civilized."

"Women like me?" Stung, she folded her arms tightly across her chest. It was so obvious that he thought she was a loose woman, lacking in morals. The moment he had touched her, she had melted into him like a wanton.

Bitterness from hurts long unhealed spilled over the wound of his rejection. "There are plenty of other women to choose from, Jack Donovan," she said stiffly.

"And every one of them is trying to get into my bed," he muttered.

"That should make your search much easier!" She turned away from him and stalked toward the blanket where her reticule lay. He had been playing the same game with her for months now, and she was tired of it. As much as being in his arms made her blood sing, her heart couldn't take any more abuse.

"Wait a minute, Sarah!"

She took out her comb and jerked it through her hair, ignoring him.

Until he grabbed the comb, and her hair with it.

"Ow!" She yanked the comb from his hand and rubbed her stinging scalp, glaring at him.

"Just listen to me, Sarah," he said. "Look, you just told me something important about your past, and then things got out of control. You know what could have happened, right here in front of the whole town?"

"What *almost* happened, you mean."

"I wanted you, and I thought you wanted me. I'm trying to do what's best for both of us."

"Which is what? To seduce me? No, thank you, Jack. I have no interest in your games." She parted her hair and rapidly started braiding.

"They're not games!" He hauled her close against him, holding her firmly to his chest. She struggled but her hands were tangled in her hair, leaving her helpless in his grasp. "Damn it, Sarah, I was trying to make you feel good, trying to give you what you need. You don't appreciate yourself enough."

"And you do? Tell me, Jack, what am I supposed to do? Thank you for taking pity on the poor ruined spinster?"

"It's not like that! You're twisting my words, Sarah."

"Then explain it to me."

He gave a growl of frustration. "Look, one of the most respected men in town wants to marry you—"

"Oh, I see how it is now!" She shoved one hand against his chest, freeing herself from his embrace. "Now that Ross Turner is interested in marrying me, I'm suddenly more desirable? I'm not some sort of prize heifer to be fought over!"

"I never said you were." He grasped her shoulders. "And I have *never* stopped wanting you, Sarah."

She jerked away from him again. "How nice for you that Ross's approval of me finally makes it all right for you to acknowledge your feelings."

"I don't think Ross is right for you, but if you're dead set on marrying him—"

"You thought you'd give me one last tumble before I marry a man you think is wrong for me? Is that what this was, Jack?" She tied off the braid and flipped it back over her shoulder.

"There's no talking to you," he said, throwing his hands up in surrender.

"I don't need your pity, and I don't need your advice," she snarled, stabbing a finger into his chest. "And I'll thank you to keep your distance from me in the future."

"It's not pity!"

"I don't want to hear your excuses. I'm done playing your games, Jack Donovan." She swept up her reticule off the blanket. "The sooner you get yourself married, the happier I'll be!"

She stormed off, leaving Donovan standing amid the ruins of the meal he had purchased for thirty dollars.

Chapter 10

Jack Donovan was a man to admit his mistakes and learn from them, but since he'd met Sarah Calhoun, it was getting to be a damned habit.

As he steered his brand-new buggy down the road, he admitted to himself that he had bungled things with Sarah at the box social. He had bought her lunch with the idea of wooing her, so she would see that he was serious and not just teasing. But then he had touched her—and all his good intentions had gone to hell.

He knew Sarah misunderstood his reasons for not wanting to marry her. And from her frosty attitude toward him over the past week, it was clear she had misinterpreted his irritation with himself as rejection.

Yessiree, he had made a mess of things for sure. But he had come up with a plan to convince Sarah that he was serious about courting her. There would be no misunderstandings this time. Whatever the trouble in her past, he would prove to her that he wasn't ashamed of her. He would make her believe that he saw her as a lady as well as a desirable woman. This time, he would do it right.

The shiny new buggy was the first step in his campaign to woo Sarah Ann Calhoun. If a man wanted to keep a wife, he figured he should keep her in style. Any woman would be impressed with the smooth ride of the carriage and the comfortable seats. And a man come a-courting, freshly shaven and wearing his Sunday best, could make even the stubborn heart of his sassy girl flutter a time or two. With a wide grin on his face, he steered toward the church, determined to take Miss Sarah Calhoun for a leisurely drive around the countryside after the service.

Whether she liked it or not.

As the bell tower of the church came into view, he smiled and snapped the reins over the backs of the twin brown geldings, anticipating an interesting afternoon in Sarah's company.

At the top of the rise, he saw something at the side of the road—a strange patch of brown that disturbed the green of the countryside. At first he thought it was a downed deer, but as he drew closer, it became recognizable as a man lying at the side of the road wrapped in a long, fawn-colored coat.

Donovan slowed the horses. The stillness of the figure bothered him. It was early enough that a man too drunk to stumble home might still be passed out where he fell. But one would think that the sound of horses' hooves almost on top of him would wake even the drunkest of drunks.

He pulled up on the reins. The fellow could come to harm lying at the side of the road like that—he ought to at least see if the man needed help. Donovan hopped down from the buggy and moved swiftly to kneel beside the prone figure.

He pressed his fingers to the man's neck and found a weak pulse. Good. Then he turned the fellow on to his back, and cursed.

Blood soaked the right side of his white shirt near the shoulder, and stained his coat. He'd been shot.

The man wore a pair of .45 Colt army revolvers, which by some miracle had not been stolen, and his clothing was sturdy and made for life on the trail. His skin was bronzed from lengthy hours spent outdoors, and his long, light brown hair was clean and streaked with strands of gold. This was no drifter, but a man accustomed to having money in his pocket as he traveled the trails for reasons of his own.

And he was slowly bleeding to death at the side of the road.

Donovan shoved aside the ruined coat and

ripped open the man's shirt. The ugly hole in his shoulder oozed blood. Donovan dug out his new white handkerchief and pressed it against the wound.

The man's eyelids flickered and he moaned softly, his breath hitching in his throat. A good sign, Donovan thought. He pulled out his knife and sliced off the sleeve of the man's ruined shirt, using it as a crude binding. Then as gently as he could, he picked up the unconscious man and loaded him into the buggy.

Swinging up into the driver's seat, he snapped the reins over the horses' backs and raced for town.

The ringing of the church bell echoed off the mountains, summoning the parishioners to Sunday service. It had been a week since the box social, and Sarah still smarted over the way the picnic had ended. Donovan had tried to talk to her several times over the past week, but she told herself that she didn't want to hear anything he had to say.

Her heart disagreed, but with an iron will, she ignored the longings of that treacherous organ.

As she walked beside her mother toward the church, she told herself it was for the best. There were volatile emotions at work between them, and Sarah knew it was safer if they stayed apart.

They could never be alone together again.

"You're very quiet," June said.

Sarah shrugged.

"Are you still angry at me for putting your basket in the auction?"

"You had no right to do that," Sarah replied with bitterness in her tone. "I told you—"

"I had every right," June snapped back. She stopped and put her hands on her hips, causing Sarah to halt as well. Oblivious to the fact that they stood on Main Street in full view of everyone on their way to Sunday service, June lit into her daughter with a tone Sarah hadn't heard since she was in pigtails. "I am sick and tired of the way you lock yourself away from life, Sarah Ann Calhoun. As your mother, I have had enough of it."

"Mama, I know you want the best for me, but I don't think you're being realistic."

"Don't you start with me, Sarah Ann. No one understands realistic better than I do. I left my family in Philadelphia to come west with your father. It was dangerous, and it was a risk. And then he died and left me alone, and I had to find a new way to go on." She paused. "You are *not* the only one who's suffered in this."

"I never meant that I was the only one—"

June went on as if Sarah hadn't spoken, her blue eyes flashing with a ferocity she only showed in regard to her children. "You were young, and you made a mistake. We all do; it's how we learn. But that is no reason to stop living."

"I haven't stopped living," Sarah replied, stunned by her mother's impassioned words. "I have a good life running the newspaper."

"Running the newspaper was your father's life, not yours. And at least he knew how to separate work and home." June took her hand, her voice thickening with emotion. "Sarah, you're my daughter, and I love you. Please don't expect me to stand by and watch you waste the best years of your life."

Sarah stared at her mother as if she had never seen her before. Why hadn't she ever noticed the steel beneath the sweet smile and ladylike demeanor? Why hadn't it occurred to her that one reason she had been accepted back into society was June Calhoun's unyielding support?

"Oh, Mama." Sarah reached out to hug her mother, and she felt the comfort of June's hand stroking her hair. "I don't want to waste my life," she murmured, like a little girl waking from a nightmare.

"You won't, sweetheart. You're my daughter, and I don't remember teaching you to give up."

The thunder of horses approaching drew Sarah's attention. Pulling back, she watched as a shiny black buggy drawn by a matched pair of Morgans sped past them and bulleted toward the church.

"Good gracious, wasn't that Mr. Donovan?" June asked, shading her eyes with her hand.

"Yes, it was." Sarah watched the buggy pull up outside the church in a cloud of dust. Donovan leaped from the vehicle and hurried inside the building. He emerged seconds later with Doc Mercer.

"Something's going on," Sarah murmured. Her investigative instincts hummed as both men climbed into the buggy. Donovan wheeled the vehicle around and dashed down the street to the clinic. He hitched the horses quickly, then hurried to the other side of the buggy to help Doc Mercer carry an unconscious man into the physician's office.

"Someone's hurt," June said.

"I'm going to go find out who," Sarah said. Lifting her skirts, she ran down the street.

"Sarah Ann Calhoun," her mother called after her, "just what do you think you're doing? You're going to miss church!"

Sarah just waved and made a beeline for the door of the clinic.

Not only was there a story brewing, but somehow Jack Donovan was at the heart of it.

"Good thing you found him when you did." Doc Mercer worked steadily on his patient as he spoke. "Bullet went clean through, but he lost a lot of blood. Much longer and he would have bled to death."

Donovan mumbled a response, his attention distracted. The doctor had shed his Sunday coat and donned a snow-white apron that was now splattered with crimson. As the short, balding man stitched the wound with his usual care and precision, Donovan had gone through the stranger's coat pockets to find out who he was. He had his answer now in the small piece of metal that he held in his palm.

"Looks like we know something, at least." Donovan threw the object on a table with a tinny clang. "He's a lawman."

Doc glanced up from his work and noted the details of the badge. "U.S. marshal," he said. "Well, well."

"A U.S. marshal?"

Both men looked up at the feminine voice. Donovan scowled. Sarah Calhoun, all done up in her brown poplin Sunday best, watched them from the open doorway of the clinic.

"Good morning, Sarah." Doc Mercer smiled and went back to his stitching. "I figured you'd be along."

She came into the room and closed the door behind her, her eyes on Donovan. "A wounded U.S. marshal is big news in Burr," she said. "Hello, Jack."

"Sarah." He gave her a nod and wished she didn't look like something in a confectionery window. His mouth watered with the need to taste.

She turned her attention to the man on the examining table and stepped closer. "How is he, Doc?"

"Weak," the physician replied. "But I think he'll pull through. His type usually does. But it's still a lucky thing Donovan here found him when he did."

"You found him?" Notebook in hand, Sarah glanced at Donovan. For an instant there was a flicker of something warm and wild in her eyes, then she was all business.

He tensed at that look, remembering it well from their encounter beneath the tree at the box social. But she was trying to ignore the sensual pull between them, so he did the same. Clearing his throat, he answered, "Yeah, I found him."

"Where and how did you find him, Mr. Donovan?"

Mr. Donovan. When he'd held her in his arms, she had called him Jack in that sweet, husky voice . . .

He jerked his mind away from that dangerous territory. "I found him on the road, just outside of town."

"Was he conscious? Did he say anything to you?"

"No, he's been unconscious since I found him."

Sarah jotted something in her notebook. "And you, Dr. Mercer? It's your opinion that he will live?"

"Yes, I believe so." The physician finished dressing the man's wound, then turned to pour water from a pitcher into a basin.

"Do we know his name or what he was doing in the area?"

"We know nothing about him other than what we told you," Donovan said. "We'll have to wait until he comes to before we can find out anything else."

"Hmmm." Sarah came over to the table and looked down at the sleeping lawman. "Who are you? Who are you looking for?" she asked, more to herself than him.

A soft moan answered her. Donovan glanced at the doc, who looked equally startled, before moving over to the table.

The lawman's eyelids flickered, then opened, and a shuddering breath escaped him. His lips moved.

"What?" Donovan leaned closer, trying to hear. "What did you say?"

The marshal's lips moved again, his voice a mere whisper. Then his eyelids slid closed and his breathing steadied.

"He's out again," the doctor observed.

"What did he say?" Sarah asked. "Did you hear?"

"Yeah." Donovan straightened. "It sounded like 'Luke Petrie.' "

"Dear God." Sarah's notebook fell from her fingers.

"Well, well," said the doctor.

Sarah gave Donovan a frightened look and bolted from the room.

Donovan picked up her fallen notebook and hurried after her.

Sarah fled to the one place where she felt safe, where she had control of her life. The newspaper office.

She slammed the door behind her and stood there for a moment, her heart pounding like that of a jackrabbit with a hound on its trail. She took comfort in the sight of her sturdy wooden desk with its collection of pens and the small glass vase of wildflowers. Her printing press dominated half of the working area, strong and powerful, grotesquely beautiful in its black steel majesty.

Here, she was secure. Here, she was master of her fate.

Slowly she untied the ribbons of her straw bonnet and hung it on the peg by the door. As she walked to her desk, the door behind her opened. She whirled with a little scream, her hand going to her bosom.

"Easy, Sarah. It's just me."

"Good heavens." Sarah slowly lowered her

hand from her thundering heart as Donovan closed the door behind him. "You gave me such a fright."

"Seems to me you're a bit on edge." He advanced on her slowly, as a man might approach a feral animal. "You left the doc's awful quick."

"Yes. Well." At a loss for words, she shrugged and looked away.

He stopped just in front of her and paused, then put a hand on her shoulder. "Are you all right?"

The gentle understanding in his tone almost undid her fragile defenses. She wanted nothing more than to step into his arms and let him tell her everything would be all right.

But she couldn't do that.

"I'm fine," she said, forcing herself to look him in the eye. "I was just startled, that's all."

"I'll say you were. Hearing that name must be like hearing the devil's coming to call."

She gave a small, wry smile. "Apparently, he is."

"You're really scared of this fella, aren't you?"

She let out the breath she didn't know she was holding. "Yes. Very. But I'll handle it."

"From what I've heard, he sounds like a nasty son of a bitch."

"Oh, he is." She pulled away from the comfort of his touch and began to pace the room.

"I suppose someone told you the whole sordid story."

He shrugged. "Bits and pieces. Enough to make me think you need some protection."

"You may be right about that." She glanced at the gun hanging on the wall with an expression of distaste. "Lordy, I hate guns."

"There are other weapons besides guns. I'd be happy to teach you. Right now, if you like."

She pondered the idea. "I'm tempted, but I don't want to muss up your fine suit. That's a lovely waistcoat, by the way."

Donovan glanced down at his attire as if he had forgotten how he was dressed. "I can always change."

"That would be a shame. You look very handsome." She frowned. "Did you have plans? We can always put this off until tomorrow."

"As a matter of fact, I did have plans to take a lady for a drive, but with an escaped convict in the area, I don't think that's such a good idea after all. I can go change and then be back—"

"You were taking a lady for a drive?" she interrupted, stunned.

"I was supposed to, but this is more important."

"You don't waste any time, do you?" she said. "Just last week you practically made love to me against that tree, and this week you're taking someone else for a ride in your new buggy." She raked a scornful glance from his head to his feet. "Planning on finding yourself another tree, Mr. Donovan?"

He moved so quickly that she barely had time to blink. Then he was close, too close, and cupping her chin in his hand. The glitter in his hell-dark eyes made her clamp her lips tightly against the sharp retort that hovered there.

"Now you listen here, Sarah Calhoun. I'm tired of you jumping to conclusions about what I think and how I feel, and we're gonna straighten this out right now. The only woman I intend to take driving is *you*. The only woman around these parts that interests me is *you*." He released her jaw. "Now, I believe you owe me an apology."

The sensual threat was there in his eyes and in his voice. "I have no intention of apologizing for what was a natural assumption," she whispered, the vestige of his touch lingering like hot wax on her skin.

"You can apologize now or later, it makes no difference to me. But you *will* apologize, Sarah Calhoun, and you'll mean it when you do. And you *will* let me help you."

He stepped back, and she wasn't sure if she should be grateful or disappointed. She drew in a shuddery breath. "I can take care of myself, Jack. I've been doing it for a long time."

"Don't be stubborn, Sarah." He hitched a hip on the corner of her desk. "Let me help you."

"I don't need any help."

"I think you do. I think you need *my* help."

"I *don't* need you, Jack." She glared at him with a mutinous twist to her lips, and he scowled right back at her.

"Fine. I can see there's no reasoning with you right now." He straightened. "I'll be back, sassy girl. And then we'll do things my way."

"Get out of my office."

"Fine." He pulled her notebook from his pocket and flipped it on to the desk. "By the way, you dropped this."

"Thank you." She marched to the door and held it open. "Good day, Mr. Donovan."

He stalked toward the door, but paused before stepping outside. "You know, when you call me Mr. Donovan in that uppity way of yours, it makes me want to kiss you till you can't remember your name, much less mine." His gaze slid to her mouth.

She stiffened. "I really don't care what you want."

He chuckled, but the sound had a hard edge to it. "Oh, yes, you do, sweetheart. But I've got cattle to see to, so you'll have to save your flirting for later." He continued despite her gasp of indignation. "I'm sending a man to walk you home at quitting time, and I'm setting someone to watch your house, too. Don't even think about arguing."

She had opened her mouth to do just that,

but changed her mind. The look in his eyes discouraged dissension.

"Smart girl." He stalked over to Sarah and pressed a kiss to her mouth, then left, slamming the door behind him.

"Arrogant jackass," she muttered to the empty room. "He'll change his mind."

She knew that he couldn't be serious about courting her. No, he was just toying with her like he always did. No matter what he said, once the old scandal got fired up again, he wouldn't want anything to do with her at all. And there was no way to avoid the talk, now that Luke was in the area.

Despair made tears sting her eyes even as fear made her hands shake. Suddenly weary, she leaned back against the door. Just when she had a chance at a normal life, just when Ross was a breath away from proposing marriage . . . She only hoped the old rumors wouldn't make him change his mind, too.

Well, she didn't care what any of them thought. Tears trickled slowly down her cheeks. She'd already proved that Sarah Calhoun didn't need anybody.

And she would prove it again, if she had to.

Chapter 11

"**Y**essiree, the boss is one lucky bastard," Art Foley said, swigging back an ale and wiping a hand across his mouth. "You can bet that bossy blond of his is one hot piece of tail."

The other five cowhands laughed, and Foley, who was Ross Turner's foreman, leered to underscore his words. One of the cowpokes banged his empty glass on the table, shouting for more liquor. Another one reached out to pinch the satin-clad bottom of one of Harve's girls as she sauntered past. The bunch of them roared with laughter as the girl squealed, whirled around, and found herself pulled into the fellow's lap. She struggled to get up, but the crumpled bills he held up changed her from a spitting cat to a purring kitten in seconds.

Donovan clenched his hand around his

whiskey glass. Normally he wouldn't have tarnished his newfound respectability by lingering in the saloon on a Sunday, but tonight was an exception. He needed information on Petrie, and this seemed the most likely place to find it.

When he had first come through the double doors of the Four Aces, he had been struck by a nostalgic feeling of homecoming. Everything seemed familiar, from the bouncing tune of the piano, to the girls all dolled up in satin and feathers, to the smell of good tobacco and hard liquor. For the first time in a long while, he knew how to walk, what to say, and what to do.

He had settled himself at a table with his back to the wall and a glass of whiskey to keep him company, automatically picking the best vantage point, where he could watch the comings and goings, yet still remain unnoticed. And where no one could come upon him unawares. He scanned the room, nursing his whiskey, his eyes missing nothing, and his ears open for any scrap of information.

He didn't like what he heard.

Art Foley and his group were known to be a little crude and a little rowdy, preferring the saloon girls to more respectable women. But this time Foley had gone too far.

"How do you know so much?" one of the

hands, a new fellow named Shorty Jenkins, challenged.

"I been around," Art stated, leaning back in his chair. "And I hear things."

"Like what? I don't think the boss'd talk to *you* about his woman."

"Nope, the boss don't talk about womenfolk. But everybody knows how Sarah Calhoun is. Heck, if the boss weren't plannin' on marryin' up with her, I'd want a poke at her myself."

"I don't believe it," Shorty scoffed.

"Why else do you suppose he's so set on her when he could have any woman he wants?" Art said with a sneer. "She spread her legs for that no-account Petrie, so you can be sure the boss ain't gonna spend any cold nights this winter. She acts all uppity like she's better'n the rest of us, but I hear tell she can tear up the sheets better'n any whore around."

"Petrie used to talk about her," another cow-puncher spoke up. "Told Foley here she had a mouth to take a man to heaven, and there was nothin' she wouldn't do."

"Maybe if we're lucky, the boss'll share her." Art cupped a hand around his crotch and made a rude gesture, sending the others into roars of laughter.

The sniggering halted abruptly as Donovan rose to his feet with a screech of chair legs on the wood floor. His gaze settled on Art Foley, his entire body tense with fury. The piano music stopped mid-tune. Conversations faded to whispers and finally to silence. Art's lewd grin faded from his florid face as he realized that Donovan had fixed that black-as-death stare on *him*.

The other hands at the table all grabbed their drinks and fled to the anonymity of the crowd. Foley slowly rose to his feet, his thumbs hooked around the belt that circled his thickening waist. He raised his chin and met Donovan's gaze. "You got a problem, Donovan?"

Donovan came forward, the crowd retreating before him like soil before the plow. He moved slowly, carefully, though rage churned in his gut. Already he felt the familiar change coming over him, as the instincts that had saved his life many times sharpened his senses. It was as if his conscience settled into the back of his mind, out of the way of the hunting wolf that broke free of the tethers of morality.

When he was like this, he could dispassionately kill a man as easily as drink with him. And feel no regret at all.

He could smell the fear emanating from Foley, could see the bead of sweat that slowly trickled down the foreman's temple. His blood thundered from the slow beat of his heart as he approached, every footfall bringing him closer to transforming into the man known as Blade.

The foreman nervously cast an eye over the

spectators, no doubt looking for his buddies. His expression of confidence faded to uncertainty and then fear as he realized that he would face Donovan alone. Donovan had noticed a few of his own men standing at the front of the crowd and knew with only a single glance that they were prepared to back him.

He doubted he'd need their help. His opponent was mean, but he was also half drunk and a little out of shape. Donovan could take him easily, if it came to that. But he had something else in mind.

He stopped an arm's length from his opponent.

"You're drunk, Foley," Donovan said softly. "Where I come from, decent men don't talk about ladies in saloons."

Foley's florid complexion turned bright red. "I heard you was sweet on the Calhoun woman," he sneered, all bravado. "In fact, I heard tell that you spent thirty dollars to have her at the box social."

"If I were you," Donovan warned, "I wouldn't be talking about Miss Calhoun like that. She's a respectable lady."

"Lady!" Foley hooted. "That gal's not much better than a high-priced whore! Hell, she gave it away to Petrie, but you had to pay for a piece!"

Icy wrath crept through Donovan's veins, but he controlled it. He slapped a companionable hand on Foley's shoulder, squeezing his fingers in merciless punishment around flesh and bone. "Like I said, Foley, you're drunk. You don't know what you're saying."

Foley swung around, trying to dislodge the painful grip. Donovan let him go, and Foley stumbled, off balance. Donovan grabbed his shirt with both hands this time, bringing him back around to face him.

"Whoa, Foley, you've really had too much tonight! Let me help you out of here before you embarrass yourself with more lies."

"I ain't lyin'!" Foley snarled, twisting back and forth in Donovan's clutch.

Donovan chuckled, but it wasn't a pleasant sound. "Now why would Luke Petrie tell *you* anything? Foley, you tell the fanciest lies I ever heard, and everybody knows it. Right?" He looked around at the crowd and to his amusement saw several enthusiastic nods.

"I ain't no liar!" Foley screamed. "Everyone knows about Sarah Calhoun—"

"Easy there, Foley!" Shielding the action from the crowd, Donovan crushed Foley's toes beneath his boot. The foreman yowled and stumbled, looking for all the world as if he were a bumbling drunk. Donovan tightened his grip on the man's shirt. "You want to lean on me or something?"

Foley spat curses and tried to take a swing at Donovan.

"Now, that's no way to treat someone who's trying to help you," Donovan said with a shake of his head. He shoved Foley away, hard enough that the foreman tripped over his own feet and crashed into the table, shattering glass and scattering poker chips. "Look at you, you can't even stand."

Donovan walked over and stopped beside Foley, then extended a hand as if to help the man up. At the same time he jabbed him hard in the ribs with the toe of his boot. "Come on, Foley. You've been telling the same lies for years now. I bet these folks are sick of it."

Foley slapped Donovan's hand away and slowly got to his feet, his cheek bleeding where a flying piece of glass had struck him. "Ain't no lies," he snarled. "Girl's as good as a whore."

A murmur of discontent rumbled from the crowd.

"You'd better watch what you say, Foley," Donovan said, indicating the throng. "Folks don't take kindly to an innocent woman being slandered like that." He fixed his gaze on the foreman's face, letting some of his tightly controlled fury into his tone. "And neither do I."

Foley flinched at the implied threat. Looking around for aid, he started to sweat as he noticed the hostility of the spectators. "But . . . but . . . everyone knows . . ."

"You hush now, Foley!" someone called

from the crowd. "You've dragged that girl's name through the mud for too long now!"

Foley gaped. "But—"

"She's a respectable girl who's had enough trouble," someone else called out. "What with her pa gettin' killed by her sweetheart, she don't need your lyin' tongue to make it worse!"

"Let the gal alone!" a third voice chimed in.

Foley seemed to realize that he had been branded a liar before the whole town. He whirled on Donovan. "This is your fault," he snarled.

"Mine? I'm new here. I wasn't even around when you started spinning those tales."

"But it's the truth!" Foley wailed.

The crowd stirred, animosity like a live thing among them. Donovan looked at the foreman in disgust. "You got something against women, Foley? How long has it been since you've been with one, anyway? Or has all your drinking dried up your pecker?"

"Lyin' bastard!" Foley took a swing at him, but Donovan nimbly stepped out of the way.

"You're a mean drunk, Foley," Donovan said.

"I ain't drunk!" Foley swung again. Donovan dodged the blow, then scowled at his opponent.

"Have it your way." He jerked Foley up by a fistful of his shirt and landed three punches to Foley's face in quick succession. A soft crunch and a spurt of blood had Foley howling in pain and stumbling backward, one hand clinging to the bar for support as the other cupped his broken nose.

"You sober yet, Foley?" Donovan asked, his fists still tightly clenched.

"You broke my nose, you son of a bitch!" the foreman cried. Shoving away from the bar, Foley charged him, and Donovan spun out of the way. The foreman stumbled onward, driven by his own momentum, and Donovan helped him along with a boot in the backside. With a crash of discordant notes, Foley smashed into the piano, groaned, and dropped to the floor to lay unmoving.

Donovan gave a short nod of satisfaction. Retrieving his hat where it had fallen during the fight, he placed it on his head and glanced at Harve. "Sorry about the mess," he said to the saloonkeeper. "I'll pay for the damage."

Harve nodded, unperturbed, well used to such happenings. The crowd shifted to let Donovan pass as he headed for the door amid claps on the back and the murmurings of the converted.

"Foley deserved it."

" 'Bout time someone made him account for them lies."

"That poor gal's been sufferin' all this time on account of him."

Donovan stepped out of the saloon and

stared up at the crescent moon, the sympathetic rumbles of the crowd following him into the night. Anger still licked at him, and he started walking fast to let off some steam. As much as he had wanted to kill Foley, he knew that what he had done was much better. He had rewritten history, even though he had revealed more about his violent side than was wise, considering this was where he intended to settle down and raise children with his sassy girl. Still, he considered it a worthy sacrifice.

A feral smile slowly spread across his face as he remembered the satisfaction of hearing Foley's nose break beneath his fist. Hellfire, it had felt *good*.

"More lemonade, Ross?" Sarah asked, interrupting the rancher's dissertation on the merits of cross-breeding cattle.

He scowled, obviously not pleased that she had broken into his lecture, but he held out his glass anyway. "Thank you kindly, Sarah."

Sarah lifted the pitcher and poured. Once the glass was full, Ross nodded at her, gulped back half the lemonade, and then continued on with his oration as if she had never interrupted.

Sarah sighed and stared out at the starry night. She had to admit it; she was bored. Ross had shown up unexpectedly this evening, and she'd had no choice but to sit with him for a spell on her front porch. Her mother was working on Betty Ames's wedding gown in the parlor, far enough away to allow a certain amount of privacy to Sarah and her suitor, but close enough to qualify as an appropriate chaperone.

She glanced at the rancher sitting beside her. Ross was good-looking enough and certainly a prime catch for any unmarried girl, yet his conversation centered around himself and his cattle—morning, noon, and night. Never once did he ask about her: what her dreams were, what she liked to do. It was as if she existed just to be an extension of him, someone to bolster his ego and add to his consequence. She imagined it would only get worse if she became his wife.

Could she really marry such a man? Could she give up *all* of her dreams to make just one of them come true?

"Evenin', Miss Calhoun," a male voice called out from the darkness.

"Oh, no," Sarah murmured. Ross spluttered to a stop as two cowhands rode up to the picket fence, rifles resting across their saddles.

"Just wanted you to know that I'm done with my shift, ma'am," said the rider who had greeted her. "This here is Sam Watkins. He's takin' over until I come back at sunrise."

"Evenin', ma'am," Sam said.

"We didn't want you to be worried when you saw a fella that wasn't me hangin' around outside your house," the first man continued.

"I'll be back to relieve Sam in the morning."

"Thank you, Clem," Sarah answered, ignoring the look of growing outrage on Ross's face.

"You have a nice evenin', ma'am." Clem tugged his hat brim, as did Sam, and both riders disappeared into the night. A few moments later hoofbeats faded into the distance, though Sarah knew that Sam now watched over the house from a short distance away.

"Would you care to explain?" Ross asked with pointed sarcasm.

Sarah stared into the ruddy face of her almost-fiancé and suddenly knew that she couldn't do it. She could never marry a man as hidebound as Ross Turner, even if he was her last hope to have a family.

"Those men are watching the house," Sarah explained. "With an escaped convict in the area, it seemed a wise precaution."

"Those are *Donovan's* men," Ross snapped. "If you needed protecting, why didn't you come to me?"

"I didn't ask him to post a guard on me," she protested. "But he wouldn't take no for an answer."

"I'll handle Donovan," Ross replied, rising to his feet. His entire body radiated with anger.

Sarah rose as well. "What do you mean, you'll handle him?" she asked, carefully keeping the annoyance from her tone. "He was only trying to help."

"You don't need help from his kind, Sarah." Ross shoved his hat on his head. "I'll put a stop to his interference once and for all."

"Ross, I think you're taking a neighborly gesture way too seriously."

"Neighborly! I know what he's up to, and let me assure you, being your neighbor has nothing to do with it." He sneered. "Even if you can't say no to the man, I can."

The insinuation hung between them for a long, charged moment.

"Just what do you mean by that?" she asked quietly.

He looked uncomfortable. "Nothing, Sarah. It's just talk."

No one knew better than Sarah Calhoun how severely *just talk* could wound. "Ross, if you've got something on your mind, you'd best say it now."

He opened his mouth, no doubt to bluster some more, but a glance at her face apparently changed his mind. His tone grew placating. "Well, heck, Sarah, how does it look, having Donovan's men watching your place when everyone knows you and I are courting? Donovan showed up out of nowhere, flaunting his money like it grows on trees. Anyone who looks at him can see he's not one of us, but those idiots still listen to him like he was some sort of god. And it's no secret he's had his eye on you. Well, he's not going to have you."

"I see. And when did you start making the decisions in my life, Ross Turner? We're not engaged, and we're not married. Why do you assume you can speak for me?"

"Now, Sarah, don't get upset," Ross said with an indulgent smile. "Women need a man's guidance. You just sit back and let me handle it."

"No."

Ross stared. "What did you say?"

"I said no, Ross. You're not going to handle anything for me. And I'm not going to marry you." She clenched her hands tightly at her waist. "I'm sorry."

"What do you mean, you're not going to marry me?" he snapped, the amiability vanishing from his face. "Of course you are."

She shook her head. "No, I'm not."

"You little tease!" he spat.

"I'm not a tease." She tried to keep her voice steady. She had expected that Ross would be stung by her decision, but she hadn't expected him to get this upset. "I've been thinking about the situation, and I've come to the conclusion that we wouldn't be a good match."

"You don't consider *me* a good match?" His eyes bulged with astonishment, then narrowed in hostility. "I was doing you a favor, Sarah. Before I started courting you, no decent man in town would have ever considered you for a wife!"

She flinched; she couldn't help it.

Ross went on, his tone tight with animosity. "I was willing to put my reputation on the line and give you my name, despite your past. Not only that, I was considering not sending my girls back east like I had originally planned. I figured that maybe you might make an adequate mother after all. I even wondered if the stories about you had been exaggerated."

"How generous of you," she murmured through stiff lips.

He leaned closer, meanness underscoring his tone. "Tell me the truth, Sarah. Are you a decent, God-fearing woman? Or is it like everyone says? That you're really just a slut who can't keep her legs closed, not even for the scum who killed her father?"

"I think it's time for you to leave, Ross," she said, meeting his eyes squarely. His accusation stung like a slap, and he obviously took pleasure in rubbing her face in the dirt of her past. But if he thought she was going to show him her pain, then he was in for a surprise.

Ross waited, but she remained impassive. With a curse, he shoved past her, but paused at the steps. He whirled back. "It's Donovan, isn't it?" he demanded. "You're throwing me over for that saddle bum!"

"This has nothing to do with Donovan."

He laughed, but it was an ugly sound. "Well, Sarah, I wish you luck. I have a feeling there's more to Donovan than anyone knows, and none of it good. He's got the eyes of a killer. And you're right in his sights."

"Get out," she hissed.

"You deserve each other," he sneered. "The saddle bum . . . and his whore."

"I said get out, Ross." His face flushed with increased temper and when he clenched his fists at his sides, she reminded him, "Don't forget, the house is being watched. You might get a bullet in your belly if I start yelling."

His startled look indicated that he'd forgotten about the guard. She wanted to laugh at his expression, but she was afraid she would cry. For a moment, she had been afraid that he would strike her.

"Fine. I'm going. Just don't expect me to come back once Donovan shows his true colors. This was your only chance, Sarah." Turning, he stormed down the stairs and headed for the gate.

"If you come back," she called after him, "I'll shoot you myself!"

He stiffened but didn't look at her, just headed around back to where his horse was corralled. Moments later he came galloping past the house at a breakneck pace. As Sarah collapsed down into her chair, she hoped he *did* break his neck.

Though it was a warm night, she was shaking as if it were the middle of winter. She folded her arms close to her body and hugged herself, trying to will his hurtful words away. But they lingered in her mind like cigar smoke at the saloon.

He hadn't really wanted *her*, just a woman who would be grateful enough to live under his thumb for the rest of her days. He hadn't even considered her fit company for his girls. And he had implied that he thought she was being intimate with Donovan. Wouldn't he be surprised, she thought with a hysterical giggle, if he knew that Donovan didn't want her as a wife? She laughed at the thought of it, laughed until she started to cry, her dreams in tatters around her.

Donovan found her that way a few minutes later, sitting curled up into herself with her eyes red and puffy from crying. He hadn't meant to let her see him. He'd just wanted to walk off some of the fury that still churned in him, and then decided to take a stroll past Sarah's place to make sure she was all right.

Obviously, she wasn't.

Her quiet sniffles bit at him like spurs on a horse. He took the steps two at a time and knelt down in front of her, touching her gently on the arm. His first thought was that Petrie had somehow gotten to her, despite the guards he had set. He glanced over her quickly, but he saw no rips in her clothing, no signs of blood.

What he did see was the aching despair in her eyes.

He cursed, scooping her into his arms and then sitting down in the chair, cuddling her in his lap. He really didn't know what to do with a crying female—but holding her seemed like a damned good idea.

She turned her face into his neck, her hands resting helplessly on his chest, as her bosom rose and fell with shuddering breaths. He could feel her trembling and tightened his arms around her. What happened? Who had done this to her? Whoever it was had better damned sure stay clear of him; he was still in the mood to pound someone.

They sat that way for a while, listening to the wind whisper through the trees and the insects chirping to each other. Finally Sarah's breathing steadied, and she raised her head from his chest.

"You can let go of me now," she said quietly.

"I don't want to." He shifted, pulling his bandanna from his pocket and wiping the tears from her cheeks. "You okay now?"

She took a deep breath that hitched in her throat, then let it out slowly and nodded.

"Good." He cupped her cheek in his palm and made her look at him. "Who hurt you, sassy girl?"

Her lips quivered, and something broke apart inside him. Lord, this woman did something to him like no one else ever had. Somehow, she had gotten to him. He stroked loose tendrils of hair back from her face with a tenderness that he hadn't known he possessed. Her eyelids slid closed, and she turned her head so that her cheek touched his hand, her expression one of utter contentment, as if all she needed was his touch to make her world complete. Emotion welled up in him, clogging in his throat and making his hand tremble against her cheek.

Sweet Jesus, was this what love felt like? This need to touch her, to hold her, to rip apart anybody who hurt her? The humbling emotion seemed so much larger than anything he had ever experienced. Part of him was scared spitless. The other part of him rejoiced. Somehow Sarah had crawled inside him, changed him. And he would never be the same again.

"I had an argument with Ross," she said. Donovan jolted at the other man's name. He'd forgotten about Turner.

"What about?" he asked, trying to sound casual.

"He was . . . angry that you had posted your men to watch the house," she explained. "He said I should have gone to him."

"You shouldn't have to go to him," Donovan said, annoyed. "He should have thought of it himself, and he would have, if he'd really been concerned about your welfare."

"I don't think Ross is interested in anything but himself."

Donovan raised his brows. Well, well. So Turner was showing his true colors, was he?

Sarah wiggled in his arms, distracting him. "You can let me go now," she said.

"You don't like me holding you?" He relished the feel of her soft bottom squirming in his lap. Another few seconds, and she was going to have him hotter than a convict after a five-year sentence.

"Your lack of social graces is showing again," she retorted with a little of her usual spirit. "This is utterly improper."

"Yeah, well, I like it. And I think you do, too."

Color flooded her face. "Can't you act like a gentleman, just once?"

"Being a gentleman is no fun, sassy girl. And if you keep rubbing yourself against me like that, I'm gonna forget everything except that I'm a man, and you're a woman."

She grew completely still, her back ramrod-straight. He took one look at her face and barked with laughter. Her expression was a comical combination of nervousness and feminine curiosity.

She scowled at him. "Do I amuse you?"

"All the time, sweetheart." He raised her hand to his lips and planted a smacking kiss on her palm. She gasped and jerked her hand away, but he noticed how her fingers curled closed, as if to hold on to his kiss.

"You're impossible," she muttered.

"Good thing you like me that way."

"Mr. Donovan, I never said that I liked you at all."

God, he loved that uppity tone of voice. "I guess you forgot what I said about my name, Sarah, and the snooty way you say it."

Her eyes widened, but by then it was too late. He cupped a hand behind her head and pulled her close for a deep, hungry kiss.

He'd been starving for this since the box social. She resisted at first, sitting rigidly in his lap. Then her mouth softened beneath his, and her fingers curled into his chest. He made a sound of pleasure and angled his head to take more of her mouth. The kiss changed, becoming softer, more intimate. Her arms slipped around his neck and he savored her, tasting her in a slow, tender blending of lips and tongue that was more than sex, more than he had ever thought himself capable of offering a woman.

She shifted in his lap, pressing her breasts against his chest and rubbing her soft buttocks against his aching erection. The blood pounded in his ears, yet he found himself cradling her against him, cherishing her rather than seducing her, enjoying the sweet torment of arousal without needing to satisfy his physical cravings.

Not that he didn't want to, but his relationship with Sarah had taken a very complicated turn. It was emotional now as much as physical. And he wasn't sure how comfortable he felt with that yet.

He broke the kiss, softly touching her face when she made a sound of protest. Her eyes slowly opened, and the sultry heat he saw there almost undid all his good intentions. He smiled at her. "Any more of this, sassy girl, and Sam out there is gonna get an eyeful."

He knew the instant his words penetrated her passion-induced daze. She gasped, color blooming in her face, and she jerked out of his arms, stumbling to her feet. He let her go and watched with affectionate amusement as she grabbed the porch railing for balance, leaning against it as she struggled for control. He waited, knowing that when she recovered herself, she'd be back to spitting and clawing just like always.

Shaken by the powerful emotions that held her captive, Sarah grappled for control of her body and mind. The desolation and hurt caused by Ross's words had faded, like a nightmare in the face of sunrise. But now she felt confused and vulnerable, and she didn't know what to think.

"I don't know what you want from me," she said quietly. She glanced at him, so dark and male on her pretty white porch. The look on his face made her heartbeat quicken. She could see the way desire lingered in his eyes, the way it tightened his sharp features. His deceptively relaxed pose couldn't hide the tension of his body or the conspicuous bulge in the front of his pants. Yet he didn't act on his obvious arousal, which only puzzled her more.

"I told you what I want," he answered. "I want *you*, Sarah."

"But what does that mean? Do you want me as a friend? A lover?" She twisted her fingers together. "I need to know."

"I want you to be my wife."

She jerked her gaze to his. "What did you say?"

He rose from his chair and came to stand in front of her. "I said I want you to marry me."

"No more games, Jack."

"I'm not playing games." He stroked the backs of his fingers over her cheek. "You're the only woman for me, Sarah. Say you'll marry me."

She started to speak, but the words stuck in her throat. She took a step back to put some distance between them. "Jack, if this is about Ross, I think you should know that he's no longer interested in me."

"He said that to you?" She nodded, and he cursed. "Did he say anything else?"

"Nothing that I haven't heard before."

Her face must have given something away,

because he pulled her into his embrace, holding her as if he would never let her go. "Don't you listen to him, sassy girl," he growled. "He's a damned fool."

Something long imprisoned broke free inside her at the conviction in his voice. Whatever else he thought of her, it was obvious that Jack Donovan didn't consider her the sordid creature that other people believed her to be. But she knew what Jack wanted in a woman, and she had only just realized this evening that she could never be that woman. She could be nothing other than herself. Anything else would be a lie.

She pulled back from his tight embrace, but he kept his arms around her waist. Comforted by the sensation of being held, Sarah allowed him that.

"You say that you want me to marry you." He opened his mouth to speak, but she held up a hand, halting the words before they left his lips. "If you truly mean that, Jack, then I should tell you that I have no intention of giving up the paper. It's too important to me."

"Keep the damned paper," he answered. "I want *you*, Sarah, just as you are. Marry me."

She could barely resist the husky longing in his voice, the fierce admiration in his eyes. But she had to be smart about this. She had almost made one disastrous mistake; she would be very cautious about making another.

"I need time to think, Jack," she replied. "I'm not saying no, but I can't say yes either. Not until I'm sure."

He closed his eyes for a moment, and she thought he might have changed his mind. Then he opened them again, and she was relieved to see that the tenderness was still there. "Take your time, sassy girl. I'm a patient man."

She let loose the breath she only just realized she was holding. "Good."

"But," he continued, taking her chin in his hand, "that doesn't mean that I'm not going to try to convince you to say yes."

She straightened her spine, knowing a challenge when she heard one. "Take your best shot, Mr. Donovan."

He smiled slowly, his expression taking on the predatory look that created butterflies in her stomach. "You can count on that, Miss Calhoun."

Chapter 12

Donovan waited until Friday before he stopped in to pay the wounded marshal a visit.

Because he had intended to set aside the day to come into town, he had put in extra hours at the ranch during the week. He hadn't even been able to slip away to see Sarah, a situation he meant to correct as soon as he was done with the lawman.

He stepped into the clinic. Doc Mercer was sitting at his desk, a large book open before him. The physician glanced at him over his glasses. "Morning, Donovan."

"Morning, Doc." He indicated the back room with a nod of his head. "How's the patient?"

"Awake and *im*patient," the doctor replied, chuckling at his own wit.

"Mind if I go back and visit?"

"Go right ahead. Just don't stay too long.

Marshal Brown is still weak and needs his rest."

"Much obliged, Doc." Leaving the doctor to his reading, Donovan stepped through the open door. The back room of the clinic boasted six beds, each with curtains that could be drawn for privacy. All of the beds were empty but one, which was in the far corner, right next to the window and farthest from the door.

The one, he thought with amusement, he would have chosen himself.

The marshal turned his head as Donovan approached, the utter picture of a very sick man. His left arm, wrapped in a sling, rested on his stomach. His right hand hung down the side of the bed, out of sight. Yes indeed, the lawman's pallor and listless pose indicated that he was ailing. But his eyes told a different story.

Donovan stopped a few feet from the bed and raised his hands at shoulder height. "I don't have a gun, Marshal," he said calmly. "And I'm not here to kill you. All I want to do is talk. I can call Doc Mercer to vouch for me if you want."

Marshal Brown's eyes narrowed, and he brought his right arm up to where Donovan could see it. He held a Colt army revolver, which he rested on his thigh. "You got a name?"

"Donovan. Jack Donovan. I own a spread outside town."

"Jedidiah Brown." The lawman sat up, wincing as he jostled his shoulder, but he kept a firm hand on the Colt. "I understand I owe you a debt, Mr. Donovan. You saved my life."

"You don't owe me anything."

Jedidiah sat up straighter. "Where I come from, Mr. Donovan, a man always pays his debts."

"That would be down south?"

The marshal nodded, a hint of respect flashing across his face. "I'm impressed. I thought I had perfected my Western accent."

"You did. But you can't do anything about that inbred Southern pride."

The lawman laughed and finally slipped his revolver under his pillow. "Pull up a chair, Mr. Donovan, and tell me what I can do for you."

"I want to ask you a few questions—about Luke Petrie."

Jedidiah's expression grew hard. As Donovan pulled a chair to the side of the bed, he was glad he had never walked on the wrong side of the law. He'd hate to face Jedidiah Brown over the barrel of a gun.

"Why are you interested in Petrie?" the marshal asked.

"A few years back he killed a man here in Burr and robbed the bank."

"I'm aware of that. That's why I'm so surprised he headed this way. You'd think he'd have better sense than to go where he'd be recognized."

"The man he killed was my intended's father. She's the one who turned him in, and I'm thinking he's got a score to settle."

Marshal Brown leaned back against his pillows. "That explains a lot. This woman, she's your intended, you say?"

"She hasn't said yes yet, but I mean to marry her, that's for sure."

"And I take it you mean to protect her."

"However I have to."

Marshal Brown sent Donovan a sharp look. "Don't take the law into your own hands, Mr. Donovan. I'm warning you."

"And I'm warning *you*, Marshal: if Petrie comes anywhere near my woman, I won't hesitate to kill him."

The two men stared at each other, at an impasse.

"The law doesn't take kindly to civilians interfering in its business," Jedidiah said finally, but it was obvious from his tone that he knew his words wouldn't be heeded.

"As long as Petrie stays clear of Sarah," Donovan said with a cold smile, "I won't get in the law's way."

"See that you don't." Jedidiah leaned back against the pillows, frowning in concentration. "You know, for a moment there, you reminded me of someone."

Alarm skittered down his spine. "Oh?"

"I just can't place who—"

They both heard the scuff of a footstep at the same time. The marshal whipped out his revolver even as Donovan leaped to his feet and turned to face the intruder, a knife in his hand.

"Gracious." Sarah stood frozen in the doorway, her hand over her heart.

"Damn it, Sarah." Donovan slipped his knife back into the sheath up his sleeve. The marshal slid the revolver from sight.

"Unarmed?" Jedidiah murmured.

"I said I didn't have a gun, not that I wasn't armed," Donovan replied just as softly, his attention on Sarah. He heard the lawman chuckle.

"The doctor said that it was all right for me to come back here." Sarah's gaze slid from Donovan to the marshal and back again. "Don't let me interrupt."

"We're through here."

"Yes, please come in," Jedidiah said, suddenly every inch the charming Southern gentleman. "There's nothing like a lovely lady to brighten up the boredom of a sickroom."

Sarah stepped forward hesitantly. As she reached them, Donovan could see the questions in her eyes. He held out a hand, feeling an absurd sense of satisfaction as she placed her fingers in his. "Sarah, this is Marshal Jedidiah Brown. Marshal, Miss Sarah Calhoun, editor of the *Burr Chronicle*."

"A pleasure to meet you." In a blatantly flirtatious manner, Jedidiah lifted Sarah's free hand to his lips. Donovan scowled at the lawman as Sarah blushed furiously.

"Marshal Brown, I'd like to interview you for the newspaper, if you're feeling up to it," Sarah said with a flustered smile.

"Miss Calhoun, in your presence, I feel no pain. Only the greatest pleasure."

Donovan rolled his eyes, but he couldn't help but notice how Sarah seemed to respond to the lavish compliments like a flower opening to sunlight. Maybe he should learn some fancy words. Since she was a writer and all, words probably meant a lot to her.

Dr. Mercer came to the doorway. "Here now, only one visitor at a time. The marshal needs to rest."

Donovan had every intention of staying right where he was, but the doctor was looking right at him when he spoke.

Marshal Brown also sent him a look. "Thanks for stopping by, Mr. Donovan. You and I can continue our conversation—later."

Forced by Sarah's highly prized social graces to take the hint, Donovan had no choice but to exit the room. As he left, he cast a glance back over his shoulder. Marshal Brown had focused his entire attention on Sarah. And his sassy girl was blushing and smiling and hanging on every word the smooth-talking Southerner said.

"Not too long now, Sarah," the doctor admonished. "I don't want my patient to have a relapse." The physician left the room, urging Donovan along with him. Donovan didn't much like being shuffled aside like a child who couldn't stay out of trouble, but he said goodbye to the doctor and stepped out on to Main Street.

"Afternoon, Mr. Donovan," Reverend Westerly said as he passed by on his way to the church.

"Afternoon, Reverend."

The preacher paused. "Say, would you be willing to judge the pie-baking contest at the Founder's Day Festival tomorrow? We could sure use the help."

"Be happy to."

"Fine, fine. The judging is at twelve-thirty. That way we can use the pies for the pie-eating contest later on." The reverend grinned.

Donovan found himself grinning back. "See you at twelve-thirty, then."

The preacher nodded and headed toward the church. Donovan stood and watched him go. All around him, the citizens of Burr called out greetings to him as they passed by. He answered them absently as a realization crystallized in his mind.

He belonged here.

No longer was he the outcast, the bounty hunter, an unwanted but necessary evil in catching criminals. He was a proper citizen of this little town, a decent man who people could look in the eye, not the fellow who made ladies cross the street to avoid him. Even though he'd always walked on the right side of the law, people had tended to shun him like they would a gunslinger.

But no longer. Now his company was sought; his advice was asked. He had succeeded in leaving his past behind, and a bright future lay ahead of him with Sarah as his wife.

He didn't know how long he stood there, lost in revelation, but suddenly the door to the clinic opened, and Sarah stepped out. She halted, then a smile stretched across her face. "I didn't know you were still here."

His first instinct was to deny that he'd been waiting for her. Then he remembered how she had reacted to the marshal's flirtation, so he smiled warmly at her and offered his arm. "I thought I'd walk you back to your office."

"Why, thank you." Her eyes sparkled as she shyly put her hand on his arm. "I haven't seen you since Sunday."

"Since I asked you to marry me, you mean."

She glanced away, her cheeks turning a pretty pink. "Yes, since then."

He'd made her blush! Lord, he wanted to

pull her into a dark corner somewhere and kiss her. This emotion that gripped him was still uncomfortable, yet he felt as proud as a rooster as he walked down the street with Sarah on his arm. How had he gotten so lucky? He'd been looking for this woman his entire life, and somehow he'd actually found her.

It was enough to make a man believe in miracles.

"How did your interview with the marshal go?" he asked as he held open the door of the newspaper office for her.

"Very well. He's a charming man." Entering the office, she stepped behind her desk and slipped her drawstring bag into a drawer.

"So I saw."

She glanced up, her lips quirking with amusement. "Heavens, Jack, are you jealous?"

"No. Well—maybe just a little." He came over and sat on the corner of her desk. "Marshal Brown seems to have all those social graces you say that I lack."

"Marshal Brown might have some social polish, but I'm not at all attracted to him. There's something about him that bothers me."

Donovan raised his brows. "You don't say."

She laughed. "I see you trying to hide that smile, Jack Donovan."

The grin escaped, spreading across his face as his heart lightened. "So tell me what bothers you about the marshal."

"You're incorrigible."

He snagged her braid and tugged her face close to his. "Is that like irresistible?"

"No, it's more like impossible."

He brushed his lips against hers. Just touching her made his heart sing. "What didn't you like about the marshal?" he persisted.

She laughed and pushed him away. "All right, I'll tell you. He's dangerous—that's what I don't like about him."

"Dangerous?"

"Yes, dangerous. He's a man who lives by the gun, and I swore when my father died that I would never again become involved with a dangerous man."

The song in his heart stopped with a clang of discordant notes.

Sarah continued, "I've seen too many widows out here, too many children without fathers. Look what happened to my mother and me, all because I got tangled up with the wrong man."

"Lawmen may fall into your 'dangerous man' category, but if they didn't carry guns, things would be a lot worse."

"I know that, and I'm not saying there isn't a need for men like that, with the criminal sorts that seem to find their way out here. I just wouldn't get personally involved with one again, even if he was on the right side of the law."

Donovan stood, suddenly too restless to sit still. "Well, sweetheart, the only man you're personally involved with is me, and it had better stay that way."

She laughed. "As if any other man would have me."

"You might be surprised."

Her expression grew thoughtful. "You know, come to think of it, everyone has been unusually kind to me this week. Even old Mrs. Meltzer, who always crosses the street when she sees me, stopped to say hello and ask about my mother just the other day."

"I'd say that's progress."

"Maybe. Or maybe her memory's failing and she forgot I was in disgrace."

He took her hand and pulled her into his arms. "Don't talk about my intended that way."

"Your intended?" She tilted her head back to look up at him. "I don't recall saying yes, Mr. Donovan."

"And I suppose you don't recall what I said about the snooty way you say my name."

Her gaze dropped to his mouth, and a sensual smile pulled at her lips. "Maybe I do and maybe I don't."

"Let me refresh your memory." He pulled her close for a satisfying kiss, more comfortable now with the simmering hunger that flooded his veins when he touched her. He wasn't as used to this need to have her in his life, but he imagined he'd adjust to it. He would convince her to marry him, and they'd live on his ranch and raise children and cattle. His dream was about to come true.

He'd just make sure she never found out about his old life. Because if she did discover who and what he used to be, he'd lose her forever.

Everyone watched the stagecoach come through town.

Outside the Four Aces, Mort, Johnny, and Gabriel paused in their checker game to stare as the Friday afternoon stage, which usually flew nonstop through town like a burning hay cart, ambled down Main Street like Cleopatra's barge floating down the Nile. Leaning back in his chair, Mort squinted to see who was inside.

"Sweet mother—!" He was so surprised at the passenger's identity that he let his chair leg fall forward right onto Gabriel's foot. While Gabe hollered and Mort stammered out an explanation, Johnny crawled on his hands and knees, searching for the checkers he'd dropped when he'd gotten a glimpse of the passenger's face.

The Tremont sisters were gossiping with Mrs. Castor by the picket fence outside their home, but when the stagecoach passed by all conversation came to a halt, then started up again in a flurry of voices.

"Did you see who that was?"

"It couldn't be her!"

"Good heavens!"

Like startled crows, the three women scattered in different directions to pass along the newest gossip.

Locking up the bank for the day, Mr. Castor glanced up as the stage passed by, just in time to see the passenger give him a smile and a wave. Stunned, he let his mouth fall open, and his cigar tumbled to the ground. His keys slipped from his hand.

The stage halted outside the mercantile, where Nate Pearson was sweeping his walk. Old Abe jumped down from the driver's seat and hurried around to open the door. Abe offered his hand to his passenger, which was enough to make Nate stare, but then she alighted, and Nate positively gaped.

Mr. Castor arrived, huffing and puffing from his sprint across the street. He cleared his throat and swiped his hat off his head. "Ma'am, as mayor of the town of Burr, allow me to be the first to welcome you—"

"Take care of my baggage, would you?" the woman said with a flirtatious pat on the arm that made the mayor stutter into silence. "There's a dear."

The portly banker found himself nodding obediently as she turned away.

"So," she said, removing her gloves one finger at a time and looking around, "I see everything's the same." Her gaze lit on Nate, and she sent him a dazzling smile that made him drop his broom. "I'll have to change that, won't I?"

With a jaunty wave she sauntered across the street to the newspaper office, leaving the three men gazing moonstruck after her.

Sarah set the type swiftly and nimbly. The click-click of the pieces was normally as soothing as a lullaby, but not today. Not since her short conversation with the marshal had confirmed her worst fear: Luke Petrie had indeed broken out of jail and was back in the area.

Terror clutched her with icy talons, making her want to rage and scream. Instead, she worked. But even as her hands laid out the first page for Wednesday's edition of the *Burr Chronicle*, her thoughts whirled in an emotional tornado. Luke Petrie. Dear God.

Her father's murderer.

Her former lover.

What did Luke want? What he was doing here? She knew Luke had never loved her, though he had certainly wanted her. She had the feeling that his return to the area could only mean trouble. And even though she knew

Donovan would protect her, even though he had men watching her house, she was still afraid. Luke Petrie was ruthless and would stop at nothing until he got what he wanted.

How had she ever believed herself in love with the man?

She laid down the type and folded her arms across her middle. Donovan was coming by the house at ten o'clock tomorrow morning to escort her to the Founder's Day Festival. As long as she was with him and in a crowd, she would be safe. She had to believe that.

Yet Donovan was another reason to be nervous.

Her feelings for the man were strange and unpredictable, and unusually strong. She wanted to believe that he was sincere in his desire to make her his wife, but she was wary of trusting him, of giving up anything of herself that she might not be able to get back. Jack Donovan had the power to hurt her in ways Luke Petrie never had.

Could it possibly work? He had said he accepted her keeping the newspaper, but what if he changed his mind? What if she let herself love him, and he decided that he preferred someone else, someone more suited to his original plans? Someone willing to make being Mrs. Jack Donovan the center of her existence?

There was every chance she was already halfway in love with the man. She didn't think she could handle one more turnabout from him.

The door to the office clicked open, and Sarah jumped. As if Luke Petrie would come strolling into the office in the middle of the day, she thought with a twist of her lips. Still, relief washed over her as a tall, statuesque woman turned to close the door. The stunning female was dressed in a fabulous cherry-red gown with black trim that showed off her incredible figure to perfection, complete with bows and ruffles. Her silver-blond hair was upswept into fashionable curls, and a natty red hat with a long, curving red feather completed the ensemble. Sarah stared, wondering what such a creature was doing in Burr.

"Hello? Is anyone here?" The woman turned to face her, and Sarah gasped. She knew those exotically slanted blue eyes, the slashing cheekbones, that bee-stung mouth, as well as she knew her own face.

"Susannah!"

"Sarah!" Her sister swept over to embrace Sarah in an exuberant hug. "Goodness, you're covered with ink!"

"Part of the job." Sarah stepped back and picked up a rag to wipe her hands, the scent of Susannah's expensive perfume overwhelming the familiar odors of ink and paper. "What are you doing here? I thought you were breaking hearts in San Francisco."

"I got bored." Susannah gave her the sunny smile that had bedazzled males throughout the territory and took both Sarah's hands in hers. "Besides, I missed this place. You and Mama. After Daddy died, I just couldn't stay here."

"I understand."

"But Mama's been sending me the newspaper every week," Susannah continued. "And it just made me homesick, I guess. So here I am."

"We've missed you. Have you seen Mama yet?"

"Heavens, no! I just got off the stage and came right here." She glanced around the office. "It looks the same as when Daddy was alive. But different." She smiled at Sarah again. "You've made the place your own, Sarah. I'm proud of you."

Sarah swallowed back sudden tears. "Oh, Susannah, you don't know how much that means to me. I'm so glad you're here. And Mama's going to be beside herself."

"I can't wait to see her!"

"Let's go right now—I want to see her face." Sarah went to the desk to fetch her reticule. "How long can you visit with us?"

"Visit?" Susannah laughed. "Little sister, I'm home to stay."

"Really?" Sarah was surprised. "What about your singing career in California?"

"I'm done with all that," Susannah announced with a wave of her hand. "I've discovered my true destiny, and I have you to thank for it."

"Me?" Sarah opened the door and stood aside to let her sister pass. "I don't understand."

"Thanks to you and your newspaper, I know what I'm going to do with the rest of my life." Susannah paused dramatically in the doorway and smiled at Sarah. "I intend to become Mrs. Jack Donovan."

She swept through the door, leaving Sarah gaping in her wake.

Susannah had come all the way from California to marry Jack? For a moment, Sarah battled a feeling of panic. Men acted like lovestruck fools when they met Suzie, and her sister had always gotten any man she wanted. Now she wanted Jack.

Many women dismissed Susannah as a pretty face without much substance, but Sarah knew her sister was warmhearted and capable of great love. And Mama had taught both of them how to cook, sew, and run a house efficiently. The fact that Suzie bought her clothes from dressmakers and ate at restaurants had nothing to do with her wifely skills. A man would be lucky to have Susannah Calhoun as his wife.

"Sarah!" Suzie called impatiently. "What are you waiting for?"

"I'm coming!" Sarah locked the office door,

then hurried to catch up with her sister. Maybe she was being silly. After all, he had already proposed to *her* and Jack Donovan was a man who knew what he wanted. She just wished she knew what *she* wanted.

Heads turned as the two women walked down the street, but Sarah expected nothing less. Wherever Susannah went, she always attracted attention.

"You seem to be doing well for yourself," Susannah said, smiling and nodding at two ranch hands who passed by.

"The paper is doing well," Sarah corrected. "And you look gorgeous as always."

A crash sounded behind them, and Sarah glanced back to see that the two men had erupted into a fistfight. Shouts of, "She smiled at me!" and "No, she was looking at me!" got lost in a clamor of pain-induced grunts and fists hitting flesh. Shaking her head, she hurried to keep step with Susannah, who hadn't even noticed.

"How's Mama?" Susannah asked as they passed the barbershop.

"She's fine. She's been busy with a lot of work since so many women have moved into the area."

"I always found it convenient to have a mother who was a dressmaker," Susannah said with a laugh.

"You would," Sarah returned with a grin, unable to resist her sister's charm.

As they walked by the clinic, a trapper paused in mounting his horse to stare goggle-eyed at Susannah. With his eyes on her, the buckskin-clad man lifted a leg and missed the stirrup, falling forward to whack his face against his horse. Sarah giggled and followed her sister around the corner toward home.

"It all looks the same," Susannah exclaimed as they approached the Calhoun house. "Everything. I didn't realize how much I had missed it until I came home."

"We missed you," Sarah said. "Especially Mama."

"The house is the same . . . but the curtains are different. And there's only one horse in the corral."

"We had to sell one."

"So many changes," Susannah sighed. She and Sarah had barely reached the porch stairs when the door flew open, and June rushed out.

"Susannah!" she cried, running down the steps and throwing her arms wide to embrace her daughter.

"Mama." Susannah closed her eyes and accepted her mother's hug. "I'm home," she whispered.

The sun hung low over the mountains, streaking brilliant shades of orange and pink across the sky. Donovan stood for a moment on the wraparound porch of his house and looked over the Triple D. His ranch. His outfit. Finally, his home.

The men had just come in from the range, and he could hear their laughter coming from the bunkhouse as they washed off the day's grime at the outside pump. In about a half-hour or so, Jasper Riggs, the cook, would have their supper on the table.

Donovan had already eaten a plate of Jasper's stew, though normally he ate at the bunkhouse with the men. It had taken a while, but his hands had finally become accustomed to having the boss sit at the table with them. But this evening he had something else to do.

He walked behind the house to a yard bare of anything but hard-packed dirt. He had always hoped that his wife would brighten up the house a bit—maybe plant a garden or set out some furniture. Watch the children as they chased butterflies. Hang the wash on the line. He couldn't figure why, but the idea of sheets drying in the sunshine when he came home in the evening just made him feel warm all over.

Maybe Sarah would do some of that. And maybe he would have to hire a housekeeper. It didn't matter, as long as he had his sassy girl lying beside him at night in that great big bed.

Sarah's safety was constantly on his mind since the threat of Luke Petrie had arisen. The town council had sent out a posse or two to see if they could round up the escaped convict, but no one had seen hide nor hair of him. Donovan had thought about offering his services, but his priority was Sarah, and he felt better staying close to her in case Petrie tried something. And he *would* try something—Donovan could feel it.

He moved to a corner of the yard and pulled his blade from the sheath on his arm. Picking a knot in the fence as his target, he hefted the knife, balanced it, and threw, all in one smooth moment. The weapon sank into the fence—directly on target—with a solid thunk. A satisfied smile on his lips, he went over and pulled the knife from the wood, wiping the blade clean with his thumb. He had survived by his instincts for too many years to dismiss them now. Petrie would try to get to Sarah.

And when he did, he would find that he had to get through Jack Donovan first.

Chapter 13

The first Saturday in June was Founder's Day, the anniversary of the day Josiah Burr had come down off the mountain looking for his lost cow and discovered gold instead. Of course, it had turned out to be fool's gold, but by the time anyone had figured that out, the town had already started to build up. Burr might have been abandoned after that, but since it was so close to the Western trail used by the cattle drovers, the founding fathers decided to stay put.

Old Josiah had died years ago, but the citizens of Burr had taken up the tradition of throwing a Founder's Day Festival every year to commemorate the establishment of their fair town. There were pie-eating contests, sack races, turtle races, more food than anyone could eat, competitions for who baked the tastiest pie and who raised the finest hog. There would be a parade in the morning, followed by a speech by the mayor, and later that night there would be dancing and fireworks.

Saturday dawned cloudless and sunny, promising a flawless spring afternoon. The citizens of Burr busied themselves with preparations for the festival, certain the day would be one to remember.

Cheered by the fine weather, Sarah gave in to an uncharacteristic impulse and dressed in her pink and white Sunday finest. This would be her first foray into society on the arm of Jack Donovan, and she wanted to look her best. So she pulled out her new pink gingham and put up her hair and ignored her mother's pleased smile. By ten o'clock, she was gowned and coifed and ready for her suitor to arrive.

By eleven o'clock, she was still waiting.

Her mother and sister left for the festival, after trying without success to persuade Sarah to accompany them. Uncertain of her feelings for Donovan, and unwilling to get her mother's hopes up, Sarah had said nothing about Donovan escorting her. Instead, she convinced them she had something to do at the newspaper office and that she would catch up with them. They reluctantly left without her.

By noontime, Donovan had still not arrived.

Jack Donovan was not a man who broke promises, so something must have happened to delay him. Maybe it was for the best, Sarah thought as she changed back into her plain brown skirt and white blouse. Perhaps this was a sign that their relationship wasn't meant to be. Maybe she *was* the wrong woman after all.

Determined to ignore the pain that twisted her heart, she brushed and plaited her hair into a practical braid. She would go finish up some things at the newspaper before heading over to the festival. After all, she hadn't gotten a lick of work done since Susannah had come home yesterday afternoon.

Her resolve lasted all the way down the stairs and out the front door. Then she saw Donovan coming up the walk.

Her heart clenched. He looked so handsome, all dressed up in his black suit with the silver waistcoat, his long legs making it easy for him to take the porch steps two at a time. He grinned as he saw her, his dimple flashing. Before she could say a word, he bent forward and stole a quick kiss. "Hello, sweet Sarah."

"Jack." Fighting to regain emotional equilibrium, Sarah took a step back. "I didn't think you were coming."

He was instantly contrite. "I'm sorry, sweetheart. Some fence was down in the south pasture, and part of the herd had wandered off. It took us a while to round them all up again."

"I knew it had to be something like that."

"Well, I'm glad you're not mad at me. I was afraid you would be." He took her hand.

"What say we get on to the festival? I'm supposed to judge the pie-baking contest at twelve-thirty."

"No, you go on without me." She tugged her hand loose and clenched all ten fingers around her purse. "I have some work to do at the newspaper office."

His grin faded, and he studied her closely. "You *are* mad at me."

"No, really, I'm not." She tried to smile. "Look, Jack, I've simply changed my mind about going to the festival. Just let it go."

"I can't let it go. Tell me what I can do to make it up to you."

"Jack, I'm *not* angry with you! I just... changed my mind is all."

"Uh-huh." He folded his arms and narrowed his eyes. "About the festival? Or about me?"

She couldn't look at him. "The festival, of course."

"You're a rotten liar, sassy girl."

She glared at him. "All right, here's the truth: I'm still not sure that a relationship between us would work. This morning seemed to only make it more obvious."

He raised his brows. "Well, I've got news for you, Sarah Calhoun. We already have a relationship. And things seemed to be going just fine to me—except for you not making up your mind about marrying me."

"I don't want to make a hasty decision," she

insisted. "I did that once before, and I've regretted it ever since. And what about you? What if I can't be the kind of wife you want?"

He advanced, his dark eyes fixed on her as if he could see right into her soul. She retreated until her back hit the door. Still he came forward, flattening his hands against the door on either side of her and leaning down until their gazes were level.

"Don't you worry about what kind of wife you'll make, sassy girl," he said, his voice low and rough. "You just say yes, and I guarantee that neither one of us will regret it."

Her heart pounded in her chest, and her lips trembled. He was so close that she could feel the heat of him. She wanted to step forward into his arms and let him take care of everything, but she couldn't do that. What if she fell in love with him, and he decided that she wasn't right for him after all? He'd break her heart.

"I need more time, Jack," she whispered.

"You can have all the time you need, sweetheart. Just don't push me away." He touched her cheek as gently as a snowflake drifting to earth, and she felt herself weakening.

"I just don't know if we should be seen together yet," she insisted, closing her eyes against the tenderness she saw in his face. She had to remain in control. "Not until I make up my mind."

"Avoiding me isn't going to help you make up your mind."

"Maybe not." Grasping at the fragments of her determination, she met his gaze firmly. "But I don't want to fuel any more gossip."

"It's not the talk you're worried about," he murmured, playing with a strand that had come free of her braid. "You're just scared that this might actually work out."

"That's ridiculous."

"Actually, it makes a lot of sense. But I'm not going to let you be a coward, sassy girl."

The gleam in his eyes alarmed her in a purely feminine way. "What do you mean by that?"

"Either you come with me to the festival like we agreed, or I'm going to pick you up and carry you there. And that will definitely cause gossip. It's your choice, Sarah, but either way, you're going."

Was she being a coward? With a sigh of surrender, Sarah nodded. "Fine, I'll go."

"I thought you'd see it that way."

It seemed all of Burr had gathered in the church square. Sarah itched to take notes, but Donovan's unyielding grasp on her hand would not allow it. Just a few moments ago, young Kevin O'Brien's turtle had won the turtle race. The youngster carried his champion around with a fat blue ribbon tied around its shell, and Sarah wanted to interview the boy for the paper. One steely-eyed look from Donovan had quelled that notion.

Just who did the man think he was, she fumed, to stop a journalist from performing her job? But deep down, she knew that wasn't it. He just didn't want her sneaking off.

She scowled at her escort, wondering how he'd seen through her so completely. But before she could start a nice, lively argument with him, Reverend Westerly hurried over to them.

"Mr. Donovan, there you are! We've been looking for you. The pie-baking competition is about to begin."

"Already?" Donovan squinted at the sky, as if gauging the time.

"Yes indeed. Are you ready to judge the contest?"

Donovan looked at Sarah, obviously torn.

She gave him a sweet smile. "Don't let me stop you."

"Oh, I won't. You're coming with me."

Before Sarah could protest, Donovan was guiding her through the crowd. He stopped beside the platform where the judging was to be done and gave her a hard look. "Stay here, Sarah. You don't want me to come looking for you."

She merely gave him a telling look and turned away to study the table, laden with pies of all varieties. He made a sound of frustration—music to her ears—and mounted the platform.

Smothering a victorious grin, she glanced around. Hopeful women crowded the vicinity, whispering and giggling. Sarah raised her eyebrows and wondered if they were more eager for the results of the judging, or for the judge himself.

"Now, ladies," the reverend called out. "Back off a bit and give Mr. Donovan some room."

The herd of skirts and petticoats shifted. Inch by inch, the ladies moved back from the platform. Finally Sarah had a clear view of Donovan.

He looked so handsome, like a gentleman desperado. He'd slicked his hair back beneath the brim of his black hat, and a few strands blew in the gentle spring breeze. His dimple flashed as he conversed with Reverend Westerly, and as he picked up the first piece of pie, she noticed how strong and masculine his tanned, callused hands looked next to the dainty white china plate.

It was no wonder the women were all panting to catch his eye.

Donovan lifted a forkful of flaky-crusted blueberry pastry to his mouth. His gaze met hers as those sensual lips closed over the fork, sliding the pie between his teeth. He chewed, his expression thoughtful, the muscles of his jaw and throat working in a way she found strangely arousing. He swallowed and nodded, then went on to the next slice of pie.

Sarah stood captivated as he slowly lifted a bite of Emmaline Tremont's lemon meringue to his mouth and slid it between his lips, his tongue dipping out to catch an escaping crumb. He sent Sarah a cocky grin, then deliberately licked the fork. Her heart did a little flip in her chest.

She couldn't take her eyes off him as he moved to the next pie. He was seducing her without laying a finger on her. No man had ever affected her like this before. And while the other women in the crowd sighed and murmured, it was Sarah he watched. It was Sarah he invited to come closer with a mere flash of a dimple and a gleam in his eye. It was only Sarah he tempted to join him in the sensual promises he made without speaking a word.

She laid a hand on her bosom, her pulse pounding. She had never imagined she could feel this way just from watching a man eat a piece of pie! She wanted that sexy mouth savoring *her*, tasting and licking her, as if she were a delicious morsel he couldn't get enough of. Her hand shook as she made notes on her pad.

At the last entry, she found herself holding her breath when he once more raised the fork to his lips, holding her gaze, and she had to close her eyes when he started chewing. Good Lord, the man would think her crazy if he knew what she was feeling! But when she looked again, he was smiling at her, and his eyes glowed with a hot need that matched her own.

By the time he ruled an ancient widow named Mrs. Pepperidge the winner of the pie contest, Sarah was ready to drag him into an alley and gobble him up like a peach cobbler.

She turned away quickly from temptation and headed across the square.

While she knew they were well-matched in passion, it was the day-to-day living that she wasn't sure of. Seeing him doing something as domestic as judging a pie contest made her sway toward accepting his proposal. But other times he got that lean and edgy look on his face, and she wasn't so sure.

She had made two errors in judgment when it came to the men in her life. With both Luke Petrie and Ross Turner, she had discovered the hard way that the relationship would not work.

She wanted to be very careful with Donovan. He mattered too much.

"Yoohoo, Sarah!" Mrs. Castor descended on her from the nearby refreshment table. Sarah turned, determined to pretend she hadn't seen the mayor's wife, but then she spotted Donovan heading for her like a bullet from the opposite direction. The look on his face echoed the hot need that throbbed through her. She whirled to face Mrs. Castor with a wide smile.

"Mrs. Castor, how are you?"

"I've been looking everywhere for you, Sarah," the mayor's wife said, just as Donovan caught up with them. "The Ladies' Auxiliary could certainly use your help at the refreshment table this afternoon."

Sarah's jaw dropped. For the past three years, the Ladies' Auxiliary for the Betterment of Burr had made it quite clear that they would sooner accept a mule as member than Sarah Calhoun. Yet here was the president of the organization herself, requesting her help with a committee project.

"Good afternoon, Mrs. Castor," Donovan said, taking Sarah's hand and firmly placing it on his arm.

"Well, hello, Mr. Donovan." Mrs. Castor's bright, inquiring gaze went from Donovan to Sarah and back again. "I was just asking Sarah if she would be willing to help out the committee. Though if you two have plans . . ."

"No, we don't," Sarah interjected, her pulse skipping from the mere pressure of Donovan's hand pressing hers to his arm. Lordy, she had to get away from him before she forgot herself and did something disgraceful—like eat him alive. "I'd be happy to help out, Mrs. Castor."

The mayor's wife beamed and clapped her pudgy hands together. "Well then, that's wonderful!"

"Sarah," Donovan said, warning clear in his tone. But Sarah merely smiled, mocking him with her eyes. Deliberately, she pulled her hand from his arm.

"Now, now, everyone should help out the community," she said, triumph underscoring her words.

"Yes, indeed." Mrs. Castor linked her elbow through Sarah's. "We're so happy to have you with us, Sarah, especially after the misunderstanding."

"Misunderstanding?" Perplexed, Sarah barely enjoyed the thwarted expression on Donovan's face as Mrs. Castor led her off.

"Yes, that misunderstanding about what happened three years ago. It's amazing how one man's lies can ruin someone's reputation."

"Isn't it," Sarah murmured, still confused.

Mrs. Castor pursed her lips. "That Art Foley's been telling tales about you all this time. But Mr. Donovan set him straight."

"Did he really?"

"Oh yes, he got Mr. Foley to confess to lying right in front of everyone in the saloon last week. Not that a lady talks about what happens in saloons—but this is just between you and me now, isn't it?"

"Of course."

"And we're all so sorry about misjudging you. But it's all water under the bridge now, isn't it? And we'd all love to make amends." Mrs. Castor patted Sarah's hand. "Not that I ever really believed any of those lies."

"Of course not." Sarah's mind was in a whirl. Donovan had done something that had somehow erased the blot on her past. How? And why?

The instant she could slip away from Mrs. Castor, she would ask him.

Escaping Mrs. Castor was easier said than done.

Manning the punch bowl for an hour was not Sarah's idea of a good time, but the mayor's wife ran the refreshment table like a general commanding the troops. Sarah found herself trapped between Mrs. Castor's watchful eye and Donovan's brooding stare.

Not that he was lacking for company.

Donovan couldn't turn around without bumping into a woman hopeful of capturing his attention. Any other day, Sarah might have enjoyed the spectacle of seeing him besieged by marriage-minded women. But today she was nagged by lustful impulses, and she felt oddly proprietory toward him—which both confused and frightened her.

What she needed more than anything was a few quiet moments to get her emotions under control. Or maybe just a few moments alone with Donovan.

She also wanted to ask him what he had done to repair her reputation.

The opportunity for retreat arrived when Buford Beaumont's prize hog escaped and disrupted the three-legged race, sending people sprawling everywhere. In the commotion, Sarah slipped away from the refreshment table. Now if she could just catch Donovan's eye before Mrs. Castor realized she was gone . . .

"Sarah Ann Calhoun, you stop right there!"

Muttering beneath her breath, Sarah halted by Doc Mercer's office and faced Susannah as her sister caught up with her.

"Are you sneaking off to work again? Heavens, Sarah, why can't you just let yourself have a good time for once?"

"I—"

"And what happened to that lovely pink dress you were wearing?" Suzie interrupted. "Do you have some sort of aversion to looking nice?"

Sarah could see Donovan looking around for her. If she could just get rid of Suzie . . . "I changed. Now, if you'll just excuse me—"

"Oh, no, you don't." Suzie stepped closer,

studying her sister's face. "Something's wrong."

"Don't be ridiculous." Sarah glanced at Donovan again. He didn't look happy that she had disappeared, and she wouldn't put it past the man to fling her over his shoulder and carry her back forcibly if he thought she was trying to escape to her office.

"You may be the smart one, Sarah, but don't treat me like I'm stupid. I can tell that something is bothering you. What is it?"

At the simple caring in her sister's tone, Sarah smiled ruefully. "I never could hide anything from you, could I?"

"No, so you might as well just start talking."

Sarah took a deep breath. "I don't know how to tell you this, but—"

"It's a man, isn't it?"

Sarah nodded. "Jack Donovan. He asked me to marry him. I'm sorry, Suzie."

"Sorry?" Susannah stared at her as if she'd grown a second head. "How can you be sorry that a man like that asked you to marry him? I'd put a banner headline in the newspaper if he asked me!"

Startled by Susannah's easy acceptance of the news, Sarah replied, "I haven't accepted yet. That's why I haven't told Mama—I don't want to get her hopes up. But I *had* to tell you."

"You had to?" Susannah's eyes widened as Sarah's words suddenly made sense. "Oh,

Sarah, you must have wanted to smack me when I announced that I intended to marry Mr. Donovan."

Sarah grinned. "It did give me a bad moment or two. How was I supposed to tell my sister that the man she came home to marry had already proposed to me?"

"Exactly the way you just did." Susannah hugged Sarah. "I'm so happy for you!"

"Well, I haven't accepted. And I may not." As Susannah pulled back to gape at her, Sarah said, "I need to be very sure about this, Suzie. I can't take the chance of being wrong. Not again."

"Sniffing all that printer's ink has finally made you crazy!" Susannah exclaimed. "The most eligible bachelor in town has asked you to marry him, and you aren't sure if you're going to accept?"

"Please understand, Suzie." Sarah bit her lip. "He might change his mind, and I'd rather find out sooner than later."

Susannah snorted indelicately. "You don't have a lot of faith in yourself, do you? Are you in love with him?"

Sarah ignored the question, too afraid of what her answer would be. "I'm just not rushing into anything. This way either one of us can back out if we feel it isn't going to work."

"You're fooling yourself, Sarah."

"Maybe. But this is the way it has to be, so

please don't say anything to Mama just yet."

"Fine." Susannah turned back toward the crowd. "Uh-oh, there's Mrs. Castor."

"Drat." The mayor's wife had noticed her, and Sarah sighed as the woman beckoned imperiously. "You know, I think I liked it better when I was a social outcast."

"Back to your punch bowl, Sarah," Suzie teased with a grin.

"I was *trying* to get to Jack," Sarah muttered. "I wanted to ask him something, but now he's surrounded, and I can't seem to escape the Ladies' Auxiliary."

Suzie shaded her eyes and peered across the square to where Donovan stood in a cluster of several women. "Want me to go chase them off?" she asked. "All's fair in love and war."

Sarah grinned. "You could do me a big favor and tell Jack that I'd like to talk to him about something. Tell him to meet me at the newspaper office in about half an hour. I should be able to get away by then."

"You've got it. And if Mrs. Castor won't let you go, *I'll* serve punch."

Sarah gave her sister a big hug. "Thanks, Suzie."

"What are sisters for? Don't worry about your man, Sarah. I'll take good care of him."

"I know you will."

Susannah watched her sister take her place back at the refreshment table, then turned a considering gaze on the crowd that had gathered around Donovan. She would not only chase them off, but would also use the opportunity to ascertain whether Jack Donovan was good enough for Sarah.

She smoothed her hair and her dress to be sure she was presentable. She even pinched her cheeks to make them rosy. Just because she was doing her sisterly duty in interrogating the man didn't mean that she couldn't look good while doing it.

"So tell me," said a low masculine voice from above. "Are you really doing your sister a favor here? Or are you planning to take her beau away from her?"

Suzie glanced up and saw a man at the window of Dr. Mercer's clinic, just a couple of feet above her head. He had long straw-colored hair, dark eyes, and a mustache, and the smirk on his handsome face made her instinctively want to smack it off.

"I don't believe that's any of your business."

"You're pretty enough to get the whole cavalry to come a-courtin'. Why don't you just leave your sister's man be?"

"You're mistaken, sir," Susannah said primly.

As she walked away, he said, "If I were you, I'd just leave well enough alone."

"Well, you're not me," she snapped, irritated at the way her pulse skittered at the sound of that slow, Southern drawl. She propped her hands on her hips. "Perhaps you should take your own advice and leave well enough alone."

He laughed, showing her a glimpse of white teeth and a strong throat. "You're something, princess. If I weren't a sick man, I'd come out there and—"

She responded with a chilly look of disdain. "You'd have to catch me first."

He narrowed his gaze. "Oh, I'd catch you all right. I'm a U.S. marshal, ma'am. And we always get our man—or woman."

"Conceited ox." Turning on her heel, she headed back toward the festival, the rascal's laughter chasing behind her.

Donovan had noticed immediately when Sarah left the refreshment table, but before he could chase after her he was cornered by the Tremont sisters.

Emmaline stood nearby, no doubt acting as a chaperone, though she turned a blind eye to her sister's obvious flirting. Donovan, scanning the area for Sarah, hardly noticed Juliana's attempts to capture his interest. He just wanted them both to go away so that he could catch up with his intended.

Finally, Sarah reappeared and took up her station at the punch bowl. She met his eyes for a moment, glanced at the Tremonts, then arched her brows.

He looked down at Juliana's proprietary hand on his arm and at once realized how the situation might look to Sarah. Suddenly hankering for a glass of punch, he tried to break free, but Juliana's grip became tighter than a bear trap. Helpless, he could only look over at Sarah, unsure how to escape without committing some grave social error. But at the militant look in his sassy girl's eye, he found himself weighing the consequences of a social blunder on his part against the gossip likely to result if his future bride were to launch herself over the refreshment table and pluck Juliana Tremont bald.

Just then, the cavalry arrived in the form of a beautiful woman.

"Well, well, Juliana Tremont. The last time I saw you, you were running the lemonade table at the church bazaar. Looks like you're still sour."

The tall, statuesque woman who had joined their group was dressed in a fancy store-bought blue dress with lace trim that showcased her curvy figure. Her silver-blond hair was done up in ringlets that looked alluring rather than childish, and her lush mouth curved in a confident smile.

"Susannah Calhoun. I'd heard you were back." From the tone of Juliana's voice, she didn't seem overjoyed over the prospect.

Donovan would have been happy to see the devil himself if it meant escaping the Tremonts. "Miss Calhoun, I'm Jack Donovan. I know your family."

"Mr. Donovan." Slanting him a seductive glance, Susannah offered her hand. Donovan took it and held it.

"You're interrupting our conversation, Susannah." Emmaline sniffed.

"Emmaline," Susannah said with a smile. "You haven't changed a bit. Such a pity." Dismissing the Tremonts with an elegant shrug, she turned back to Donovan. "Mr. Donovan, I find myself in need of an escort for the pie-eating contest."

"Allow me." Donovan offered his elbow, but Juliana still held his other arm. Both Susannah and Donovan stared at Juliana until she removed her hand. Donovan nodded at the Tremonts. "Ladies."

"But—" Juliana spluttered.

"So nice seeing you again," Susannah said with an insincere smile as Donovan led her away.

Donovan dared not say a word until they were out of earshot; then he started chuckling. "Masterfully done, Miss Calhoun. I'm in your debt."

"There's nothing I like better than having a handsome man in my debt, Mr. Donovan." Susannah sent a sharp look to a pretty young girl who stood nearby, staring moon-eyed at Donovan. The girl started, blushed beet-red, and hurried away.

"You're very good at that," he remarked.

"Practice. While you're with me, none of them will bother you." She arched one perfectly curved eyebrow. "Unless you want to be bothered."

"There's only one woman I'm interested in," he declared. "And that's your sister."

"Well." Susannah's lips curved. "That puts me in my place."

"I'm sorry, Miss Calhoun. You're a beautiful woman, but—"

"No, no." Susannah waved a hand and cut him off. "I'm glad to hear it. My sister has never been lucky in love, Mr. Donovan, but I'm hoping you might change that."

"I'm trying to. I intend to marry her."

"I see." Susannah stopped to admire a quilt that was being raffled off, the proceeds of which would go toward the school fund. "Sarah's made some bad decisions in the past."

"I don't care about the past."

"But I do. She's been hurt, Mr. Donovan." Susannah slanted him a look that, had she been a man, would have had him reaching for his gun. "I intend to see that she doesn't get hurt again."

"I have no intention of hurting her."

"Good. Then you won't mind answering a few questions—to put an older sister's mind at ease."

Donovan recognized the steel beneath the tone and respected it. Had Sarah been his sister, he would have done the same thing. "Ask away, Miss Calhoun."

"Please, call me Susannah." With a sweet smile, she launched into an interrogation that would have made any military commander shudder.

Standing by the punch bowl, Sarah smothered a smile as she watched her sister extract Donovan from the clutches of the Tremont sisters.

The two seemed to be in deep conversation. Sarah frowned, wondering how long it took to deliver a message. She tried to catch Susannah's eye, but her sister was deliberately ignoring her. Sarah groaned, realizing that Suzie was probably questioning Jack about his background.

Between her mother's efforts to throw Sarah at any likely bachelor and her sister's determination to protect her, Sarah sometimes wished she were both an orphan and an only child.

The next shift for the punch bowl arrived, and Sarah handed the ladle to the woman with relief. For a moment she was tempted to go rescue Jack from Susannah's interrogation, but then she saw Mrs. Castor bearing down on her with determination. Beating a hasty retreat, Sarah set off for the newspaper office to wait for Jack.

Going around back so that no one would see her, she unlocked the door to the office and stepped inside. Sinking into her desk chair, she shook her head. Only yesterday, the Ladies' Auxiliary had done their best to ignore her existence. Today they seemed determined to include her in every one of their activities— because of something Jack had done.

How had he done it? How had he managed to make a three-year scandal disappear? And why had he done it? For her, or because he didn't want her past to reflect on him once they were married?

She wanted to believe him when he said that he didn't give credence to gossip. But she was so used to men disappointing her that she couldn't help but wonder.

Still, Jack Donovan seemed to be different from the other men she'd known. He had even offered her a chance at her dream of a family without forcing her to sacrifice her career. Not many men would make such a concession.

Good Lord—she was in love with him.

The truth of her own feelings scared her to death even as it bouyed her heart. Leaning back in her chair, she stared up at the ceiling.

Why him? Why a man who brought out the carnal side of her that made her so uncomfortable? A man who confused her by rejecting her one minute and proposing to her the next?

But love him she did. She loved his looks. His walk. That single dimple that creased his cheek when he smiled. She was fascinated by the many layers of the man inside, lured by his dreams and his secrets.

Something happened when they were together. Something more than the physical attraction between them. It was as if Donovan saw through the polite mask she showed to the rest of the world to the real woman hiding within her. And something told her that she did the same thing with him. Between them there were no pretenses, no polite words that hid true feelings. The essence of each of them was laid bare before the other, without inhibition.

So where was he?

She rose from her chair and paced to the front window. Looking outside, she noticed for the first time that thick rain clouds had moved in. The swollen gray clouds cast early darkness over the town, heralding a coming storm. It looked like Founder's Day was going to get rained out, though the dance tonight would simply be moved indoors.

The thought of the dance reminded her of the first time Donovan had kissed her, at the spring dance in May. When he had told her that she wouldn't suit him as a wife.

Yet now the man she loved had asked her to marry him—so why was she hesitating? If it turned out that they had made a mistake, they could work things out from there! She wasn't about to give up the chance to be with the man she loved, despite her lingering feelings of uncertainty. Her decision was made: she would tell Jack Donovan that she would love to be his wife.

If he ever arrived.

A knock came at the front door of the office. Smiling, she unlocked it and swung it open.

But it wasn't Jack.

The man on her doorstep had dark hair that was short and neatly trimmed beneath his wide-brimmed black hat. A thin, black mustache accented his handsome face. Ever the natty dresser, he wore fawn-colored trousers, a matching coat, and a solid vest in a darker shade of brown, complete with pocket watch. On his feet were shiny black boots.

And his eyes were steel-gray, merciless and purely evil as he stared at her over the barrel of the Remington revolver he aimed at her heart.

"Hello, Sarah," he said with a nasty smile.

"Luke," she whispered.

Then he raised his hand, and with a jolt of pain, everything went black.

Chapter 14

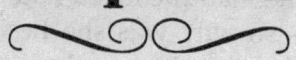

Sarah came to slowly, her head throbbing. For a moment she fought through the painful haze of confusion, until she remembered.

Luke.

She opened her eyes and found herself leaning against a large boulder at the side of the road. Luke knelt a few yards away, digging a stone from the hoof of a brown horse.

She had to get away from him.

Silently, she climbed to her feet, never taking her eyes from him. Guiding herself with her hands, she edged around the rock. He continued to work on the horse, muttering under his breath.

She might make it. A glance identified the terrain as a stretch of road not far from Miller's Pond. Though she was sure it had taken them only thirty minutes or so to get out here on horseback, it would take a couple of hours to get back to town on foot. But she didn't care. She would have gladly walked the path to hell barefoot as long as it meant getting away from Luke Petrie.

Suddenly, Luke's head came up, and he looked right at her. She froze. His gaze was flat and cold, like a rattler about to strike. He got to his feet with a shout.

The woods, she thought with panic, taking off like a startled deer. If she could just get to the woods, she would be safe. She could hide.

"Sarah!" He pounded after her in pursuit.

She didn't dare look back, her goal the copse of trees that promised sanctuary. Suddenly needles of pain exploded across her scalp as he grabbed her by her braid, yanking her to a halt.

"Not so fast, my dear," he snarled.

Bile rose in her throat as he whirled her around to face him, holding her with a strength that belied his slender build. She shoved against his chest, but she couldn't budge him an inch.

"You're not going to leave before we have a chance to talk about old times, are you?" The slow drawl she had once found charming now only nauseated her.

"I'd rather forget I ever knew you," she snapped, seeing him clearly with the wisdom of maturity. Once she had considered him handsome, this former tutor from Savannah who had come west in search of adventure. Handsome, debonair, and dazzling with his wit and smooth Southern manners, a man well versed in social graces.

He was as different from Jack Donovan as night was from day. How had she ever considered herself in love with him? How had she missed the meanness in his eyes? The rot in his soul?

"Forget you ever knew me?" He laughed in a way that sent chills down her spine. "I've come a long way to find you, Sarah Calhoun."

Fear shot through her, but she held his gaze steadily. "We have nothing to say to each other."

His expression twisted with cold menace. He pulled out the gun, holding it against her temple. "I beg to differ. You and I have unfinished business."

She wanted to argue with him, but his weapon made her hold her tongue.

"You always were a smart one, Sarah," he said, approving of her silence. Lowering the revolver, he dragged her to where the horse stood waiting, then crowded her back against the animal with his body. "Yes indeed, you've always been smart. Not to mention a wildcat in bed, my dear."

"Don't call me that." Her heart pounded. Fear froze her limbs as he nuzzled her hair.

"I'll call you anything I want, *my dear*. And

you'll like it." He jabbed the gun painfully into her side. "Won't you?"

She nodded because she had no choice, but her stomach churned with revulsion.

With a thought of snatching the gun in mind, she slid her hand down her side.

Like a snake striking, he grabbed her wrist. "What are you up to?"

"My hands are sweaty," she lied. "I was just wiping them off on my skirt."

"Excited?" Leering, he pressed a kiss to her palm. "You're just about the hottest piece I ever took to bed, my dear. I can't wait to have a taste of you again."

She gave him a sickly smile. "Right here in the middle of the road?"

He laughed. "Of course not! I've got a nice little hideout that'll make a sweet love nest." His expression grew cruelly serious. "You have something I want, Sarah. And I intend to collect."

He dropped her hand and stepped away from her to grab the horse's fallen reins. As he reached for them, Sarah felt the gun move away from her side, and she snatched her chance. She shoved him into the horse, then yanked her skirts to her knees and ran for her life.

"Sarah!" he shouted, then bellowed several colorful curses. "Come back here, you bitch!"

She sped for the trees.

"Sarah!"

Two gunshots sounded. Dirt exploded from the ground in front of her, and she froze.

"Come back here." Though his tone was low, when she turned, she saw that his gaze burned with fury. He pointed the revolver straight at her heart. "Come on, now."

Thunder rumbled as he grabbed her arm and pushed her toward the road. Clouds darkened the sky, and the thunder crashed louder, eliciting a nervous whinny from the horse. Luke shoved Sarah between the shoulder blades, sending her stumbling ahead of him.

"Move along, my dear. I don't want to get caught in this storm."

"I'm going," she snapped.

"Easy now, Sarah," he said in a low voice that made her skin crawl. "I sure would hate to shoot you before I'm done with you."

Lightning split the sky, followed by another roll of thunder. As they neared the road, Luke grabbed her arm and twisted it painfully behind her back, and she whimpered. The wind kicked up, whipping at her skirts and blowing strands of hair into her eyes.

A fat drop of rain hit her cheek. Luke cursed ripely as the heavens opened up, and rain pounded the ground. He flipped the reins over the horse's neck and jerked Sarah over to the animal's side.

"Up!" he snarled.

Releasing her arm, he shoved her toward the saddle. What she saw in his face scared her down to her soul.

He meant to kill her. It was right there in his eyes.

She screamed and leaped at him, clawing at his eyes with her nails. He swore, fell back, and dropped the gun. While he rubbed furiously at the reddening scratches, she bolted.

She fled down the road, not caring where she was going. The rain pounded down in torrents, turning the world to gray-toned shadows. She knew he was behind her; she could feel it. She thought she heard the thunder of hoofbeats, but the rumble of the storm made it impossible to tell.

She zigzagged to throw him off the track, but ended up getting herself all turned around. The driving rain obscured everything. What if she was heading toward him instead of away? She whirled, intending to bolt in the other direction. A shadowy figure on a horse loomed before her, and she screamed.

"Sarah!"

The rider slid off the horse. She darted to the right and kept on running across the field. The woods—somehow, she had to find the woods. Wet brush slapped at her skirts, and she gulped air into her burning lungs, anticipating capture at any second.

"Sarah!" Hands closed over her shoulders.

She shrieked and whirled, clawing at him once more with the only weapon she had—her bare hands. He grabbed her wrists with a strength she hadn't expected and shook her, once.

"Sarah, it's me! It's Donovan."

She kicked his shins before the words sank into her panicked mind.

"Goddamnit, woman!" he roared.

"*Jack?*" Hardly able to hope, she looked up. He'd lost his hat, and the rain plastered his black hair against his head. Rivulets of water streamed over his cheekbones and trickled off his jaw. His dark eyes blazed at her as he clenched his teeth in pain.

"Of course it's me. What the heck were you doing, whacking my leg like that? Damnit!"

"Oh, my God!" She threw her arms around him and clung hard. "It was Luke—he's here someplace."

"I know. I saw him take you, and I followed." Donovan grasped her upper arms. "Where is he?"

"He had a gun! He had a gun, and he was going to—"

"Easy, sweetheart," he murmured, pulling her close.

She accepted the comfort of his arms with relief. "Just hold me," she whispered, shivering.

"All right." He stroked his hand over her

sopping wet braid. "Where is he now?" he repeated.

"I don't know. I scratched his eyes and ran. I thought you were him."

"That's my girl."

"I was so scared—"

"I know you were," he soothed her.

She jerked away from him. "He might still be here, Jack! We have to get away!"

"You're right." His mouth thinned, and the wildness of the wolf entered his eyes.

Grabbing her hand, he led her at a run across the field and back to the road, the rain hammering down around them and thunder booming off the mountains. Lightning forked across the sky, but Sarah saw nothing but Donovan. And safety.

They reached the road, which had turned into a quagmire of mud. Through the driving rain they could see Senseless, hitched to a bush, tossing his head nervously at the storm.

"I don't see him," Sarah shouted over the howl of the wind. "Maybe he took off?"

"I don't want to take any chances." Donovan unknotted the reins from the branch. "Let's get you safe. Then I'll deal with Petrie."

Thunder resounded above their heads, and lightning spiked across the sky to strike a tree somewhere in the woods. The resulting crack of a limb and the scent of smoke made Senseless roll his eyes and shriek. He reared up, jerking the reins from Donovan's hand, then took off at a gallop down the road.

"Senseless! Get back here!" Donovan whistled, but the horse disappeared into the pounding rain. "Damn you, horse!" Thwarted, he glanced around, his posture alert with tension. "We've got to get out of here."

Sarah moved closer to Donovan, expecting Luke to pop out of the storm at any moment and shoot them on the spot. "There's an old shed nearby, at Miller's Pond. We can at least wait out the storm there."

"Good girl." He reached beneath his coat and pulled out his throwing knife, then he took her hand. "Let's go. If Petrie's still around, I'll take care of him."

Sarah glanced from the knife to his face. Her wolf was back, and the weapon he held with such confident skill seemed to be more a part of him than the gun he wore strapped to his thigh. As she followed him into the woods, she was glad he was her protector. She had not the slightest doubt that Jack Donovan would make a very dangerous enemy.

The shed was barely that, merely a space old man Miller had used to store his plow and other gardening tools. They stumbled into it, soaking wet. There were a couple of leaks in the roof, but for the most part it was dry, though dark. Donovan left the door standing open to take advantage of the fading light. It had been almost sunset when the storm had blown in.

"Lucky they built this thing on a rise, otherwise we'd be up to our ankles in mud," he said, poking around the shed. He discovered a wagon cover lying in the corner, and under it, a treasure. "I found a lamp. It looks like there's a little oil left. And a tinderbox."

Sarah didn't respond. He took the tinderbox and struck a flame, then lit the ancient lantern, setting it on the dirt floor. A soft glow filled the shed, revealing weathered wood walls with spiders' webs in the corners. Ancient tools hung from rusted nails, and a pile of what had once been blankets rotted in a dark corner.

"Home sweet home," he murmured, turning to Sarah with a smile.

The smile faded as he looked at her. She stood trembling in her dripping clothes, her arms folded tightly around herself. Her eyes were wide with fear and misery.

"Sarah?"

"It's all my fault," she whispered. The despair in her voice tugged at him.

"None of this is your fault, sweetheart," he said soothingly.

"Yes, it is. He came back for me. Someone else could die because of *me*."

"Sarah . . ." He touched her arm, but she lurched away from him.

"You don't understand!" Her expression twisted with pain and regret. "My father died because of me. Because I wouldn't listen when he told me that Luke was no good. I was young and foolish; then *he* came along and made me feel special—wanted. But he was just using me." Her voice broke.

Donovan approached her slowly, knowing only that he had to comfort her somehow. "Sarah, you're drenched," he said quietly. "You're going to get sick if you don't get out of those clothes."

"How could you ask me to marry you?" she tossed out, her face pale and her eyes fierce, lost in a world of bitterness and grief. "I have blood on my hands."

Something snapped in him. "That's bullshit," he snarled. He gripped her arms and stared into her eyes. The depth of pain he saw there made him hurt just as she was hurting. "*He's* the killer; not you, sassy girl. You didn't do anything wrong."

His blunt words seemed to reach her as the calming ones had not. She took a deep, shuddering breath. "He used me," she repeated, her voice less shaky than before. "I used to ... meet him ... in the woods. I thought he loved me. But he used me to get information so he could rob the bank. My father knew something was wrong and caught Luke in the act. And Luke killed him."

Donovan pulled her into his arms, holding her as if he could somehow absorb the anguish of the past. He had seen this before, during his days as a bounty hunter. He knew that she had been victimized, and that she had to say it, all of it, in order to begin healing. She had to face what had happened and accept it before she could move on with her life.

But knowing that didn't make it any easier for him to bear as she struggled with the words.

"I held my father's hand while he died," she continued, her voice muffled against his chest. "And Luke stood there and told me how he hadn't had any choice . . . that my father was going to stop us. That he still wanted to marry me." She snorted with disbelief. "He would have said anything at that point. He probably would have shot me, too, except the gunshot had woken up the sheriff, and he came running down the street to see what had happened. Luke lit out, but I told the sheriff where to find him—at our special place, out in the woods. They got the money back, and they put Luke in jail. But last week he managed to get away—and now he's back. For revenge." She sniffled, fighting back the tears. "When everyone found out that I had been . . . meeting . . . Luke, my reputation was ruined. It was only the newspaper that made them accept me."

"I'm sorry, sweetheart."

She finally cried then, a torrent of healing tears. He simply held her, wishing he had gotten the opportunity to do some damage to the bastard who had hurt his woman.

Outside, the storm railed, and rain splattered against the old wooden structure. Sarah's sobs lessened as Donovan held her close, stroking his hands over her back and hair. Finally she raised her head and stepped away from his embrace. His arms dropped to his sides.

"I'm sorry," she whispered, her cheeks flaming red in her wan face. "I didn't mean to fall apart that way."

"Don't worry about it, sweetheart. You've been through a rough patch tonight." He shrugged out of his coat and shook the water from it. "This thing kept me fairly dry, but I can't say the same for you. You'd better get out of those clothes."

"Excuse me?"

Her shocked tone made him smile. This was the Sarah he knew. "You need to get those wet clothes off before you get sick. You can wear my shirt."

Sarah gaped. She had just spilled her secrets and her tears all over him, and he wanted her to take off her clothes? Didn't he care about what she had just told him? Or didn't he realize what it meant? "I'm fine," she insisted, watching him with a puzzled frown.

"Don't be stupid," he retorted, unbuttoning

his shirt. "This is about survival. But if you want to preserve your modesty, I'll turn my back."

She hesitated. He didn't glance up from his buttons. This was even worse. Had she repulsed him? The Jack Donovan she knew would have at least tried to steal a kiss in this kind of situation, yet now he wouldn't even look at her.

Had she ruined everything by telling him the truth?

A shiver wracked her, and she realized that it would be the height of idiocy to come down with a chill while she tried to puzzle out his motivations. "I would appreciate the loan of your shirt," she replied with prim dignity, turning her back as he did the same.

No more words were spoken. Only the rasp and slap of wet material against skin broke the silence between them. "You can look now if you want," he said finally.

She glanced back over her shoulder, and his shirt hit her in the face. As she spluttered and tried to untangle herself, he issued more orders.

"Get out of your skirt and shirtwaist. Take a couple of those tools down and hang your clothes from those nails in the wall. You can keep your camisole and bloomers on if you've got a mind to, for modesty's sake."

"Your knowledge of women's undergarments is shocking and inappropriate, Mr. Donovan," she said with a sniff.

"Inappropriate, hell, *Miss Calhoun*," he retorted. He pulled out the wagon cover he had discovered earlier and spread it on the ground. "What it is, is plain good sense. Now get out of those wet clothes, sassy girl, before I come over there and strip you myself."

He looked up then. For an instant, something stretched between them, an unspoken dare. Her heart pounded. His eyes narrowed. Then he clenched his hands and turned his back again. Unsettled by the sudden tension, she retreated to a corner of the shed. Not that it was a far distance; a man could lie on the floor and touch one wall with his hands and the other with his toes.

As she stripped off her wet garments, Sarah periodically glanced over her shoulder at Donovan. He busied himself arranging a tidy bedroll for the two of them, and didn't even glance at her. Strangely disappointed, she hung her clothes on the nails as he had suggested, then turned to face him just as he went over and shut the door. Dragging an old plow blade over, he propped it under the latch and then piled more rusted tools at the base of the door.

"What are you doing?"

"Making sure no one gets in here without us knowing," he answered. Swiping the dust from his hands, he finally faced her.

Her pulse skipped as he scanned her from head to toe. She followed his gaze, noticing the way the wet material of her bloomers clung to her legs and displayed glimpses of the flesh beneath. She had buttoned his shirt up to the neck, and the tails hung well over her thighs, but she still felt as if she stood before him stark naked.

When his eyes met hers, she saw a hunger there that staggered her.

He still wanted her.

She glanced at the makeshift bed he had laid out for them. The lure of spending the night pressed against Donovan made her want to give in to that side of her that was wild and spontaneous. She wanted to close her eyes and surrender to the fire that lived inside her, the slumbering coals that Donovan had stoked to life.

Could she trust him with the passion that simmered inside her? Or would it end in disaster? Did she dare take the risk?

He was a man who had protected her, a man she respected and loved. She wanted to lie with him, to feel his strong hands touch her and his body join with hers. Tonight, she wanted to become Donovan's woman.

And if the way he watched her was any indication, he wanted that, too.

She lifted both hands and smoothed her wet hair, very much aware that the shirt rode up with her movements. He swallowed hard, and tenderness swelled inside her. Heady with feminine power, she lowered her hands and smoothed the shirt over her chest and belly, watching him carefully. His jaw clenched, and his hands fisted.

"Sarah." His tone was rough, his eyes hot with need. But his words were gentle. "You've had a bad scare. You need to rest."

"I'm not scared."

"By the time this rain lets up," he continued, as if she hadn't spoken, "it's going to be dark. There's no way we can get back to town tonight."

"All right." She tugged at the hem of the shirt, then smiled at him.

"Damn it, it's not all right!" He kicked an old ax handle, sending it flying to land in the heap at the door. "It wasn't supposed to be like this. I courted you properly. I asked you the right way. Yet now your reputation is going to be ruined again."

"You saved my life, Jack."

He glared at her. "I'll be damned if I'll stand by and watch them rip you apart again, sassy girl."

"I can handle it."

"I don't want you to have to handle it!"

"Let's worry about that tomorrow." She took a deep breath, twisting her fingers together. This was it. She was about to take a step that would either be the smartest decision she had ever made in her life—or the greatest mistake. "I want to be with you tonight, Jack."

"What?" The quiet word seemed to echo like thunder in the tiny shed.

"I said I want to be with you."

He stared at her. "You're upset. You've had a shock."

Her determination wavered. "If you don't want me, just say so, Jack."

His expression softened. "How could I not want you, sassy girl?"

"Then—"

"I just don't want to take advantage of you. You're vulnerable right now."

"I'm hot and bothered right now!" Her ardent words startled both of them. She flushed and he grinned.

"Hot and bothered, huh?" He chuckled. "Sweetheart, I had no idea you even knew that expression."

Sarah took a deep breath. "The rumors are true, Jack—I'm not a virgin."

"So? Neither am I."

She made a sound of exasperation. "You know very well that it's different for a man."

"For people who care about things like that." He stepped toward her. "I know you, Sarah Calhoun. You're passionate, but you're not a whore."

She flinched at the word. "The town doesn't agree with you."

He smiled with grim amusement. "They do now."

"I heard something about that. What did you do, Jack?"

"Nothing at all. And neither did you, according to the current gossip."

She shook her head, and a chuckle escaped her. "I don't know what to do with you, Jack Donovan."

"Just love me, Sarah. The way I love you."

Her smile faded, and she stared at him. "What did you say?"

He shifted uncomfortably. "I said I love you, damn it."

"Oh, Jack." She raised a trembling hand to her mouth. He loved her? After everything she had just told him? "Are you sure?"

"Of course I'm sure!"

She took a step toward him. Hesitated. "I don't know what to say."

"Say you'll marry me." He opened his arms. "I need you, sassy girl."

"Yes!" She flew into his embrace. "Yes, I'll marry you."

"About damned time," he muttered. Then he kissed her, and passion erupted with a force that shook both of them.

Chapter 15

Sarah gave herself up to his kiss, her heart singing with the joy of revelation. He loved her!

"Sarah," he panted, breaking the kiss. "We should stop."

"Why?" She twined her arms around his neck, feeling gloriously alive. "This has been coming for a long time, Jack."

"It's about to get out of hand."

"Maybe I want it to."

He groaned, closing his eyes and resting his forehead against hers. "Maybe isn't good enough, Sarah. We can stop here and wait for our wedding night. That's what we should do."

She smiled, doubts and fears melting away like brown sugar on the tongue, leaving only sweet passion behind. "Since when does either one of us do what we're supposed to do?"

He tightened his fingers on her waist. "Be sure, Sarah. I don't think I can stop this time."

She leaned up and brushed her lips against his. "I'm sure. I want to be with you, Jack. No regrets."

"No regrets," he repeated.

This time when he kissed her, she met him halfway.

No man had ever stirred her like this. No other man ever would. She pressed herself against him, longing for his warmth, hungry for the taste of him. His arms were strong and sure as he held her close, his mouth deliciously demanding.

Arousal simmered, slow and hot, as the rain battered their tiny haven. She thought she knew what to expect, but she was so wrong. Nothing had prepared her for the tenderness of his hands as he slowly peeled the damp clothing from her body. Nothing had warned her how her knees would weaken at the way he looked at her, as if she were something rare and precious. Nothing in her wildest imaginings had hinted at the slow, drugging desire that flowed through her like hot wax when she finally stood naked before him—and he touched only her cheek.

Her limbs trembled as he cupped her face in his hands and kissed her with exquisite sweetness, as if nothing existed for him but her mouth.

"Sarah," he murmured, nipping at her lower lip. "You're mine."

She made a soft sound of assent. He lifted his head and looked at her, stroking his hands down her neck and over her shoulders. Holding her gaze, he continued downward until he cupped her breasts in his palms. Desire spiked through her as he rubbed his thumbs over the nipples. She didn't try to hide her reaction from him. She couldn't.

"You're beautiful," he said softly. "Every inch of you, inside and out."

"Jack . . ." His touch utterly devastated her.

"I need your hands on me, Sarah." He guided one of her palms to his chest. She flattened her fingers against the broad expanse, then flicked open one of the buttons of his long underwear. A glance at his face made her smile, and she popped open another button. He leaned back against the wall, his hands resting on her hips, letting her set her own pace.

Finally she had unbuttoned down to the waistband of his trousers. Spreading the edges wide, she smoothed her palms over the hair-roughened muscles. He simply watched her, his eyes slitted. Then she leaned closer and pressed a kiss to his chest. He groaned, and his eyes slid closed.

Such power. Her lips curved in a smile, and she dragged her nails lightly down the exposed flesh. He shuddered, sending a thrill through her. She scored him again with her nails, enjoying the way her lone wolf gritted his teeth and quivered beneath her touch. She did it again and again until he grabbed her wrist.

He opened his eyes, and she almost stepped back. Her wolf had returned all right, and he was hungry.

Taking her hand, he led her to the pallet he had made.

She lowered herself to the makeshift bed, sitting back on her heels and watching as he stripped off his garments. His boots went first, tossed carelessly to the foot of the bedroll. Then he stripped off his trousers, sending them flying after the boots. His long underwear hid nothing, his arousal stretching the white cotton to the limit even as he ripped open the buttons. One popped off and zinged across the shed. In moments, he was as naked as she.

He came to the edge of the bedroll and looked down at her for a long moment. She waited, her heart pounding. Donovan without his clothes was a sight to behold. His body was solid and lean, marked here and there with scars. She longed to kiss each and every one of them. Here was a man who had lived hard and survived. Here was a man she could trust with her heart.

He knelt on the bedroll, shifting until their knees touched. She stretched up to meet his descending mouth, linking her hands around his neck once more. With a groan, he clasped his arms around her, pulling her against him with desperate strength. Wrapping her braid around one hand, he tugged her head backward, breaking the kiss and holding her prisoner while he nipped at her neck and sent her senses soaring.

"I need you," he muttered against her throat. "Let me love you, Sarah."

"Yes," she whispered. And again, "Yes."

He released her hair and cupped one hand possessively over her bottom, urging her closer. His erection pressed into her belly, hotly insistent. She slid her hand down, closed her fingers around him. His guttural moan urged her to stroke him. Their mouths met in reckless greed. He squeezed her bottom, stroked her back. She smoothed her hands over every sleek muscle she could reach, always coming back to the hungry flesh between his thighs. He returned the favor, parting her legs and caressing her with a tenderness that hinted at his tenuous control even as it edged her to the boiling point.

"Jack." Mindless with need, she reared up and bit his earlobe. "Jack, please."

"God." He shuddered, still stroking the slick heat between her thighs. "You're so ready for me, sweetheart."

"Yes." Trembling, she dug her nails into his shoulders. "I want you so much."

"Sweet Sarah." He tumbled her backward, cushioning her with one arm until she lay fully beneath him. She didn't even care about the rough blankets against her skin. Her world was filled with Donovan. She stroked her hand over his forehead, combed the sweat-dampened hair back from his face. Dropping a kiss on her breast, he shifted, hooking his elbows beneath her knees and spreading her wide for him. "I love you, Sarah," he murmured against her mouth. Then he slipped into her.

A sound of startled enjoyment escaped her lips. There was no pain, only a slow, satisfying stretching as he pressed insistently forward until he filled her completely. There he paused, waiting for her body to adapt to the sensual penetration. Her loins clenched instinctively, little ripples of adjustment that wrung a surprised groan from him. He began to rock his hips in response, and she clung to him, her movements echoing his as he plunged harder, faster, deeper. Nothing else felt like this, the pleasure and the heat, the instinctive rhythm of loving. She met his kiss eagerly, her tongue teasing his, imitating the age-old mating dance.

When he buried his face in her neck and called her name, she tumbled right behind him into rapture.

The door crashed open with a clatter of rusty tools. Donovan sat bolt upright, his knife already in his hand. With a sleepy murmur, Sarah snuggled closer to him, flinging an arm over his thighs.

"Here they are!" Mort peered into the shed, Gabriel just behind him. Amos pushed them aside and stuck his head in.

"There ya are, boss!"

Sarah stirred, no doubt disturbed by the commotion.

"Ya had us right worried," Amos continued, entering the tiny edifice as if he owned it. "When your horse come back without ya, we thought something awful had happened to ya. Shoulda known better."

"Keep your voice down," Donovan said. He tucked the blanket around Sarah's shoulders as she settled into slumber once more.

"That gal must be plumb tuckered." Matt wandered in, his rifle in hand, followed by Mort and Gabriel. The four men looked at Donovan with raised brows.

"She was attacked by that bastard, Petrie," he said in response to the unspoken question. "My horse ran off, so we had to bunk down here. *End of story.*"

Amos rubbed his chaw-stained beard and glanced at Matt. "Well, boss, I reckon there's something we ought to tell you . . ."

"I heard the commotion," said a new voice from the doorway.

Donovan met the newcomer's gaze squarely. "Morning, Ross."

"Donovan." Ross's gaze slid to the slumbering Sarah and then back to Donovan. His mouth thinned.

A rustle of the tarp drew everyone's attention. Sarah sat up, rubbing a hand across her eyes and yawning.

"Jack?" she said in a sleepy voice. Then her eyes focused, and she cried out, jerking the blanket to her chin. Her face flushed redder than a tomato as she glanced from one man to another.

"Good morning, Sarah," Ross said. He looked at Donovan. "I think we'd *all* better wait outside while Sarah gets dressed."

With a sigh, Donovan got to his feet, grateful he had slipped back into his trousers sometime before dawn, and followed the posse outside. Ross brought up the rear, his expression grim and his fingers tight around the rifle in his hand.

The instant the door to the shed closed behind him, the rancher turned to him. "I hope you know what you're doing."

"What's that supposed to mean?" Donovan asked, his tone deceptively mild.

"Your horse showed up at the Calhouns' last night, right around the time Mrs. Calhoun was asking around about Sarah. The whole town knows the both of you were missing all night."

"Bet they'll be glad to know we're alive," Donovan said sarcastically. "People should be more concerned about Petrie running loose than whether or not Sarah and I are going to get married. Which we *are* going to do, by the way." He scanned each man in turn, as if daring them to protest. But instead, their bodies relaxed as the worry left their faces.

"I sure am glad to hear that," Amos said, voicing what was obviously a shared opinion. "I like that gal. Didn't want to see her get hurt again."

"I take care of what's mine." Donovan looked at Ross as he spoke.

Ross nodded once in understanding. "Then it looks like I'm not needed here anymore. I've got cattle to see to."

"Turner," Donovan warned as Ross mounted his horse. "I expect to see you dancing at my wedding."

The two men held each other's gaze for a long moment. Then Ross gave him a jerky nod. "Tell Sarah I'm sorry for the other night," he said. "And that I hope she'll be happy."

"She will be," Donovan assured him.

With a nod to the other men, Ross kicked his horse into a gallop.

"Sure hope he can dance," Amos mused. He spit a wad of tobacco juice into the hoofprints left by Ross's horse.

The door to the shed opened. "Please take me home, Jack," Sarah said.

Donovan came to her and took her hand, pressing her trembling fingers over his heart. "You are home."

One week later, the entire town of Burr attended the wedding of Sarah Calhoun and Jack Donovan. After the ceremony, everyone rode out to the Donovan spread for an enormous wedding reception.

Sarah clung to her new husband's hand as they walked among the guests, greeting them and being congratulated. The yard was overflowing with people in their Sunday best. Trestle tables covered with white tablecloths had been set up for dining, and a steer was slowly being roasted over an open fire. A line of tables alongside the house sagged with the weight of hot corn and potatoes, biscuits and gravy, and dozens of other delectable foods. Smack in the center of all this bounty rose a three-tiered wedding cake, baked by Honoria Westerly and her daughter, Marianne.

A bunch of Donovan's hands had built a wooden dance floor outside the white picket fence surrounding the huge yard. Mort, Johnny, and Gabriel had taken their places atop the dais and kicked up a foot-stomping tune. Someone handed Sarah a plate full of food and she even sat down with it, but she couldn't eat. Donovan, however, ate heartily, accepting congratulations and slaps on the back with sociable good humor.

Sarah made an effort to pick at the delicious offerings on her plate, but finally she just pushed it aside. She was too edgy to eat anything. Every time someone came up behind her, she jumped, expecting to see Luke's leering face. She had spent the week before her wedding expecting him to step out of some corner and threaten her again.

As if he sensed her turmoil, Donovan reached over and took her hand without pausing in his conversation with Matt and Amos. He caressed her fingers with his thumb, and she found herself relaxing. Even if Luke was still around, she was safe with Donovan.

Comforted by her husband's soothing presence, she took more of an interest in her surroundings. Donovan's yard was little more than hard-packed dirt, and she envisioned how it might look once she took the gardening in hand. Perhaps a trellis on the side of the house. Rose bushes maybe, or petunias. Someone laughed, breaking her free from her imaginings.

At the next table, Mr. Castor stuffed his mouth with beef while arguing politics with Harve Heinman, the owner of the Four Aces Saloon. The cattlemen crowded in a corner of the yard, glasses of whiskey in their hands, debating the vagaries of the cattle market. Across the way, the Tillis family sat with Katie O'Brien and the Westerlys amid the bedlam created by their collective children. The Tremont sisters sat with their uncle Mortimer. Sarah's eyebrows rose in surprise as she noticed Ross Turner fetching lemonade for a blushing Emmaline.

Over near the house, Susannah was surrounded by most of the eligible young males of Burr. She handled the crowd of eager suitors with the casual aplomb that Sarah had always envied.

Just a few yards away, her mother was engaged in a lively discussion with Mrs. Castor and two other matrons. She positively beamed with happiness as she described the making of her daughter's wedding gown, a fantastic creation of white satin, snowy lace, and seed pearls that was the culminating achievement of her career as a seamstress. Having one of her daughters marry the most eligible bachelor in town had made June Calhoun the envy of her contemporaries.

She noticed Doc Mercer and his wife in deep conversation with the Pearsons, and sitting with them was Marshal Brown.

He seemed fit enough now, she thought, though his arm was still in a sling. He was tall and lean, with wheat-colored hair that fell to his shoulders and a mustache of the same color. His dark eyes scanned the crowd, a habit, no doubt, from years of having to watch his back. He looked personable enough in a white shirt and fawn-colored pants with a matching coat, but the way he held himself made her think that he could move quickly in any direction at a moment's notice.

Just like Jack.

As if he heard her unspoken words, the marshal turned his gaze on her new husband. He watched Donovan with a measured thoroughness that made her edgy.

She knew Jack had a past. Only now did she wonder whether it had been a *legal* one. But what could Donovan have possibly done to draw the attention of the authorities? She glanced at her husband, who was talking to Ned Gorman and Amos. He had told her that he wasn't wanted anywhere, and she believed him. But Donovan had definitely seen some dark times in his past.

Frowning in concentration, she glanced back at the marshal and jolted when she realized that the lawman was now looking at *her*.

Her deductive instincts sprang to life. Rising, she headed for the marshal, determined to get some answers.

Donovan knew he was being watched.

He continued to converse with Ned and Amos as if nothing was wrong, even as his senses pricked with the knowledge that he was the object of intense scrutiny.

His first thought was Petrie. Had the bastard managed to sneak up on them after all? He shifted so that he could get to the knife in his boot if necessary, silently cursing his decision not to wear his gun. But he'd known Sarah would object if he showed up at the church with the obvious weapon.

To the casual observer, he appeared relaxed. Smiling and bantering, he slowly turned his head until he could see his stalker out of the corner of his eye.

Marshal Jedidiah Brown.

Several conversations with the man over the past week had indicated that the lawman was excellent at his job. Donovan's keen instincts told him that the marshal's interest stemmed from more than the worry that Donovan might take the law into his own hands and go after Petrie.

But there were important reasons why he had left Blade behind, Donovan thought. Blade had been ruthless, a cold-blooded tracker of men. He had lived on the edges of society, alone. He had no friends, no wife, no lover. No family. And while those circumstances had made it possible to survive, he had grown tired of living in shadows.

He'd taken back his real name. He had changed his appearance—cut his hair, shaved his mustache and beard—to leave Blade far behind and make a new start as Jack Donovan.

And he was tired of being alone.

He was happy to let his legendary past self fade into Western folklore. But there were some people who wouldn't be content with that—people who had been tracked by him, or simply wanted to kill a legend to make a name for themselves. He could handle whatever ghosts from his past rose to challenge him. But the innocent people that surrounded him—friends, family—would be endangered. And that he could not allow.

Sarah was his wife now, and so precious that he would die to protect her.

For a moment he felt a twinge of guilt that he hadn't told her the whole truth about himself, but he knew what would happen if he did.

I swore when my father died that I would never again become involved with a dangerous man ... even if he was on the right side of the law.

As long as nobody knew where to find Blade, no one would come to Burr looking for him. And Sarah would never know.

But Marshal Brown's interest made him wonder if the lawman had already figured it out.

"Marshal Brown, I don't believe you've danced with the bride."

Jedidiah Brown gave Sarah a smile that was

surprisingly sweet. "I don't reckon I can dance much with this arm, ma'am."

"Now, Marshal, I simply won't take no for an answer." Sarah touched his shoulder with a flirtatious grin. The man hadn't said two words to her the entire ten minutes she'd stood there talking to the Mercers; it was obvious she was going to have to arrange things to get him into a private conversation.

"Go ahead and dance, son," Doc Mercer said with a laugh. "It's your shoulder that's wounded, not your feet!"

Sarah took his free hand and tugged playfully. "Come now, Marshal. You know you're supposed to listen to your doctor."

"I suppose so." The lawman rose gracefully and allowed Sarah to lead him to the dance floor.

"You do know how to dance?" Sarah asked.

"Yes, ma'am," he answered. He took her hand in one of his. "Why don't you put your other hand on my shoulder there, and try not to squeeze too tight."

"All right." Once positioned, she barely had time to smile at him before he whisked her into step.

"Good heavens, Marshal." she laughed. "You surely *can* dance!"

"My mama would turn over in her grave if I couldn't."

"Where are you from, Marshal?"

"Jedidiah, please. And I'm from Charleston."

Sarah smiled up at him. "And how do you like our little town?"

"Bunch of nice folks," Jedidiah replied. "And you sure do make a pretty bride, Mrs. Donovan."

Sarah laughed. "Be sure to call me that a few times so I get used to it."

"Guess it takes a while to settle in." At her quizzical look, he clarified, "I mean getting married and all. Especially to a man as prominent as your husband."

Sarah's senses sharpened at the mention of Jack. "He is that," she agreed.

"You two know each other long?"

"Long enough."

"I'm only asking because he seems familiar to me somehow."

"Really?" Her flesh prickled with the sensation that a disclosure was imminent. "Perhaps he resembles an acquaintance from Charleston."

"No, that's not it." He fixed her with a steady stare. "It'll come to me."

Sarah swallowed hard and glanced away from that implacable look. "I'm certain it will."

A disturbance among the dancers drew her attention, and she saw Donovan approaching them through the crowd.

She had to keep him away from the marshal.

"Excuse me, Jedidiah," she said with a pretty

smile. "My husband is looking for me. Thank you for the dance."

Jedidiah barely had time to nod before she broke free and hurried to Donovan.

Her husband smiled at her as she came up to him and took his hand. "Is it possible for me to claim my own wife for a dance?" he teased.

"Absolutely." Without hesitation, she went into his arms and allowed him to guide her into the rhythm of the music. To her dismay, his gaze drifted to Marshal Brown, who stood at the edge of the dance floor.

"Good. I was worried he might upset you with talk about . . . Well, I was worried that he might upset you."

"He didn't mention Luke," Sarah assured him. "It was quite an unremarkable conversation, all in all. Did you know he's from Charleston?"

"Is he?"

"He's a very nice man." She paused, then said casually, "He thought you looked familiar. I suspect you must resemble someone he knows from home."

Donovan's muscles stiffened beneath her hands. "Maybe I have one of those faces," he said. The indifference of his tone indicated that he couldn't care less, but the tension of his body told another tale.

Sarah's investigative instincts tingled to life.

The only reason for his concern would be if he had something to hide. But what?

Now, because she loved him, she was afraid of that past that he refused to talk about. She was worried that the marshal might know something of Donovan's former life, and that it would rise like the devil from hell and steal their happiness.

She would not let that happen. She would keep Jedidiah Brown away from Donovan until the lawman left town. Then everything would be fine.

It had to be.

Donovan's slow caress up her spine scattered every rational thought. She met his gaze and almost melted from the heat reflected there.

Pulling her more snugly into his embrace, he lowered his mouth close to her ear. "I can hardly wait to get you in my bed, sassy girl," he whispered. "This has been a long week."

His bed: that huge walnut four-poster that had haunted her dreams and fantasies ever since she had first laid eyes on it. Tonight she would be sleeping there.

Or not sleeping.

Hunger rose in a wave, a surge of desire too long denied. She remembered that day beneath the tree at the box social—every touch, every kiss, every whispered promise. And in the shed at Miller's Pond—where every secret had been revealed, every dream fulfilled. Her knees weakened at the thought of what would happen tonight, on her wedding night, in that bed.

Tonight she would finally be able to lie in the arms of the man she loved without fear of gossip or consequences. Tonight she could openly show her love and trust Donovan with her passion.

Donovan smiled down at her, the gleam in his eyes showing he had guessed the direction of her thoughts. "Come on, sweetheart," he murmured, guiding her toward the edge of the dance floor. "Let's see if we can find a nice dark corner for a minute or two."

Her limbs tingling, Sarah followed her husband away from the crowd. But as they slipped away, she was aware of Marshal Brown's enigmatic gaze following them.

Chapter 16

"**W**ell, aren't you just the picture of the happy newlywed," Susannah drawled, seated at the table in the Donovans' huge kitchen.

Sarah laughed as she finished preparing two cups of tea. "I am happy," she said, balancing the delicate china cups and saucers in her hands.

"That's obvious." Susannah ignored the tea placed in front of her as Sarah sat down. What she saw in her sister's face satisfied her immensely. "So I take it you aren't worried about being married to Donovan anymore? Things are working out?"

"Better than I thought." Sarah perused the plate of cookies on the table and selected one. "Jack and I have negotiated a compromise of sorts. I make sure I get home from the paper in time to cook supper, and he sometimes does a chore or two that I can't get to. Right now, everything is going along wonderfully."

Susannah tapped a finger on her saucer. "Sarah, as glad as I am to hear that everything is going well, I feel obliged to remind you that you've only been married for two weeks."

"Two wonderful weeks."

"You're bound to have a fight eventually."

"We've fought before, and we'll probably fight again," Sarah agreed. "But the thing I was worried about—the day-to-day living—hasn't been a problem at all."

"Well, good." Susannah reached for her tea.

"I am worried about Luke, though." Sarah took a gulp of her tea. "He's still out there, and sometimes I expect him to just show up and ruin everything."

"I'd say your husband can handle him."

"But that's another thing." Sarah wrapped both hands around her tea cup, her expression serious. "Suzie, I want you to keep what I'm about to tell you to yourself."

"Oh, and I was just itching to run over to the undertaker's and tell Juliana Tremont all about it," Suzie drawled.

"All right, I'm sorry I insulted you. But this is important—it's about Jack."

Susannah grinned. "I love the way you call him 'Jack' when the rest of the town just calls him 'Donovan.' Even me."

"I just can't see myself addressing my husband by his last name," Sarah said primly, making Susannah chuckle. "It sounds too much like calling the dog."

At that, Suzie burst into laughter. "All right, what's this big bad secret?"

"When I first met Jack," Sarah began, "I knew he wasn't exactly what he appeared to be."

"What do you mean by that?" Suzie leaned forward. "Is he wanted somewhere?"

"He says he's not, and I believe him. He's too honorable a man to put people around him in danger if he was wanted by the law."

"You're so naive sometimes, Sarah." At her sister's disapproving look, Suzie held up her hands. "All right, let's say he's telling the truth. What's bothering you about the situation?"

"At the wedding, Marshal Brown said that Jack looked familiar to him. And I'm getting a bad feeling about it."

"The marshal said that to you? On your wedding day?" At Sarah's nod, Susannah started to fume. "That man has no sensitivity whatsoever!"

"I've always found Marshal Brown to be very charming," Sarah responded, obviously puzzled by her sister's outburst. "If he hadn't been the sort of man that he is, I might even have been attracted to him."

"What do you mean, 'the sort of man that he is'?" Susannah asked.

"You know, a dangerous sort of man. One who lives by the gun and is constantly surrounded by violence."

"He's a lawman, Sarah. He has to be dangerous in order to catch criminals."

"I know that." Sarah folded her hands on the table. "But I swore after Papa died that I would never again become involved with a man like—"

"Luke Petrie," Susannah finished. "Sarah, just because a man wears a gun doesn't mean that he's going to be like Luke. I met lots of lawmen in San Francisco, and most of them— the good ones who knew what they were doing—took a lot of trouble to keep violence out of their personal lives."

"Rationally, I understand that," Sarah said. "But I just can't—" She stopped, clenching her fingers more tightly.

"All right, don't get upset. Lord knows, Marshal Brown isn't worth it."

Sarah raised her brows. "Why, Suzie, don't you like him?"

"I do not. The man's a lout."

"That wasn't my experience."

"Well, he's probably scared of Donovan, so he was nice to you." Suzie waved her hand dismissively. "Let's get back to your concern. So the marshal says he thinks he knows Donovan, and that worries you." Sarah nodded. "Why?"

"I have no idea what's in Jack's past, Suzie. And I'm worried that something might come to light someday that could destroy everything we've built."

"I can't see Donovan letting that happen."

"He might not be able to stop it."

Susannah weighed the facts for a moment. "My advice is to not worry about it so much. Right now everything is going well for you. Don't borrow trouble."

Sarah took a deep breath, then nodded. "Perhaps you're right. Maybe the marshal just thinks that he knows Jack. It might not be him at all."

"And maybe the marshal is just a nosy busybody." Susannah took a sip of her tea, then rose, taking up the frilly parasol in tearose yellow that matched her tailored walking dress. "Well, I've got to get back to town. Mother will be looking for me."

"Give her my love." Sarah stood as well.

Susannah followed Sarah through the foyer to the front door. "And you stop worrying about the marshal. The fool is probably addled from his injuries."

Sarah laughed. "All right, I'll forget about it."

"Good." Suzie gave her sister a hug. "Take care of yourself, and give Donovan a big kiss for me, won't you?"

At Sarah's blush, Susannah laughed, then

went down the front steps to her wagon. She managed to get herself into it despite her numerous petticoats, then waved to Sarah before starting down the drive.

So Marshal Brown thought he knew Donovan, did he? And he'd had the bad manners to mention it on her sister's wedding day? Suzie set the horse to a faster pace. She would have a word with Marshal Jedidiah Brown—and she would see just what he thought he knew.

And what he didn't.

Sunday afternoons tended to be rather lazy out at the ranch, and Sarah found herself at loose ends once Susannah had departed. Donovan had disappeared into the barn as soon as Susannah's wagon had been spotted coming up the drive, to give her some privacy with her sister.

Could a woman ask for more?

A smile curving her lips, Sarah left the house and crossed the deserted yard to the barn. She smelled the musky scent of animals as soon as she stepped into the shadowed building. Senseless whuffed in greeting as she paused by his stall to stroke his nose.

"Jack?" she called. "Are you in here?"

"Just a minute," came the muffled reply.

Senseless nudged her, sniffing for treats. "Sorry," Sarah said with a laugh, gently pushing the horse's muzzle away. "No goodies today."

"Does that go for everyone?" Donovan asked, stepping out of a stall with a pitchfork in his hand.

"Well, ah . . ." Her voice deserted her as he stepped closer.

Silhouetted against the sunbeam that streamed in through the open barn doors, his broad, bare shoulders were gilded with sunlight. His arm muscles rippled as he leaned the pitchfork against a stall, and again when he raised both hands to push back his hair where it curled over his forehead and around his ears, clinging to his neck in damp strands. Sarah swallowed hard, not daring to look down where his Levi's clung to his lean waist and long legs.

"Cat got your tongue, sassy girl?" he teased, coming closer for a kiss. His lips barely brushed hers, then he stepped back. "I'm covered with grime or else I'd kiss you properly."

"You look fine to me." Even she heard the hint of longing in her voice.

Ever since they had been married, Jack had made love to her every night in his majestic bed, treating her with almost reverent care that was very satisfying. While she enjoyed his tenderness, she often longed for the sweet, wild passion that had claimed them both that night at Miller's Pond.

Since she had become the respectable Mrs. Jack Donovan, passion had developed into a nightly ritual that always took place in bed with the lights off.

But here in the barn, enveloped by the very basic scents of livestock and sweat and man, she sensed that things could be different. The bare simplicity of her surroundings called to that primitive side of her, the part of her that tossed inhibition to the wind and laughed as it blew away. She was beginning to accept that side of herself—especially since Jack not only enjoyed her erotic impulses, but encouraged them.

She wanted Jack, right here and right now, with an uncivilized passion that would have scandalized the members of the Ladies' Auxiliary for the Betterment of Burr.

"Are you all right, sweetheart? Problem with your sister?"

She realized that she had been lost in the fog of her awakening desire. The tender concern on his face made her want to snuggle closer, even as she contemplated how to get him naked as quickly as possible.

"I'm fine, Jack." The smooth skin of his chest glistened with perspiration, and she reached up to stroke the firm flesh, captivated by the way he shifted beneath her hands.

Funny, she had never imagined how appealing a half-dressed, sweaty man could be.

"Sarah?"

"Yes, Jack?" She traced his ribs with her fingers, then followed the line of a scar that curved below them and disappeared into the waistband of his jeans. Her husband had many scars. He never mentioned them, and neither did she, but they fascinated her.

"Sarah." His tone roughened, and his hands clenched into fists. "Sassy girl, what are you doing?"

"Don't you know?" She slanted a look at him as she played with his belt buckle.

"Sweetheart, let me go inside and get cleaned up a little."

"Why?" She took pity on him and moved her hands away from his waist, caressing his powerful arms and shoulders instead. "You look fine to me."

"I'm all sweaty."

She touched her tongue to her upper lip. "I noticed."

"And dirty."

"I've been dirty before."

"Sarah—"

"What is it, Jack?" She linked her arms around his neck, stepping close enough so that their bodies touched—his, hot, sweaty, and bare, and hers, clad in immaculate blue gingham that smelled of soap and sunshine. "Do you think that I don't find you attractive this way?"

He shifted, putting an inch of space between them even as his hands closed on her hips. "Something like that."

"I don't know why you think I'm so priggish," she said, tangling her fingers into the hair at his nape.

Donovan closed his eyes. Her fingers caressing the back of his neck were making him crazy. *She* was making him crazy. He fought a nearly uncontrollable impulse to pick her up and carry her into the nearest stall, to lay her down in the straw and let passion take them. But he was dirty and covered in perspiration from mucking out stalls, and he probably didn't smell too pretty either. Sarah deserved more than a hot and sweaty tumble in the barn. She was his wife, not some saloon girl.

"Have I done something to make you think that I'm a prude?" Sarah stepped closer to him again and rubbed her nose against his chest. "I like the way you look right now. The way you smell. And the way you taste." She pressed a kiss to his neck, and he felt the touch of her tongue on his flesh. He nearly groaned.

Lust tried to claw its way free, but he managed to contain it—barely.

"Sarah," he said hoarsely. "Let's go up to the house."

She looked up at him with those big blue eyes and slowly shook her head. "I don't think so, Jack. It seems to me that you're harboring some misconceptions about your wife that we need to talk about."

"I'm not." The words came out strangled as she started nibbling on his neck again. He closed his eyes and thought of an ice cold mountain stream. "I know who you are and what you like."

She tipped her head back. "Do you, Jack?" Slowly she brought one hand from behind his neck, sliding it over his shoulder and down over his chest. "Or did you just put me in a little box in your head that's labeled 'Wife' and filled with all sorts of wrongheaded notions?"

"You are my wife." He took a deep breath that shuddered out again when her hand made its way back to his belt buckle. "My wife," he repeated. "Not some loose woman that I met in a saloon."

"That doesn't mean I don't have the same needs as those women."

"You're a decent woman," he said. "You deserve better."

"Wrong, Jack," she whispered, her fingers slipping past his belt buckle to press against his aching erection. "I'm a decent woman, but I'm not made of china, Jack. Though I love you all the more for treating me as if I am."

He dug his fingers into her hips, pulling her tightly against him. "You telling me you want a tumble in the hay, sassy girl?"

She smiled. "That's exactly what I'm telling you."

He heard the excitement in her voice, felt the hardness of her nipples pressed against his chest through the thin material of her dress. But still he hesitated. "I don't want to hurt you, sweetheart."

"Jack, the only way you could hurt me would be to say no."

"God help me, sassy girl, I can't deny you anything." He cupped her face in his hands, gazing into her beautiful eyes. "You tell me if I do anything you don't like."

Her smile was slow and seductive. "I promise."

He held out a hand, and she took it.

He led her to an empty stall, then stole the breath from her lungs by pressing her up against the wall and kissing her with a slow heat that set every nerve humming. She lifted her hands to link them around his neck, but he caught her wrists in her hands and pinned them to the wall on either side of her head. Her heart thudded in her chest. She felt helpless in the face of his greater strength, exposed and unable to defend herself.

And so excited she was amazed her legs were still supporting her.

She moaned beneath his mouth, the sound one of both hunger and surrender. He broke the kiss for an instant, scanning her face for signs of distress. What he saw must have satisfied him, because a predatory gleam came into his dark eyes. So slowly that she wanted to scream, he started brushing kisses against her cheeks and forehead. He lingered near her ear, nibbling the lobe. At the same time he brought his full weight against her.

She couldn't move; couldn't reciprocate the hot caresses that made her knees weak and her bones melt. He nipped at her throat, and she tipped her head so that he could have better access. When he let go of her wrists, she rested her palms on his shoulders while he reached behind her and unbuttoned her dress. With each button that came free, he took her mouth in an unhurried kiss, his tongue stroking hers and stoking the fires of arousal higher.

By the time he tugged the dress from her shoulders, she could barely stand. She clung to him, gripping his arms while he knelt and helped her to step free of the garment. He draped it over the door of the stall, then took her hand and knelt in the straw.

"Come here, sweetheart," he murmured, tugging at her hand. She tumbled into his lap, and he grinned.

Then he bent over her and sank his teeth gently into her throat, one hand sliding up her torso to clasp her breast. He toyed with the plump flesh, squeezing it gently until her breath came in pants. Sarah drew his head down until he took the nipple between his teeth, dampening the material of her chemise. She moaned at the intense pleasure, undulating her hips in unconscious response. He groaned and raised his head.

"You've got too many clothes on, sassy girl." With a swiftness that made her gasp, he stripped her of every garment except the chemise. At her questioning glance, he grinned like an outlaw. "That's to protect your modesty in case someone comes out here."

"What!" Sarah struggled to get up, but Donovan held her firmly, maneuvering her until she straddled his lap.

"Oh, no, you don't," he growled, holding her firmly around the waist. He could feel the heat of her naked loins against him even through the thick material of his Levi's. "You started this; you're going to finish it. You had your chance to make love like civilized people in a bed."

"But if someone comes . . ."

"Someone will," he teased with raw humor that set her cheeks aflame.

"That's not what I meant, Jack!"

"Don't fret, sassy girl. You let me take care of everything." He tugged down the straps of her chemise until her breasts were bared to the sunlight that filtered into the barn. "Now, that's a pretty sight."

"Jack, I . . . oh, my God." The words lingered

on a moan as he took one nipple into his mouth and sucked strongly, then all coherent thoughts flew from her head. If the entire town of Burr had shown up in the barn at that moment, she wouldn't have cared.

His hand came up to knead her other breast while he suckled the first, and she speared her hands into his hair to hold his head firmly against her. When both nipples were hard and aching and damp from his mouth, he took her face between his hands and kissed her as if she were the main course at a carnal banquet. While he fed on her mouth, she combed her hands through the hair on his chest, tracing his flat male nipples with wondering fingers.

"Feels good," he murmured. "Give me your hand." She put her hand in his, and he pressed her palm against the obvious hardness below his belt buckle. "Open it, Sarah."

The sensual command sent a thrill streaking through her. Eagerly, she tugged at the belt. It took her a few tries, but she finally managed to loosen it. All the while he played with her bare breasts, as if he were in no hurry whatsoever.

"Open my Levi's," he said when she'd gotten the belt undone. His dark eyes had narrowed to slits as he leaned back against the wall of the stall, his strong, sun-tanned hands kneading her pale breasts. Her fingers trembled as she finally succeeded in getting his pants open. "Now touch me, Sarah."

He wasn't wearing anything underneath, she realized, scandalized and excited at the same time. She trailed her fingers along the velvety smooth flesh of his hardness, delighting in the way he responded to her touch, the way the muscles of his flat belly rippled as she stroked that very sensitive part of his body.

"You're driving me crazy," he muttered, watching her through nearly closed eyes. He kept playing with her breasts, his thighs like iron beneath her bottom. "I've got to get inside you."

"Yes," she replied, kneeling. He tugged his denims down to his thighs, then took her hips in his hands, holding the chemise out of the way, and lowered her slowly onto his hard shaft.

"That's it," he murmured. "Take all of it, sweetheart."

She braced her hands on his shoulders and shifted, each movement bringing him deeper inside. Finally he was fully seated within her, and she settled back down, her thighs spread wide over his. He took her mouth in a slow kiss as he started to move.

Sarah moaned, leaning her head back. She met each hard thrust with equal strength, riding him like a prize stallion. He kissed her breasts, nipped at the nipples, then gripped her hips and vigorously plunged deep inside her over and over again.

"Jack!" she moaned, digging her nails hard into his shoulders. Tension swelled inside her, and she bit his neck, not caring that she left marks. His mouth found hers, and he swallowed her scream of release as orgasm ripped through her.

She melted against him, her body a boneless mass of tingling pleasure, as he continued to move deep inside her. He gave a long, guttural moan, his back arching and his head hitting the wall behind him as he gripped her hips and followed her over the edge.

They stayed like that for long moments, until their heartbeats slowed and the perspiration dried on their skin.

"Jack?" Sarah said, her words muffled against his bare chest.

"What, sweetheart?"

"Don't treat me like china anymore."

He chuckled and kissed the top of her head. "My pleasure, sassy girl."

Susannah had worked herself into a royal temper by the time she made it over to the clinic. She burst into the infirmary and found herself looking down the barrel of a revolver held by the steady hand of the man standing in the middle of the room.

"Oh, for heavens sake," she said with exasperation. "Put it away, Marshal. I'm unarmed."

Jedidiah Brown lowered the weapon and scanned her figure with male appreciation. "Well, Miss Calhoun, I wouldn't exactly say that."

Despite herself, Susannah felt a flutter in the vicinity of her heart. She took refuge in anger. "You dare to flirt with me? You are an impossible man."

"So I've been told." The marshal went over to the bed and slipped the weapon back under his pillow, then turned and regarded Susannah with interest. "Now, Miss Calhoun, to what do I owe the pleasure of your visit?"

"I've come to have a word with you about your incredible lack of manners, Marshal Brown."

"Is that so? My mama would be right disappointed."

"Don't you dare joke about this," Susannah snapped. "What possessed you to upset my sister at her wedding?"

Jedidiah frowned. "Mrs. Donovan is upset? Why?"

"Don't play games with me, Marshal. Better men than you have tried."

"Really?" His eyes took on a bold gleam that made her want to take a step back. But she would die before she moved an inch. "I'll have to try harder then."

Susannah let out an exasperated sigh. "I

want my sister to be happy. But you and your innuendoes about Donovan upset her, and at her wedding, no less!"

"You don't say." His expression grew shuttered. "I do apologize. I wasn't aware that my observations had caused the lady distress."

She sent him a glare that had been known to freeze men where they stood. "Any woman would be distressed if a stranger started hinting that he knew secrets about her new husband at her wedding!"

"You have my word that I will apologize to your sister at the first opportunity," the marshal said smoothly. "Now that you've said what you've come to say, shall I show you out?"

She managed to look down her nose at him, though he was a head taller. "You disappoint me, sir. I had expected this discussion to be more . . . stimulating."

"You mean you expected an argument. Sorry to disappoint you."

"Marshal, it seems that you are destined to disappoint me."

"Oh?" He moved so swiftly that she missed it just by blinking. Suddenly he was there, taking her chin in his hand. "Stick around for a few more minutes, Miss Calhoun, and things will definitely get 'stimulating'."

She hated the way her pulse sped up. "You, sir, are an ill-bred lout."

He caressed her lips with his thumb. "You've got a tongue like a razor blade."

She narrowed her eyes. "And you've got the intellect of a blade of grass. Now release me at once."

"Of course." His hand dropped to his side, but an arrested expression appeared in his eyes. "A blade of grass, you say?"

"That's what I said," she sniffed.

"Just what are you trying to tell me?" he murmured.

She rolled her eyes. "I thought it was obvious. You truly are a difficult man."

"Only to my enemies, Miss Calhoun." As if he had all the time in the world, he lifted her hand and pressed a kiss to her palm, his sherry-colored gaze holding her captive for a long, breathless moment. "Now, did you really come here about your sister, or did you come to me for another reason?"

She stiffened even as her pulse sped like a runaway train. "Marshal Brown, I came here solely on my sister's behalf. Perhaps I should speak more slowly so that you can understand."

"I understand what you're saying. Now let's see what you're not saying." He leaned forward and pressed his mouth to hers in a slow, easy kiss that she could have broken without effort. Yet she didn't move, trapped in the spell of his mouth on hers. When he pulled back and looked at her, she had the feeling that he'd been places she'd allowed no other man, seen things that she didn't want anyone else to see.

He licked his lips as if still savoring the taste of her. "It's a crying shame I can't stick around these parts and see where this is going."

She jerked back the hand he still held. "*This* is not going anywhere. And I, for one, will be most happy to see the back of you."

He laughed. "I'd like to see *all* of you, princess . . . But my duties take me all over the territory, and I can't afford to be tied down."

"You presume too much, Marshal." Her cheeks burning, she scalded him with a look of contempt. "I merely came here to deliver a message."

"I know why you came here, princess. Probably better than you do."

She clenched her fingers, tempted to slap the amusement from his face. Glancing at her fisted hands, he raised one tawny brow, and his eyes hardened to chips of ice.

"I wouldn't," he warned.

For a moment she was tempted to ignore his advice. But something about his battle-ready stance made her back off. Eyeing him as if he were a particularly nasty bug, she said regally, "Since your manners show no signs of improving, I have nothing more to say to you. Good day, Marshal."

"Allow me to escort you to the door." He

took her arm, all but dragging her along.

"Marshal—" Unused to being dominated, Susannah dug in her heels simply out of principle. As much as she wanted to leave the irritating man's company, she would do so when she desired to and not a moment before.

"Give my regards to your mother and sister." He jerked open the door.

Susannah braced herself in the doorway, using her parasol to prop open the door when he would have shoved her through it. "Marshal Brown, never in my life have I—"

"I'm astonished to hear that, princess." His lips quirked in a roguish grin. "I would have presumed that a woman of your looks and temperament *would* have by now."

She gasped as his innuendo sank in, but before she could respond, he pulled the parasol from her hand and flung it through the door. "Are you mad?" she exclaimed. "That parasol comes all the way from Paris!"

He shoved his face close to hers. "You want to argue about it? Or maybe you're not so anxious to leave after all."

Her breathing hitched as she realized that his lips were mere inches from hers. "Don't you dare kiss me again," she whispered.

He looked at her mouth and seemed to be considering her words. Susannah's blood thundered in her ears. There was nothing in the world she wanted more than for him to kiss her again. And nothing in the world she feared more.

Her body started to tremble as the tension grew. She moistened her lips and glanced at his mouth. Would he kiss her again?

Suddenly he straightened and gave her a charming smile.

"I never disappoint a lady."

Yanking her away from the doorframe, he shoved her into the hall, then swatted her on the bottom for emphasis. Slamming the door, he leaned back against it, disregarding her screech of outrage from the other side. Flirtations aside, Susannah had managed to convey her message successfully.

"Blade," he said with a slow grin. "I'll be damned."

Chapter 17

Monday morning, Sarah set the type for the newest edition of the *Burr Chronicle*. She hummed as she worked, more content than she had been in a very long time. She had left the door standing open to enjoy the sweet June breeze, and only moments before, she had seen Emmaline and Juliana hurry by. She had thought it was odd that they didn't stop in, as was their usual habit, but then she realized why they hadn't.

They had nothing to gossip about.

She was a happily married woman now, and that had restored the respectability she lost three years earlier. Or had it been her husband who had done that? Either way, the Tremont sisters no longer had the ammunition to keep firing their nasty barbs. It was a welcome change.

The sound of booted footsteps made her look

up from her work as a thrill shot through her. But her heart slowed as she realized that it was Marshal Brown who had come to see her, not Jack.

"Good afternoon, Mrs. Donovan," the marshal said, removing his hat. "I wonder if I might have a moment of your time."

"Of course, Marshal." Sarah put down the type and picked up a rag, wiping the smudges of ink from her fingers. "What can I do for you today?"

"Well, first of all, I'd like to remind you to call me Jedidiah. And secondly, I'd be obliged if you'd put a notice about Petrie in your paper. I want all the folks in the area to be warned about him."

"Already done, Jedidiah. I wrote the article myself."

"Well, then." The lawman hesitated. "Mind if I close the door, ma'am?"

Intrigued, Sarah shrugged. "Go ahead."

The marshal went to the door and glanced outside before firmly shutting it. Then he came back to Sarah.

She frowned at his odd behavior. "Jedidiah, whatever is going on?"

"I just wanted to have a few words with you, Mrs. Donovan, to let you know how sorry I am about what happened on your wedding day."

Sarah sat on the edge of her desk, dread

knotting in the pit of her stomach. "What about my wedding day?"

The marshal fingered the brim of his hat. "I understand that I upset you, ma'am, and I'd like to apologize. I imagine that your husband doesn't want it to get around that he used to be a bounty hunter. People tend to react funny to that sort of thing."

Stunned, she replied. "Yes. Yes, they do." A bounty hunter? Jack?

The marshal slipped his hat back on and sent her a grin. "But at least you can rest easy about Petrie, ma'am. I can't see him coming up against Blade and winning. Funny, I always figured him to be a myth. Guess there's a grain of truth in every legend."

"I guess so," she murmured. Her mind didn't seem to want to absorb what she was being told. Had the marshal actually said that *her husband* was the bounty hunter known as Blade? Or had she misunderstood?

Something must have shown on her face, because the marshal's expression turned to one of concern. "But don't worry, Mrs. Donovan," he soothed, "your secret is safe with me. After all, it's not as if Blade is a wanted man or anything. He always worked within the boundaries of the law."

He kept talking about Blade as if she knew the notorious tracker personally—and that could only mean one thing. She squeezed her eyes closed as if she could shut away the truth. Somehow she, Sarah Calhoun, had married the most ruthless bounty hunter ever to ride the trail. For one wild moment she hoped it was a mistake. But the marshal kept talking, confirming her worst fears with every word.

"So anyway, Mrs. Donovan, I thought I'd just stop by and put your mind at rest. No one will ever know from me that Jack Donovan was once Blade."

Put her mind at rest? Dear Lord, the man had just uprooted the very foundations of her marriage! But she couldn't let him know how he had shocked her. No one could know. This was between her and Jack.

She forced a smile to her lips. "That's very reassuring. Thank you for coming by, Jedidiah," she said. "Now, if you'll excuse me, I need to get back to work."

"Certainly, ma'am." Jedidiah Brown put on his hat and went to the door to flip open the locks. "Good day now."

"Good day." When the door had closed behind the lawman, Sarah got up and locked it again. Then she slowly returned to her desk and sank into the chair.

Jack Donovan was Blade. He was a man who had lived by the gun, walking barely on the right side of the law. A hired tracker. A man who hunted other men for profit.

A killer.

She had always known there was something dark about Jack, but never had she expected this.

Clenching her hands tightly in her lap, she concentrated on breathing steadily. Part of her was confused and disbelieving. Another part of her wanted to weep.

And part of her was furiously, painfully hurt.

Why hadn't he told her? He knew how she felt about violence—she had told him herself. And she had confided in *him*—confessed her whole past, sins and all, on the night they first made love at Miller's Pond.

But he hadn't revealed one single thing to her.

The more she thought about it, the more infuriated she became. She had agonized through every word of that confession, certain that he would withdraw his marriage proposal once he knew the truth. She had bared her soul to the man to whom she had given her heart, only to find that her husband had hidden critical information about himself from her.

And now she was married to the kind of man she despised, one who had killed for profit and thrived on violence.

How many men had he killed? And how had he killed them? Did he care whether the criminal he pursued was guilty, or did he just care about getting paid for the job?

Just who *was* Jack Donovan? The tender man she had come to love? Or a ruthless killer?

Clearly he wanted to start anew, but a man didn't put that part of himself away, never to return. At the very least, a man who had lived by violence would have made many enemies. How long would it take for one of those enemies to track him down and perhaps kill him? They had been married only two weeks, and already Jedidiah Brown, a perfect stranger, had discovered Jack's secret.

She took her reticule from the drawer and headed for the door. Only one person could answer all her questions, and that was Jack himself.

Jack knew there was trouble when he saw Senseless galloping up the drive as if pursued by a swarm of angry bees. He broke off his conversation with Matt and strode up to the house, reaching the front steps just as Sarah slid off the horse.

"Sweetheart, is there something wrong?" He reached for her arm, but she dodged his touch.

"In the house. Now." Blue eyes glittering with fury, she turned her back on him and stomped up the steps.

Donovan stared after her for a moment, then signaled to one of the ranch hands. The man came and took the horse's reins, and Donovan slowly entered the house.

Sarah wasn't in the parlor or the kitchen. He was just about to call out to her when he heard footsteps overhead. Heading for the stairs, he winced as other sounds reached his ears—slamming, banging, muttering.

His wife was in one hell of a temper about something.

He found her in the bedroom, pawing through the wardrobe. A pile of her clothes was heaped on the bed, and an empty trunk stood open in the middle of the floor. A twinge of alarm crept over him.

"Sarah?"

She whirled to face him, a pale pink gown clutched in her hands. "I'm leaving you," she said, then flung the garment on the bed with the others.

"Leaving? What are you talking about?" He came over to her and placed his hands on her shoulders. "Tell me what's bothering you."

"Don't touch me." She shrugged him off and sent a glare over her shoulder that made him step back a pace. "I may not like guns, Jack Donovan, but I certainly know how to use one—and I will if you lay your hands on me again."

Her words sparked his own temper. "Don't threaten me, Sarah."

"You don't scare me, Jack," she scoffed, turning to pile some shirtwaists on the bed. "What are you going to do? Kill me?"

"Don't be ridiculous," he snapped. "Now tell me what's going on."

"I told you. I'm leaving you."

"Why, damn it?" he roared. "What the hell have I done?"

She paused and gave him a level, pain-filled look. "It's what you haven't done, Jack ... if that's even your real name."

"What?" Fear streaked through him. She meant it—she was leaving. He grabbed her before she could take another garment from the wardrobe, tightening his grip as she struggled. "What did you mean by that?"

She twisted in his grasp, trying to peel his fingers from her arms. "You know exactly what I mean, *Blade*."

Stunned, he stared at her. His grip loosened unconsciously, and she broke away from him, rubbing at her upper arms. "What did you call me?"

"Don't insult me by pretending ignorance," she sneered. "You know exactly what I called you. And why."

He sighed with resignation. "Yes, I do know."

"What's this? A confession?" With a brittle smile, she went to the bureau and yanked open the top drawer. "You're a little late, Jack."

"How did you find out?"

"Oh, I have my ways." She dumped a handful of stockings on the bed. "You might have told me yourself."

"I didn't see that it mattered."

She spun to face him. "How can you say that? I told you everything about me—*everything*—before we got married. Didn't it occur to you to do the same?"

"Sassy girl, listen to me—"

"Don't you 'sassy girl' me," she snapped. "I bared my soul before I ever said yes to your proposal, because it was important to me to clear the air before we got married."

"I told you straight out when we first met that I wasn't going to talk about my past, Sarah."

"I'm your *wife*!" she shouted. "I have a right to know."

He clenched his jaw to keep back the stinging words that rose in response to her outburst. "You said you would leave it alone, Sarah. You said that you weren't going to dig into my past anymore. Was that a lie?"

"I have never lied to you, Jack Donovan. Never."

"Then how did you find out?"

"None of your business." She scooped a bunch of clothes off the bed and dropped them in the trunk. When she turned back for more, he was there, blocking the way.

"It *is* my business, sweetheart," he said with

soft menace. "Now I suggest you tell me how you found out."

She looked at him with a hint of fear in her eyes, and he wished he could call the words back. "The marshal told me," she said quietly. "And when he leaves town, he had better leave unharmed, Jack. Now please get out of my way."

He stepped aside without another word and watched her as she jammed two dresses in a leather satchel, then squeezed the rest of her clothes in the trunk. She slammed the lid shut, ignoring the lacy sleeve of a nightdress that hung out, and flipped the fastenings closed.

Donovan stared at that strip of ivory lace and remembered how surprised and delighted she had been when he had presented her with a new wardrobe as a wedding gift. How he had enjoyed picking out the clothes for her. How she had shyly worn the ivory nightgown on their wedding night, and how he had taken great pleasure in removing the garment an inch at a time.

But now she was leaving.

"Sarah," he said softly. "I'm not going to hurt Jedidiah. Can't we talk about this?"

"We should have talked about it a long time ago," she replied. Her shoulders sagged, and she kept her back to him. "Jack, you knew how I feel about violence. Why didn't you tell me?"

"I suppose because . . . I know how you feel

about violence." He took a step toward her. "Sarah, I didn't want to lose you." He heard her sigh, saw the way her head bowed, and felt hope. "Sarah." He stroked one hand cautiously over her braid. "Sweetheart, surely it's not that important."

Her head came up, and she slowly turned to face him. The tears welling in her eyes hit him like a full load of buckshot to the gut. "Jack, how can it not be important? Your past made you the man that you are. You can't just put it aside like an old shirt."

"I seem to have done all right." When her face fell, he hurried on. "Don't you see? No one cares who I was. It's who I am now that counts."

"And just who is that?" she demanded. "Jack Donovan is an orphan from Kansas with a lot of money. Blade is a notorious killer. Yet somehow, you are both of them."

"Being a bounty hunter doesn't necessarily involve killing—"

"Are you trying to tell me that you've never killed?" She held his gaze, her expression challenging. "Tell me that you've never killed a man, Jack, and I'll stay."

"I can't tell you that, Sarah."

She closed her eyes tightly, one tear trickling down her cheek. "Then I have to go."

"Damn it, Sarah—I love you!"

"I know you do. But I can't live with violence, Jack. It always comes back to haunt me. Just like Luke did."

"Sassy girl, please don't leave me." He took her hands in his when she would have reached for her satchel. "We can make this work."

Her fingers curled around his, then she pulled away from him. "I don't think we can."

"Damn it, Sarah, I don't deserve this!" He swung around, fists impotently clenched, and stalked the length of the room. "I wasn't a criminal. I was a tool used by the law when they needed help."

"But you've still killed, Jack. And that's something I need to come to terms with."

"Don't expect me to apologize for choices I made years ago. Living is what matters, Sarah," he said fiercely. "I did what I had to in order to survive. Does that mean that I don't deserve to build a life for myself now? I realized a long time ago that nothing's black and nothing's white. Most people are somewhere in the middle."

"I don't know, Jack—"

"What about you, Sarah? You had doubts about this marriage working because you wanted the paper, and I wanted a helpmate. But somehow you've managed to be both." He gestured to himself. "I'm the same way. I'm not going to apologize for Blade, because he got me here. But I will apologize for not telling you. I was afraid that I would lose you."

"Oh, Jack." She looked away.

"Tell me one thing, Sarah." He strode across the room and cupped her face in both his hands. "Do you still love me?"

She closed her eyes and pressed one hand against his, cradling it against her cheek. "I'll always love you, Jack. But I may never be able to live with you."

"Sarah . . ." He turned his hand and stroked the backs of his fingers down her cheek. They came away damp as her tears started to fall.

"I have to go." Reluctantly, she stepped back. His hands fell to his sides as she took up her satchel. "I'll be staying at the newspaper office."

He frowned. "Not your mother's house?"

She shook her head. "No. I need to think this out on my own, and Mama would spend twenty-four hours a day trying to talk me into coming back here."

He gave her a weak smile. "Like I said, how about your mother's house?"

She laughed, but the tiny chuckle quickly became a sob. "Send my trunk to me at the *Chronicle*, all right?"

"Sure." It was all he could do not to grab her and hold her to him. "I'm going to send one of the boys out to watch the newspaper office. And don't even think about arguing."

"I won't." She let out a soft sigh. "Actually,

that would make me feel safer. Thank you, Jack."

"Glad you're being sensible. One last thing, sassy girl."

She paused in the doorway of the bedroom. "Yes?"

"If Petrie tries to hurt you again, I just might kill him. So ponder that, too, while you're doing all that thinking." At her startled look, he said, "You wanted me to be honest."

She swallowed hard, then gave him a shaky smile. "Funny thing is, I don't think I could hold it against you if you did. Guess that makes me a hypocrite." She looked away. "I appreciate your honesty."

"My pleasure."

Then she was gone.

The emptiness crashed down on him as he looked around the bedroom, now absent of her presence. The enormous bed, covered with Sarah's wedding ring quilt from her hope chest, loomed like a mockery of his dreams. Once he had thought to found his dynasty in that bed.

But now all he wanted was Sarah.

He walked to the trunk and knelt before it. Slowly he undid each brass fastening, then lifted the lid and pulled out the lace nightdress he had bought for his wife. He closed the trunk again and locked it up tight. Then he sat on his magnificent bed, the fragile silk and lace clenched in his fingers, deploring the past he could not change.

And grieving for the future that might never be.

Chapter 18

The Fourth of July marked three weeks since Sarah's wedding to Jack Donovan, and one week since she had left him.

The air was full of laughter as everyone prepared to ride out to the town holiday picnic at Miller's Pond. Sarah had resisted all appeals from her mother and sister to attend. There was no way she could stand to spend the day where she and Jack had first made love. The memories would be too painful.

So she busied herself with the paper, and when she ran out of articles to write and type to set, she started cleaning out the back closet.

Anything to avoid remembering.

The gossips were having a wonderful time, of course. The rumor mill had been running continuously since the word spread that there had been a split between the newlyweds. The Tremont sisters had been in twice during the week, and Mrs. Castor was a daily visitor. But Sarah was numb to it all. She wanted things to go back to the way they had been before Marshal Brown had stopped by. Back to when she had been a deliriously happy bride who was thoroughly in love with her new husband.

She still loved him.

She looked at the pile of junk she had pulled from the closet and wondered what had possessed her father to keep such things. Old clothes from when he used to stay overnight at the newspaper; blankets and tarps; a broken broom and a wooden crate filled with mismatched and defective type. She would have a lot more storage space once she discarded most of the stuff.

The door to the office opened, and she looked up, swiping her sleeve across her perspiring forehead. Then she slowly lowered her arm.

"Afternoon, Sarah."

"Hello, Jack." He looked wonderful. He was dressed in his black Sunday suit, his hair slicked back except for the cowlick that resisted all attempts to tame it. The stubborn lock of hair fell over one temple, giving him the look of a mischievous boy.

But it was no boy who watched her with barely leashed hunger burning in his velvet-brown eyes.

"You coming to the picnic?" he asked, breaking the silence.

"No." She shook her head. "No, I can't."

"Come on, Sarah," he coaxed, stepping around her desk. "It's a holiday. Can't we spend it together?"

"Jack, this isn't going to work."

"What isn't?" He kept approaching, and she kept retreating until he had backed her up against the wall.

"Nothing has changed," she insisted, breathlessly aware of his nearness. "There's no use in trying to pretend that everything is all right."

"I know everything's not all right." He reached out and stroked his thumb along her jaw. "I miss you, sassy girl."

Her flesh tingled in reaction to his touch. "I miss you, too, Jack," she whispered. "But nothing has changed."

"Let's see." He lowered his head, his gaze on hers as if waiting for her to refuse him. But she couldn't. Her eyes slid closed as his warm mouth covered hers, and she reached up to cling to his arms with shaking hands.

No, nothing had changed, she thought as the power of his kiss swept through her. She still loved him, and he could still reduce her willpower to ashes with one heated touch. But he was also still the man who had once been Blade, and she still didn't know if she could live as his wife.

Torn between confusion and desire, she reluctantly broke the kiss.

Donovan stepped back. "Nothing's going to change as long as you hole up here instead of coming home with me," he coaxed. "Come on, Sarah. Let's work this out."

"Don't you see that I *can't*?" she cried. She was so tempted to step back into his arms and pretend that it would all go away. But if she didn't make the right decision now, she would regret it for the rest of her life. "I can't come home with you until I figure this out on my own. And I'm trying, Jack."

His face grew impassive. "You were afraid to marry me to begin with," he said flatly. "Maybe this just gave you an excuse to run."

"And maybe being a bounty hunter just gave you an excuse to kill!" she lashed out.

Silence stretched between them.

"You just can't get past that, can you?" he said finally.

"I'm trying, Jack. I really am." She took a deep breath. "Why don't you tell me about it?"

He gave her a chilling smile. "You don't really want to hear, do you, sweetheart? All the men I've killed?"

She lifted her chin and tried to see past the predator to the man she loved. "Maybe I'd better. I know you, Jack—or I thought I did. You didn't seem the type of man to kill easily."

"Killing is never easy."

"For some men it is."

"Not for me. I only killed as a last resort—only when there was no other option. You want examples, I'll give you one.

"On my last job there was a fellow who liked fire. Or I should say, he liked to burn down houses, with the people still in them. That was after he robbed them and tied them up so they couldn't escape."

"Jack, you don't have to—"

"The last house he burned down belonged to a widow and her three little girls. One of the girls managed to escape, but she had to sit and listen to the screams of her mama and sisters as they burned to death."

"Oh, my God." Sarah raised a hand to her mouth, horrified.

"But she'd seen the fellow, you see. And she pointed him out to the sheriff. Turns out he was a peddler who'd just been passing through. That little girl's testimony made certain he was convicted."

"What a horrible story."

"I'm not done yet. This fellow burned down the jail and got away. Then he grabbed the little girl for a hostage and ran for the hills. That was when they called me." His voice roughened. "Blade isn't the kind of man most people feel comfortable around, but they sure are glad to see him when they need him. I tracked that bastard into the hills and cornered him in a canyon. He shot my horse out from under me, but I kept coming. I could hear that little girl crying, and I was determined to get to her."

He paused and took a deep breath. Sarah stepped forward and placed her hand on his arm, massaging the rigid muscle beneath her fingers. "Jack, you don't need to finish this."

He sent her a searing look of torment. "You wanted the truth, Sarah, and I'm giving it to you. This fellow finally realized that I wasn't going to leave without him, so he decided to make a break for it. But first he needed me to be distracted. So he set the little girl on fire."

"Dear heaven!"

"Heaven had nothing to do with it," he said bleakly. "I got to her as fast as I could and managed to put the flames out, but most of her body was burned. She was sobbing from the pain and calling for her mama, and though I tried to be so careful while I carried her, every time I touched her, it hurt.

"Anyhow, I guess that bastard figured he was going to shoot me in the back, because he came up behind me. I had my arms full of this little girl, so I took the only choice I had. I flipped her over my shoulder, knowing I was hurting her by doing it, and I threw a knife at him—got him through the heart. Then I left him there for the wolves and brought the girl to the doctor as fast as I could."

"Dear God, Jack. What happened to the little girl?"

"She lived, but she'll be disfigured for the rest of her life." He lifted his anguished gaze to hers. "Should I have dropped that little girl so I could wrestle hand to hand with that son of a bitch and bring him back alive? Or maybe just let him get away to do it all over again to another child? Sometimes I've *had* to kill, sassy girl—and each time took a piece of my soul. I had to leave it all behind before I lost myself completely."

"Oh, Jack." Giving in to impulse, she hugged him fiercely. "I'm so sorry for you. It's amazing you can still feel anything for anyone."

His arms tightened around her. "Can you forgive me for not telling you, sweetheart? The past fifteen years have been full of violence and death and the terrible things people do to each other. And that's why I don't like to talk about it."

"I can understand that, Jack. But I still need time." She pulled out of his embrace. "What if someone from your past finds out where you are and comes after you? I've heard of gunslingers who want to make a name for themselves by killing famous men. What if someone like that comes out to the ranch one day and starts shooting? What if we have a little girl of our own someday who might get caught in the crossfire? I need to be certain I can live with the risks if we're going to make this work."

"I've done everything I can to be sure that something like that doesn't happen, Sarah. Blade disappeared, and I plan on him staying gone."

"The marshal knew you," she pointed out. "It only took a little time for him to connect the face with the name."

"No one can predict the future, sweetheart. You're thinking of throwing our marriage away on a bunch of what-ifs." He leaned closer to her, his expression fierce. "Well, here's a what-if for you. *What if* nothing happens, and you and I miss out on fifty years of love and happiness? Consider that while you're doing all your thinking, Sarah."

He spun on his heel and headed for the door.

"Jack!" He stopped and looked at her, his expression distant. "I love you, Jack. Whatever happens, please believe that."

He gave her a bitter smile. "Oh, I believe that you love me. You just don't have enough faith in either of us. And with all that I've seen in my life and all the mistakes I've made, at least I've never lost faith."

Then he left, closing the door behind him, leaving Sarah alone with her pile of old junk and her memories.

Her next visitor was not so polite.

Susannah burst into the office at about nine

o'clock that night, looking bright and pretty in her leaf-green dress with the satin bows. She gripped her matching parasol like a sword and stormed into the spare room that Sarah now called home.

"Sarah Ann Calhoun, I can't believe what you are putting that poor man through!"

Seated in an old rocking chair, Sarah looked up from the book she was reading. "My name is Sarah Donovan now."

"Well, I'm glad to see that you remember you're married! You're certainly not acting like it."

Sarah sighed and closed the book. "Suzie, you have no idea what you're talking about."

"All I know is that your husband is miserable. You should have seen him at the picnic, Sarah. He barely said two words to anyone—though he did talk to that rude Marshal Brown for a while," she added, crinkling her nose in distaste.

"He talked to Marshal Brown? Did he seem angry?"

"No, they actually seemed to be getting along," Suzie replied. "I can't understand it, myself."

"Good." Sarah breathed a sigh of relief. A few words with Jedidiah had confirmed that his discovery about Jack had been purely accidental. And he hadn't compounded the problem by sharing the true story with Susannah.

"But Sarah, you had better start thinking about your marriage. The vultures are already circling."

"Vultures?"

"There are a number of women in this town who would love to 'comfort' your husband."

Sarah rose from the chair, closing the book and laying it on the padded cushion. Folding her arms around her as if to ward off the cold, she turned toward the cot that served as her bed these days. "It's up to Jack if he wants comforting," she said quietly.

"Sarah, I cannot believe you just said that!" Susannah exclaimed. "If it were up to me, I'd—"

"Well, it's not up to you," Sarah snapped. "This is between me and Jack. I asked him for time, but if he decides that this marriage is over, then maybe it's for the best."

"You can't just give up!"

"Suzie, you don't understand."

Susannah plopped down in the rocking chair. "Then explain it to me."

Sarah hesitated. "I can't give you details. Let's just say that Jack didn't tell me a few things about his past."

"Important things?"

"Yes."

Susannah tapped her fingers on the arm of the rocker before nodding. "All right, then. I guess I would be upset, too, under the same circumstances."

"Thank you, Suzie," Sarah said, glad her sister wasn't pressing for more.

"But I still think you need to do something about your husband, Sarah. If you don't claim him, one of those other women will."

"I'll think about it."

A thunderous boom exploded into the night, followed by crackling and hissing. A flash of green fire lit the sky outside Sarah's window.

"Fireworks!" Susannah squealed.

The sisters crowded together at the window as brilliant colors lit the sky. The wooden walls of the office shook each time an explosion rent the air, and they giggled like children with each new blossom of fire that discharged above them. Sarah's thoughts turned to Donovan, and she wondered if he was up at Miller's Pond watching the fireworks, too. Did he think of her? Did he imagine her with him, his arms around her?

Was he as lonely as she was right now?

She pressed her lips together tightly as her volatile emotions threatened to escape in a torrent of tears. She missed Jack lying beside her at night. She missed the way he teased her and the way he touched her. Had she been wrong in not trusting him to protect his family from his past? Was she too cowardly to take a chance on them?

Maybe Jack was right. Maybe she hadn't had enough faith—in either of them.

If she had been absorbed in the fireworks, she wouldn't even have heard the squeak of the floorboard behind them. But since she was distracted with her own thoughts, the noise grabbed her attention, and she turned her head.

Luke Petrie smiled over the barrel of the gun pointed at her. "Hello, Sarah."

Donovan arrived home to an empty house and an empty bed.

Shirtless, he stood at his bedroom window and watched the dazzling display of color and sound as fireworks lit the night sky. He had gone to the picnic merely because he felt obliged to, but he hadn't enjoyed himself. Juliana Tremont had spent most of the day trying to monopolize him, Mrs. Castor had tried to worm information from him, and Susannah had alternately glared at him or stared in sympathy.

Damn it all to hell, he was sick to death of women and their confusing emotional storms.

How was a man supposed to change what he had been? He couldn't erase the past—though he admitted now that he'd been trying to do exactly that. He couldn't escape who he'd been and what he'd done. Without Blade, the boy he had been long ago might have not made it to adulthood.

But Blade had also cost him the woman he loved.

He raked a hand through his hair. All this circling around was bound to drive a man insane. What he needed was a good night's sleep.

He peeled off his clothing and climbed into his lonely bed. The cool sheets were a bleak reminder of how Sarah used to warmly cuddle up against him, her legs tangled with his. It was also too quiet. He missed the way she mumbled in her sleep. Sometimes he would have a conversation with her, asking questions that she would sleepily answer, and then laugh in the morning when she couldn't remember any of it.

God, he missed her.

Tomorrow he would bring his sassy girl home, he decided. Whether she liked it or not.

"What's this all about?" Susannah demanded.

Luke's face twisted into an expression of pure hate. "Well, well, if it isn't Sister Sue."

Knowing the longtime enmity between Luke and her sister, Sarah stepped in front of Susannah. "It's me you're here to see, Luke. Leave Susannah out of this."

"Now, that's not fair, Sarah." Luke reached

behind Sarah and yanked Susannah forward. "I can't play favorites, you know."

"Let me go, you maggot." Susannah tried to twist away, but froze as Luke shoved the revolver before her eyes.

"I suggest you stay very still, Sister Sue—unless you want that pretty face messed up like that guard outside."

"Luke," Sarah said, trying to distract him, "what do you want?"

"I just want what's mine, Sarah."

"She doesn't owe you anything!" Susannah snapped.

"Shut up," Luke growled. He pulled Susannah close to him and jabbed the gun into her ribs. His desperate gaze met Sarah's over Susannah's shoulder. "And *you* had better stop playing dumb and give me what I want, my dear."

"There's nothing I would like better, but you're talking in riddles," Sarah replied carefully. "What is it that you want, Luke? Money? Me? What?"

"You? You think I came all this way just for a woman?" Luke laughed. "You overestimate your charms, my dear."

Sarah's cheeks burned, but she held his gaze steadily. "Then what is it, Luke? I can't read your mind."

A smile stretched across his face. "You really

don't know, do you? Your father never told you what he did to me."

"He died before he had the chance."

"I didn't mean to kill him, you know. I thought it was that feeble sheriff following me into the bank. I wouldn't have killed your father, Sarah. At least not until he told me what I wanted to know."

"And what was that?"

Luke's face tightened. "Where he had hidden my plates."

Sarah frowned. "What plates?"

"The good china?" Susannah sneered.

"I've heard enough from you," Luke snarled. He raised his arm and struck Susannah on the back of the head with the butt of his gun. She slid to the floor in an unconscious heap of leaf-green dimity and silver-blond ringlets. Sarah cried out and rushed toward her sister, but Luke swung around and pointed the revolver in her direction. "Hold it right there, Sarah."

"Luke, please! Let me go to her."

Holding the gun steady, Luke poked Susannah with the toe of one shiny black boot. "She's still breathing, my dear. And if you wish her to continue to do so, you will listen to me very carefully."

Sarah fisted her hands at her sides. He looked almost happy to have hurt her sister. A kind of demented joy lit his eyes, as if he took pleasure from the pain of others. "I'm listening."

"Your father was very protective of you, my dear. He suspected that my motives for courting you were not pure, and indeed, he was right. I did need you, Sarah, but not for your female companionship—though you proved to be a surprisingly hot piece of tail. I wanted you for your printing press."

"What?" Sickened by his crudeness, she could only stare. "What are you talking about?"

"I had acquired some rather authentic-looking plates for printing stock certificates. Ah, now you see," he said with a malicious grin as her eyes widened at the revelation. "Yes, Sarah, I needed you so I could have access to your printing press. I had a brilliant plan to sell false stock in the railroad to the unsuspecting. People would have paid good money to be a part of such a growing enterprise, and by the time the fools discovered they'd been tricked, I would have been long gone. But your father disrupted my plans."

"Did he?"

"*Yes,*" Luke snarled. "And you needn't look so happy about it. Your father paid for stealing my plates and hiding them from me, didn't he? I decided to rob the bank so that my time in this dismal town would not have been wasted, but he managed to ruin that, too. I'm *glad* I shot the old fool!"

With effort, Sarah repressed the harsh words that she longed to fling at him. He would only kill her, and Suzie as well. That she had ever allowed such a man to touch her revolted her, but that she had actually considered Jack to be like Luke really sickened her.

The two men could not be more different, she realized with bitterly clear hindsight. Jack had killed, but in the name of justice and only when absolutely necessary. Luke killed on a whim—and enjoyed it.

"What do you want from me, Luke?" she asked quietly.

"My plates," he said. "And you."

"Me?" Bile rose in her throat. "I thought you said that you hadn't come back for me."

"I didn't. But I intend to have my revenge, Sarah." His eyes narrowed. "Don't think I don't know who led the sheriff to me last time. But first, I want the plates."

The menace in his tone made her skin crawl. "I don't have them."

"Your father did. You find them, Sarah." He crouched down and hooked his arm around Susannah's waist. Rising, he dragged her sister with him like an old blanket. "You find those plates, Sarah, and then you bring them to me. You have two hours."

"Wait!" she cried as he edged toward the door. "Where should I meet you?"

"Do you think I'm stupid?" he sneered, shifting Susannah until she hung like a sack of flour over his shoulder. "Do you think I'd tell you where I am so you could send the law after me again? If you want your sister to see the sun rise tomorrow, you'll find me." He grinned, his eyes gleaming with malice. "Though part of me hopes that you won't make it, Sarah. It would give me *such* pleasure to shut her mouth—permanently."

"I'll be there."

"I know you will." Luke shifted his grip on Susannah. "And do come alone, my dear. I'd hate to dispose of your sister . . . prematurely."

He flung open the door and slipped outside. Briefly he was illuminated by the fireworks as he flung Susannah across the pommel of the saddle and climbed onto his horse. Then he kicked his mount into a gallop and disappeared into the night.

Thunderstruck, Sarah listened to the sound of the retreating hoofbeats with a sense of unreality. Every conviction by which she had lived her life for the past three years had been wrong. Every assumption she had made—wrong. Every decision—*wrong*.

She glanced at the clock hanging on the wall. It was nearly ten o'clock, and Luke had said that she had only two hours. She had to find where her father had hidden the plates—if he hadn't destroyed them—and then find Luke's hideout and save Susannah.

She knew she wouldn't be able to save herself; Luke would kill her for certain. But if she managed to get Susannah to safety, the sacrifice would be worth it.

Sometimes in a desperate situation, there wasn't time to be careful about who lived and who died. And sometimes there just wasn't a choice. Jack had tried to tell her that, but she hadn't listened.

She knew now. She would happily pull the trigger on Luke herself if it meant that her sister would live.

She could accept who Jack had once been, because it had made him the man he was now. A good man. A strong man. A man whose priorities centered around his family. He would have made a wonderful father for their children. They could have been happy, if only—

A flicker of an idea broke through the soul-deep regret. An idea that might just give her the chance to have the life she wanted. But in order for it to work, she had to believe in Jack, and she had to believe in herself. She had to have faith that their love for each other was stronger than the past.

And she had to trust in Blade—a man she knew to be dangerous, but a man she loved nonetheless.

She needed Jack. She needed Blade. She needed *both* of them.

She glanced at the clock again. Five minutes after ten. She had little time to set her plans in motion. If all worked out, Donovan's secret might be in danger of exposure. But, she hoped, they would all be alive to argue about it.

With new hope blooming in her heart, she started tearing the newspaper office apart in search of the missing plates.

Chapter 19

***

I n the end, it was almost too easy.

Sarah sat on the floor amid the junk from the closet and looked down at the printing plates in her hands. They were of high quality—too high to be fakes. Obviously, Luke must have stolen them. No wonder he wanted them back.

She had found them buried at the bottom of the box of old type that she had dragged from the closet earlier that day. How lucky that she had decided to clean out the office only that morning—she might never have found them otherwise.

She slipped the two gleaming plates back into the soft leather bag that had held them and rose to her feet. The search had taken nearly an hour, and now she had just over an hour left to find her sister. But she was confident that she would make the deadline. Luke wanted the plates, which meant that he *wanted* her to be able to find him—so he wouldn't have hidden someplace difficult. She already suspected where she might find him.

Her only worry was that his dislike for her sister might tempt him to do away with Suzie before Sarah could locate them.

She closed up the office and quickly walked over to her mother's corral. Slipping the plates into her saddle bags, she mounted Senseless, a strange calm settling over her like a cloak of confidence. She knew there was every chance her plan would fail, and that she could die tonight. But at the same time, she had faith in the man she had come to know so well. If there was anyone who could help her survive this, it was Jack Donovan.

She took a last look at the house where she had lived for so many years. She had been blessed with loving parents and a nice home. Not all people were that lucky.

Jack hadn't been.

Yet despite her happy childhood, tragedy had found her, just as it had found Jack. Fate didn't discriminate when it handed out the heartache, and people did what they had to in order to survive.

Jack had become Blade. She had turned to the newspaper. And in trying to get through, they had found each other—and love.

She was depending on that love now, not

just to save her life, but for her sister's as well.

Sarah said a silent farewell to the house she might never see again and swiftly headed toward town.

Main Street was fairly deserted, but at the Four Aces, lights still burned and music and laughter carried out into the night. She spotted the familiar figure of Mort leaning back against the wall outside the saloon. Johnny and Gabriel sat nearby, setting up the checkerboard. Sarah reined in before the trio.

"Evenin', Mrs. Donovan," Mort greeted her. "Awful late for a ride, wouldn't you say?"

"I need your help," she replied with no preliminaries. "Luke Petrie kidnapped my sister, and I'm going after them. I need one of you to go fetch Jack right away."

The legs of Mort's chair hit the wooden sidewalk with a thud. "The hell you say!"

"Ma'am, wouldn't it be better to wait for your husband?" Johnny asked hopefully.

"There's no time," she said urgently. "Will you help me?"

"We'll rustle up a posse to go fetch your sister back," Gabriel said.

"That's a very good idea, but I'm still going," Sarah said. "Tell Jack I'll be at Stony Ridge." She kicked her horse into a gallop, leaving the three men in the dust of her departure.

*   *   *

Donovan was already up and dressed when Mort knocked on his door. Despite his best attempts, sleep had eluded him. Maybe it was because Sarah wasn't beside him for the seventh night in a row. Maybe it was the kiss earlier today that had made him realize that he couldn't last another night without her. Whatever the reason, after an hour of tossing and turning, he had risen from his bed and pulled on his clothes, determined that he would not spend another night without his wife beside him.

Even if it was on that cot in the back room of the *Chronicle*.

Yet now Mort stood on his doorstep with news that chilled his blood. Petrie had kidnapped Susannah, and Sarah had gone after them.

Alone.

"Marshal Brown's forming a posse," Mort continued. "But Mrs. Donovan told me to come and fetch you."

"My wife sent you?" At Mort's nod, Donovan let out a deep sigh. Finally, Sarah had given him an indication that she had faith in him. But the cost might be her life. "I'll be there directly. Tell Marshal Brown not to leave without me."

Mort nodded and hurried down the steps to his horse.

Donovan shut the door. Already the change

was coming over him. That dark, quiet part of himself that produced the deadly Blade had awakened, pushing aside the frenetic emotions that could tangle a man's thoughts during the hunt. The only thing that lingered was his love for Sarah. It was so much a part of him that he could not put it aside, even though it could distract him, and cause him to make a mistake at a crucial moment.

But he would not let that happen. He would keep his emotions in check and take care of Petrie once and for all.

It was time for Blade to ride again.

Sarah pulled Senseless to a halt and stared at the rocky precipice known as Stony Ridge. The mountain was riddled with a series of caves, left from the long ago meanderings of a river that no longer existed. A few years before, there had been a brief resurgence of the gold rush that had led Josiah Burr to found the town. The "gold strike" lasted only as long as it took to verify that the gold was pyrite again, and then died down. But one prospector, Horace Plunkett, had stuck it out. Until the day he died three years ago, he had been convinced that he would strike gold on Stony Ridge.

When Sarah had seen the words "Property of H. Plunkett" printed on the bag that held the stolen plates, she had known exactly where Luke held her sister hostage.

Sarah got off Senseless and tied him to a tree near the base of the mountain. Slowly she unfastened the saddlebags. As she lifted them from the back of the horse, the contents clinked together, making her stomach knot. She knelt in the dirt and opened one of the bags, reaching inside to pull forth the cold metal from within.

The derringer gleamed in the moonlight.

She reached into the pouch again and pulled out the ammunition for the tiny pocket revolver. With shaking fingers, she loaded the weapon as her father had taught her long ago. Then she slipped it into the pocket of her heavy brown skirt.

Sarah knew she might not survive to see the morning. But this might even the odds.

Quickly, she closed up the saddlebags and, slinging them over her shoulder, took the horse's reins, and headed for the path that led up the mountain. As she wove her way along the rocky track that led to Horace Plunkett's old cabin, the sky was cloudless, and the stars bright.

She hoped the clear weather would help Jack find her in time.

The marshal was organizing search parties by the time Donovan got to town.

As he rode down Main Street, he saw the faces of his neighbors and friends grow wary as he passed them by. Mothers clutched their children to their skirts. Men took on a challenging stance.

Blade had returned.

As he brought his horse to a stop near Marshal Brown, he felt as isolated as if he had never lived these past few months as Jack Donovan.

Maybe it was the buckskin pants or the long, dark brown duster or the wide-brimmed black hat that sat low on his forehead. Maybe it was the six-inch bowie knife at his waist or the revolver strapped to his thigh or the two rifles fastened to his saddle. Or maybe it was just the look in his eyes. But somehow the people of Burr recognized him for what he was.

Dangerous.

Jedidiah looked up as Donovan dismounted. "Glad to see you, Donovan," he said as casually as if the entire town were not staring at their neighbor in uncertainty. "I imagine you'll want to help plan this operation."

"You imagine right." Even his voice had changed, had taken on that low, emotionless cadence that had served Blade so well. "That's my family he's got—my wife, my sister-in-law."

"We can certainly use your help. You ride with my group, Donovan."

"I was going to." Donovan glanced at the men who were going to help him get his wife back. "I'm obliged for your help," he said in an attempt to bridge the chasm he felt forming between them. Never again did he intend to walk that lonely path between decency and vice, cut off from society on both sides of the scale.

At this glimpse of the man they knew, some of the stiffness immediately left the expressions of the other men in the posse.

"Mort," said the marshal, "did Mrs. Donovan say where she was headed?"

"Stony Ridge," Mort answered immediately. "But how do you reckon to find her in the dark? Even in daylight, her trail would be hard to read up there in those rocks."

Donovan turned his head to fix Mort with a steady, certain stare. "I'll find her."

"I bet you will," Mort replied.

"Let's get started," Marshal Brown said and headed for his horse.

Sarah approached the cabin as quietly as she could, but Luke must have been watching for her. The door to the building opened and he leaned against the door frame, the revolver in his hand and a smile on his face.

"Glad to see you could make it, Sarah."

"Where's my sister?" she demanded, grateful that her voice didn't tremble. The weight of the derringer was heavy in her pocket.

"Sister Sue is right inside. We've been having a little visit," he sneered.

"If you hurt her—"

He straightened. "Don't threaten me, Sarah." The firelight from inside the cabin played over his face. With his fine-boned features, thin mustache, and short black hair, he looked like Satan on a holiday. She fisted her hands to stop their trembling.

"You said if I brought you the plates, then Susannah would go free."

"That's the deal," he agreed.

She reached into the saddlebag hanging over her shoulder and pulled forth a cloth-wrapped bundle. "Here they are."

He arched his brows. "Really, Sarah, how foolish do you think I am?"

Shrugging off the saddlebags, she pulled open the leather bag and drew out the plates. The metal gleamed in the moonlight. "There. Satisfied?"

"For the moment." He gestured with the gun. "Bring the plates over here, Sarah."

She didn't budge. "No, you bring my sister out here."

"Sarah . . ." he warned.

She slipped the plates back into the bag, then hefted it in her hand and extended her arm backward, poised to throw. "Bring my sister out here, or I fling these off the mountain."

"Don't be stupid," he snapped impatiently.

"I could shoot you before you had the chance to do it."

"You might miss." She stretched her arm back a little more. "Would you like to take that chance?"

He hesitated, then said, "You'll pay for this, Sarah."

"I know I will," she muttered.

"Wait here." He disappeared inside for a moment, then reappeared with Susannah, who was conscious but unsteady on her feet. Sarah felt a pang of pride as she saw how her sister struggled to maintain her balance, rather than depend on the man who held her captive to support her weight. Luke grabbed a handful of Suzie's hair and jerked her sister's head back, pressing the gun to her temple. A whimper of pain escaped Susannah's lips.

"Let's have those plates, Sarah," he demanded. "You know it would give me the greatest of pleasure to shut your sister's mouth permanently."

"All right." She knew better than anyone what atrocities Luke Petrie was capable of committing. "I have what you want right here; just don't shoot."

"Bring the plates, Sarah."

She came forward hesitantly, holding the neck of the bag with a firm grip. Two steps . . . then one . . . and she'd be ready to make her move.

She saw the half smile on Luke's face as he gloated at having her in his grasp. She remembered that he had worn that same expression right after he had taken her virginity. At the time she had thought it was a smile of pleasure, but now she knew it was one of conquest.

This time, Luke Petrie would *not* win.

She reached them. This close, Sarah could see how pale her sister was even in the moonlight, and how she trembled. Fury rose, but she squelched it. If they were to escape alive, she couldn't give in to emotion. Still, the very real feelings made her performance all the more authentic as she gasped with alarm and reached out a hand to Susannah. Luke turned his head, a snarl escaping his lips, and swatted her arm away. At the same time, Sarah swung the bag of plates around with her other hand, slamming him solidly on the side of the head.

"Run, Suzie!" she screamed. She shoved at Luke with her body, breaking his hold on Susannah. Suzie stumbled forward a step, then swayed on her feet. "Suzie, run! Get help!"

Luke raised his arm, blood trickling from his temple, and pointed his revolver at Susannah. Sarah gave a shriek of rage and brought the bag of plates down hard on his gun arm. The shot fired harmlessly into the dirt at Susannah's feet.

"*Run, Suzie!*"

The gunshot apparently got through to Susannah as Sarah's screams hadn't, and she took off at an unsteady run.

"Bitch!" Luke roared, turning his gun on Sarah. She swung the bag around again, but he was ready this time and deflected it with a blow to her arm that numbed her fingers. The bag dropped into the dust at their feet. Luke seized her with his arm around her neck and dragged her back against him, pressing the gun to her temple as Susannah disappeared down the rocky incline.

"The only reason I haven't killed you yet," he rasped, "is because I want you to take a *long* time to die. I want you to *suffer* for what you've done to me!"

With one hand, Sarah clawed at the arm that was cutting off her air supply. With the other, she reached down to the pocket of her skirt.

Suddenly her throat was free. She spun to face him, but his hand closed over her wrist as she pulled the derringer from her pocket. Despair swamped her as he easily took the weapon from her.

"What's this? Were you going to kill me, my dear? How very bloodthirsty you've become." He tossed the derringer over the cliff, and with it, Sarah's greatest hope for survival. Then he grabbed her braid and used it to drag her face close to his. "You'll wish you had it back by the time I'm done with you," he hissed, the promise of pain shining in his eyes. "You'll want to kill me—or yourself."

With a nasty laugh, he jerked her around and shoved her into the cabin.

Donovan and the search party sat looking up at Stony Ridge.

"They could be anywhere," Mort was saying. "Them mountains are full of caves and ravines where a body could hide for months, as long as he had enough food."

"What about water?" Donovan asked.

"There's plenty of water. Streams all through the caves."

"Damn." Donovan glanced at Jedidiah, whose expression was grim. "We know she stopped here."

"But where did she *go* from here?"

Donovan dismounted and walked slowly around the area. He knelt where they had found the hoofprints from Sarah's horse, then got up and walked around some more, his gaze directed to the ground. Finally, he knelt again, this time by a break in the trees. "Here. She went this way."

"There's a track off that way," Amos said. "Goes up the mountain to some of those abandoned mines."

"Then that's where we're going." Donovan mounted his horse and picked up the trail.

*   *   *

"Do you know how long I've waited for this moment?" Luke asked softly. "Do you have any idea what it was like in that filthy prison, constantly on guard against the scum that inhabited that place?"

Sarah said nothing, since any words that passed her lips would only set off his temper. She sat on the bare dirt floor in front of the fire, which was where she'd landed when he shoved her. Luke stood just inside the door with his gun pointed at her and the bag of plates in his hand.

"Do you have any idea," he continued, "how I used to dream of getting you in my grasp again? First your father interfered with my plans, and then *you* sent the sheriff after me! Every night in that stinking prison I imagined what it would be like to make you pay for that little betrayal, just like your father paid. And now I have my opportunity."

He slammed the door with a suddenness that made her jump. She watched him warily as he came toward her, prepared for him to make a move in her direction. Instead he sat down on the bedroll he had spread on the floor close to the fire. Tucking the plates safely in his saddlebags, he waved the gun at her. "Stand up, Sarah."

Her limbs shaking, she got to her feet. Would he simply kill her now?

As if he read her thoughts, he leaned back and gave her a cocky grin that she had once found roguishly charming. "Don't worry, my dear, I have no intention of killing you—*yet*."

She licked her dry lips. "What do you want, Luke?"

"To start?" He traced a finger over his slim mustache and watched her with unreadable pale gray eyes. "To start, you can take off your clothes."

Her legs lost all strength, and her stomach knotted. "What?" she asked hoarsely.

"Take off your clothes, Sarah. I want you dressed like the whore you are while you cook my supper."

"Cook your supper?"

"You always were the wifely sort." The smile faded. "Take off your clothes. *Now!*"

She flinched at the unyielding command and raised trembling fingers to the buttons of her blouse. This could buy her some time, she realized as she slowly unfastened the first button. Perhaps she could draw out the process . . .

"That's it, my dear." A half smile of pleasure tugged at his thin lips. "Do it slowly, as if you were a slut I've paid to please me."

She moved to the next button, and the next, her nerves becoming more and more frayed with every second she stood as slave to that steady, unrelenting regard. The only thing that kept her from losing control was the knowledge that Jack was coming for her.

All she had to do was stay alive long enough for him to find her.

Chapter 20

Donovan held up a hand to halt the search party. "I hear something." He pulled a rifle from his saddle.

Jedidiah rode up beside him, the Colt in his hand. "What is it?" the marshal murmured.

"Someone's up ahead," Donovan answered in the same barely audible tone, lifting the rifle to sight down the barrel.

The marshal signaled to the rest of the posse, and Donovan was satisfied to hear the quiet snicks of weapons being cocked. They had the advantage, since they were at the edge of the woods right before it opened up at the base of Stony Ridge. To make it to the safety of the concealing trees, whoever was ahead of them would have to leave the shelter of the rocks and cross a bare, flat clearing that would leave that person vulnerable.

Donovan hoped it was Petrie coming down

the rocky path. He wanted nothing more than to put a bullet in the bastard who had taken Sarah from him.

A horse and rider cleared the rocks. Donovan recognized Senseless immediately, and his heart leaped as he saw the blond hair flowing over the back of the person who clung precariously to the saddle.

If Petrie had hurt her—

"Susannah!" Jedidiah shouted.

Susannah. Donovan saw the differences even as the marshal galloped from the cover of the trees to assist Sarah's sister. The silver-gilt hair that should have been honey blond. The fancy green dress that should have been a practical shirtwaist and skirt.

Not Sarah.

Rage made him want to howl, but he needed to keep calm. If he gave in to his emotions now, Sarah was as good as dead.

If she wasn't already.

That thought made him spur his horse forward. Jedidiah had pulled Sarah's sister off Senseless and was now cradling her in his arms on his own mount. Susannah had to be hurt, Donovan thought grimly, otherwise she and Jedidiah would have been into one of their near-famous arguments by now.

"She's almost unconscious," Jedidiah said as Donovan pulled his mount alongside the lawman's. "But she insists on talking to you. Won't let us take her to the doctor until she does."

Donovan looked down at Susannah, frowning as he saw evidence of hard treatment in the bruises that marred her skin. Her eyes were closed, and he wondered if she were even conscious. "Suzie," he said, using Sarah's nickname for her sister, "it's Donovan."

Her eyes opened, and he could tell from the dullness of her blue gaze that she was in a lot of pain. Her lips formed his name, a mere breath of sound.

"I'm here, Suzie."

"Luke ..."

"Luke has Sarah. I know that. But *where*, Suzie?" He stroked a hand gently over her cheek. "Tell me where."

"Plunkett," she rasped, wincing. "Up ... Plunkett." She made a weak upward gesture with her hand, then with a whimper, she passed out.

Jedidiah cradled her close, his gaze meeting Donovan's with implacable resolve. "I've got to get her to Doc Mercer's."

"Go." Donovan clapped a hand on the marshal's shoulder in farewell, then turned to the search party as the lawman galloped toward town. "She said Plunkett," he announced. "Does anyone know what that means?"

"Horace Plunkett," Amos answered, spitting a wad of tobacco juice into the shrubbery. "Crazy old prospector who used to live up the trail. Filthy son of a gun. Used to stink like an outhouse."

Everyone turned to stare at Amos.

With a defensive scowl, he snapped, "I take baths once a month just like the rest of you!"

"Amos," Donovan said, drawing the old man's attention. "Do you know where this place is?"

"Sure do," Amos replied, sending another wad of brown spittle into the trees. "Horace's shack is up the trail a ways. Real easy to find, if you're looking for it."

"Then you ride with me. The rest of you, get ready to surround the place when we get there. No one fires a shot until Sarah is safe."

With Amos at his side, Donovan started up the trail.

Barefoot in her camisole and bloomers, Sarah wished Luke Petrie to hell with every fiber of her being.

She could tell that he enjoyed humilating her. He had made her take off everything but these last garments, and he made her do it in such a way that she felt like a harlot putting on a performance for a paying customer—just as he had wanted her to feel.

"You've got a real talent for this sort of thing," Luke drawled, his gray eyes narrowed with meanness. "I think you missed your calling, Sarah."

She didn't give him the satisfaction of a response.

He merely laughed. "Take off the rest of it, my dear. I want to see if your body is still as lovely as I remember."

"No."

She hadn't planned on saying it, but when she saw the surprise that flashed across his face, she was glad that she had.

"What did you say?"

"I said no." Grateful that he had been too startled to shoot her, she straightened her spine proudly. "I refuse."

He sprang to his feet, and it was all she could do to hold her ground. "Do you want to die, Sarah?"

"You're going to kill me whether I do what you ask or not," she replied. "I'd rather die with my clothes on."

"So you want to choose how to die?" He gave a nasty chuckle. "Let me help you then."

He came to her and cocked the gun. Bile rose in her throat as she felt the deadly steel pressing against the pulse that throbbed at her temple. "I could shoot you in the head," he said. "Very quick death. Or perhaps . . ."

He slid the gun down the arch of her cheek and along her jaw, leaving a trail of chilly fear prickling her flesh, until the barrel touched her lips. Her panicked exhale misted over the cool metal. "This would be quick, too," Luke mused, "but messy."

She didn't dare take another breath until he moved the revolver away from her mouth. Once more the weapon glided along her flesh, tracing a path down her throat to rest snugly between her breasts.

"Heart shot," Luke whispered, the thrill of power in his tone. "Again, quick, but messy."

Not taking his eyes from hers, he reached up and deliberately caressed her breast with his other hand. A shudder of revulsion shook her, and he laughed.

"There was a time when you moaned my name when I touched you like that," he taunted. He squeezed her breast until a gasp of pain escaped her lips. Grinning in enjoyment, he moved the gun down her torso until it nudged her abdomen. "Gut shot," he whispered close to her ear. "Very painful, and a *very* slow death."

She bit her lip to keep from crying out. His face was so close that she could see clearly how much he relished her terror, and she resolved not to give him the satisfaction of hearing her beg for her life.

Whatever atrocities he committed on her person, if she just stayed alive, then Jack would find her.

"Sarah, you always were stubborn." He grabbed her hair and jerked her head back, the gun pressing against the vulnerable flesh under her chin. "You can keep being stubborn if you want, but it won't do you any good in the end."

"Why don't you just take the plates and go, Luke?" she whispered. "You know they're going to come looking for me."

"They'd kill me as soon as I hit the trail. But as long as I have you, my dear, they'll have to give me safe passage."

"The search party could be here at any minute," she pointed out. "What if they surround the cabin?"

Luke just laughed. "No one in this backward town is smart enough to find us. The only one who ever managed to outwit me was your dear, departed father."

"I found you," she said.

"But I wanted you to find me." He tugged at the tie of her braid; then he combed his fingers through her loosened hair, spreading it over her shoulders. "You're not as smart as you think you are. After all, I fooled you three years ago, didn't I?"

"Yes," she agreed bitterly. "You did."

He stepped back, finally removing the revolver from her abdomen and uncocking it. "You know, you were right, my dear. You look very tantalizing like this, in your undergarments with your hair loose. It lets the anticipation build. I'll have my supper now, Sarah."

He gave her a hard look that made her skin prickle with disgust. "And then I'll have you."

Horace Plunkett's old shack looked deserted, except for the wispy curl of smoke that flowed from the small chimney. Donovan gathered the men together.

"After I get Sarah, then you all go for Petrie. Surround the building. I don't want him getting away."

Everyone nodded, and Donovan turned toward the shack. Keeping to the shadows, he soundlessly crept closer. Petrie wasn't stupid; except for the smoke, it was impossible to tell that anyone was here. He'd closed all the shutters on the windows, and no doubt he had his horse tied up in the trees nearby. But the shack was old, and it hadn't been well-built to begin with. Donovan hugged the wall and came up beneath a window where the shutters didn't close all the way. There was just enough space between the warped wood for him to see into the cabin.

A small fire burned in the grate. Near it, Petrie lounged on his bedroll, his revolver pointed at Sarah, who was cooking something over the fire. Aside from the fact that she was in her undergarments, she seemed unharmed.

He intended to see that she stayed that way.

*   *   *

Sarah stirred the stew in the pot, but every instinct was centered on Luke. He acted as if he had all the time in the world, but she wouldn't put it past him to pounce when she least expected it. The waiting was making her nerves raw.

It had been over an hour since Susannah had escaped. She had to have gotten back to town by now. And Jack *must* be on his way. Sarah had to believe that. And because she believed that, she planned to turn the tables on Luke Petrie and get away before he decided it was time to end her life.

She stirred the stew one more time and then banged the metal spoon on the side of the pot to get every drop off the utensil.

"Is supper ready?" Luke drawled. The smug expression on his face echoed the light of malice in his eyes.

"Yes, it's ready." She wrapped a cloth around the handle and took the pot off the fire with both hands.

"Good. I'm starved." Luke sat up, resting the revolver on the ground beside him within easy reach of his hand.

Sarah smiled, then flung the contents of the pot at her former lover's face. He shrieked with pain, raking the scalding stew away from his eyes with his fingers. Sarah dove for the gun, but he anticipated her and knocked it aside with one blind swing of his hand. It skittered across the hard-packed dirt to the far corner of the room. She scrabbled after it.

Cursing beneath his breath, Luke lunged at her just as her fingers brushed the stock of the gun. She landed hard on her stomach, Petrie on top of her, just as something crashed through the window. She felt the gun beneath her hand and managed to close her fingers around it even as Luke grabbed her wrist.

He jerked her arm toward him, and she rolled with the motion, coming to rest with the gun an inch from his nose and her finger on the trigger.

He froze.

"Get off me," she snapped. For a moment she thought he was going to ignore her. His face, reddened from the hot stew and still dripping broth, tightened in an expression of thwarted fury. "*Off*," she insisted, pressing the barrel of the gun right up against his forehead. "Or I'll shoot you first and *then* shove your dead carcass off me!"

"I suggest you listen to the lady," a familiar voice said. Looking like an outlaw in his long duster and black hat, Donovan, his eyes hard and deadly, aimed his rifle at Petrie.

"Who the hell are you?" Luke demanded.

"I'm the one with the gun. Now get off the lady."

Glowering, Luke pushed himself back onto his haunches. Sarah slid out from beneath him, holding her gun steady. It would be just like Petrie to grab her as a hostage to try and get past Jack. Once she had regained her feet, she continued to aim the weapon at Petrie's head.

"Sarah," Donovan said, "I've got him covered. The cabin is surrounded. He's not going anywhere."

Sarah didn't look away from Luke. Her arms started to shake, but she held the gun steady with both hands. "Is Susannah all right?"

"We found her. Jedidiah took her to Doc Mercer's." He lowered his rifle and came to her, keeping an eye on Petrie. "She's going to be all right."

"He was going to kill her. He was going to kill Suzie."

"But he didn't." Holding the rifle with one hand, Jack closed his other hand over hers where she gripped the revolver. "Sarah, give me the gun."

"He was going to kill me, too," she whispered.

"Look at me, sassy girl."

"I can't. He'll get away."

"He's not going anywhere." He squeezed her fingers beneath his. "Sarah, you've fought so hard not to bring violence into our lives. Don't give up now."

She closed her eyes and released the gun to his grasp. "You're right. I don't know what came over me."

Donovan pulled her into his arms. "Survival, sassy girl. But luckily, you didn't have to cross that line today."

"Oh God, Jack, I would have shot him. I planned to shoot him." She buried her face in his shoulder, shuddering from the storm of emotions that suddenly washed over her.

Still holding the rifle, he slid one strong arm around her. "Hush now, sweetheart," Donovan murmured, slipping the revolver into the pocket of his duster. "He's not going to hurt anyone anymore."

A soft scuffle reached her ears. Donovan obviously heard it at the same time, because he shoved her behind him as Luke charged. In a blur of motion, Jack raised his rifle and fired. The shot caught Petrie in the shoulder, sending him tumbling backward to land slumped against the wall.

"Stupid," Donovan said.

Pressing a hand to his bloody wound, Luke glared. "Who the hell *are* you?"

Sarah stepped from behind him to glare at Luke. "You can call him Blade." The fear that filled Luke's eyes gave her much satisfaction.

"Sweetheart, why don't you get dressed and then stick your head outside and get the men in here," Donovan suggested. He sighted down the barrel of the rifle, his target Luke's chest. "I'll keep an eye on Petrie."

"Don't leave me here with him!" Luke screamed, terrified.

Donovan glanced at Sarah, a twinkle in his eye. "Go ahead, sweetheart. As long as he doesn't move, he'll still be alive when you get back."

Sarah averted her face so that Luke didn't see the grin she couldn't suppress as she headed for her discarded clothing. "Then can we go home?" she asked, sounding exasperated.

Donovan smiled, his dark eyes tender. "You bet we can, sassy girl."

Chapter 21

Glowing with the pleasure of being home, Sarah snuggled closer to Donovan beneath the wedding ring quilt on his enormous bed. His arms tightened around her, and his hand stroked possessively over her naked hip.

"It feels as if we were apart forever, but it was only seven days," she murmured.

"It was seven days too long," Donovan replied. "I couldn't sleep without you, sassy girl."

She shifted up onto her elbow so that she could see his face. His hair was a dark tangle and his morning beard shadowed his jaw, making him look quite disreputable. But she knew better. Jack Donovan was the most honorable of men, despite his notorious past.

"I'm sorry for doubting you—for doubting us," she said, brushing the cowlick from his temple. "I was so worried about your past coming back to haunt us, yet it was *my* past that almost ruined everything."

Donovan took her hand and held it against his heart. "Don't fret about it anymore, sweetheart. Petrie is in custody, and Jedidiah is going to make sure he doesn't slip out of the hangman's noose this time. He should have swung months ago for murdering your father."

"But I was wrong not to trust you to protect us."

"We were both wrong. I tried to forget my life as Blade, but you were right when you said that I couldn't just put it aside. It doesn't work that way." He threaded his fingers through her loosened hair. "You know, we'll probably argue some more over the next fifty years or so."

"Probably," she agreed.

"But sweetheart, I don't think I could stand it if you ever left me again."

His voice roughened at the end, and she leaned forward to kiss him. "That will never happen," she promised, undone by the love she saw simmering in his eyes. "I've learned that you and I are stronger together than we are apart. Together, we can get through anything."

"I was used to being alone," he murmured, tracing a finger down her cheek.

"You'll never be alone again. You're a part of this town, Jack Donovan. And you're a part of me."

Their lips met in a slow, lingering kiss that echoed the powerful emotions of their hearts.

Then Donovan leered and patted her bottom. "I like being a part of you, sassy girl."

"Jack!" She blushed despite herself.

"In fact, I think I'd like to be a part of you again." With a playful growl, he rolled over, trapping her beneath his fully aroused body. "And again and again."

She pressed her hands against his chest and grinned up at him. "I knew you were dangerous the first moment I saw you."

"Lucky for you."

"Very lucky for me." She linked her arms around his neck and arched her brows coquettishly. "So, I hear you're the best around with a blade. Feel like demonstrating?"

The slow, wolfish grin that spread across his face made her heart leap and her blood thunder through her veins. "My pleasure, sassy girl."

Epilogue

New Founder's Day Tradition Brings Prosperity to Burr

***The Burr Chronicle*—June 15, 1883**

This year, the town council's idea to have local residents dress up as famous Western legends proved a huge success. Present at the Founder's Day Festival were Nate Pearson and George Tillis as Frank and Jesse James, Jacob Mercer as Billy the Kid, Harve Heinman as Sheriff Pat Garrett, and Matt Gomez as the bounty hunter Blade.

To the thrill of the spectators, a mock bank robbery by the James brothers and Billy the Kid was foiled by Pat Garrett and Blade. Our heroes performed great feats of horsemanship and sharpshooting. This new addition to the festival brought people from miles around, making it the most successful Founder's Day Festival in the history of the town.

The Ladies' Auxiliary for the Betterment of Burr is pleased to announce that the profits from the refreshment tables will easily pay for the textbooks for the school.

Dear Reader,

What a wonderful group of books are coming your way next month! First, fans of Sabrina Jeffries are going to be thrilled that *The Dangerous Lord*, her latest Regency-set, full-length historical romance, will be in bookstores the first week of March. Sabrina's known for sexy, sweeping love stories. Her heroes are unforgettable, and her heroines are ripe for love. You won't want to miss this exciting love story from one of historical romance's rising stars.

Rachel Gibson has tongues a-waggin'! She is quickly becoming known as one of the authors to watch in the new millennium, and with *It Must Be Love*, Rachel has once again proven she gets better and better with each book. Here, a ruggedly handsome undercover cop must prove to be his latest suspect's boyfriend—but when he begins to wish that this young woman really *was* his very own, complications ensue . . . and romance is in the air.

Suzanne Enoch's spritely dialogue and delicious romantic tension have captured her many fans and *Reforming a Rake*, the first in her "With This Ring" series, is sure to please anyone looking for a wonderful Regency-set romance.

And lovers of westerns will get all the adventure they crave with Kit Dee's powerfully emotional *Brit's Lady*.

Happy Reading!

Lucia Macro

Lucia Macro
Senior Editor